Butterfly Pit Crew

Shawn Michael Bitz

C.A. BRUCE
PUBLISHING

Editing: Written Dreams/Brittiany Koren
Cover art design/Interior layout: ENC Graphic Services/Ed Vincent
Cover photgraphs @ Shutterstock.com

Category: Mainstream Fiction/ Men's Action and Adventure Fiction

ISBN-13: 978-0-9971505-0-6

First printing 2015

0 1 2 3 4 5 6 7 8 9

For Julia

"Comfort the afflicted, and afflict the comfortable."
—Finley Dunne

Chapter One

Diresk Webster would have been an unstoppable poker player had he not detested cards. I knew him better than anyone and he could consistently bluff me. All those years spent worshipping him without an inkling my cards could ever beat his.

You know something? I don't even play cards.

He was my gang. My pack. My only best friend. Christopher and Diresk, together on adventures. That was us. I continue to carry pieces of him tucked away in soul-crevices or stacked somewhere on shelves in my mind though he has been gone many years. I sometimes hear his laughter in places we frequented or while I'm driving alone in my pickup. I swear I catch glimpses of him in my bathroom window.

Not his ghost, I assure you. Diresk would never consider returning after having ascended to greater adventure, even as much as he loved me. He would continue to explore the cosmic reaches as those like him will conquer new frontiers for each of us to visit.

Was he a modern knight who grew tired of timid dragons, predictable pastures, and a world without sorcerers and stolen maidens tucked away in fortresses of blackened stone?

Pleasing conjecture, but I rather doubt its validity. His truth was buried beneath layer upon layer of pristine gauze and I am not certain I ever wish to go there. Had he asked, I would have readily pledged my life for his and would have offered to align and hold the blade myself... but at the last second, I would have pulled away when time came for the plunge.

That is the truth. I *would not* have and *could not* have died for anyone. I doubt I could today.

As I walked beside him, always behind him a little, my focus was invariably pointed on me. Always, and that has been so very hard to swallow. So very hard to forgive.

My best friend taught me to taste pure passion. How could I have misjudged him for so many years? Why did I need for him to be so invincible and vibrant? To always be my hero?

If you could have seen us then, stubborn weeds growing together in a garden of colored petals and incense, you would have laughed. We fancied ourselves rebels and harmless thieves, benefactors of the unaccepted and impoverished. We pretended to love everyone. We pretended to love ourselves. How untrue and strange and ironic it all seems now.

And sad and typical.

Somehow, the "young and foolish" alibi no longer fits the puzzle. I crave so much more understanding, more knowledge and insight.

But really, none of it means anything anymore. I just miss my best friend and the days we rode side by side upon furious stallions, snorting smoking ashes into the flying dirt clods, cut by their sharpened hooves. The mighty Diresk and his faithful servant who simply wished for valor to win in the end. I wanted nothing more than to be close to him from the day we first crossed paths. As the memories stir and flash through my mind, I know this sketch must be done. If only for me, the story must be written. Diresk was my teacher and I was so very blessed to have shared my life with his.

There is pain in my heart as I write of him. I find it puzzling to have not experienced this feeling in such a long time. Once, I believed this pain would never diminish, let alone disappear on occasion. Time has its way with all of us, and only so many bags may be carried on this voyage.

Diresk's spirit has ran ravenous with the blood in my veins. He found me hiding in tall grass and absolutely insisted I learn to fly with the angels he swore hovered in our midst. I find myself wondering if he was proud of me. *Was he?* I must insist he was in order to further honor him in my memories. And my hope is that I will learn to love myself with the intensity and passion I so eagerly offered him. That would have pleased him. To have heard me say that.

I first met Diresk on a playground in Custer, South Dakota in 1971. We were fifth-graders at the time. I had moved to town the previous June and had managed to establish little rapport with any other children in my neighborhood or class at school. My mother had recently remarried and accepted a position with an insurance company in the *majestic* logging community. My new step-father assumed the helm of the junior high mathematics department and I abhorred him for disrupting the balanced control I held over Mother, and for distancing me from my grandfather's attentions. My maternal grandfather had been the only father figure I had ever known, and though his affections had been noble, I now believe them to have been intrusive enmeshment. Oh, the wonders of psychotherapy!

My grandfather attempted to protect me from any harm and managed to, with Mother's assistance, insulate me from several truths I would be forced to address in later years. My palace had been overrun by a step-father and my kingdom thrown into alarming chaos and dishevelment. Spoiled blood had been spilled and I was not a happy prince! I begged my mother to move back to Rapid City where I had friends and was a mere forty minute drive from Grandpa's protective embrace.

But she refused.

And so, I eventually learned to move on...

My happiest childhood memories are drives I took with my grandfather in his elongated, blue Buick Centurion on the dusty back roads that framed the little town of Spearfish, and hunting for wild imaginary bears, escaped criminals, and Indian arrowheads. I wore out a spot on the car seat from hours of standing next to him as he took me from adventure to adventure. We would walk the streets of Spearfish on spring and summer mornings as Grandfather made his extended social visits to the business community, finding without fail, lost dollar bills that would find their way into my eager fingers. I could never understand my failure to locate such treasures on my own.

Everyone in town knew Clifford Hanson, the man who owned and operated the Holiday Motel where I happily spent years as a child. He was the first flickering light that had shown itself in my tunnel. To this day, I am struck with childlike enamor of any motel or hotel stay. I truly wish I could live in one.

I hate Custer! I thought, and I missed my grandfather desperately. I was frightened and my precarious esteem left me wandering aimlessly through life. The endless bickering and jaded bantering between my mom and my step-father did nothing to diminish my fears, but merely perpetuated the storm already crashing upon my inner shores. I shall never forget their argument regarding my mother's wish to purchase a wedding gown immediately following their engagement.

"You're not going to spend a ton of money on that dress, and that is final!" my step-father had screamed. "I wouldn't spend five hundred bucks on a gun I was only going to shoot once."

It would be the beginning of an endless battle between my parents, and would open a tremendous wound that continues to fester to this day. Memories of hiding in my room, a pillow thrown over my head to muffle their raging voices, are etched into my mind's window. I can still trace them with my finger.

Yes, as far back as I can remember, fear ruled my life with a tyrannical fist from deep within my stomach. It was a terrible burden for me as a child (or anyone else) to carry. I began to adopt measures designed to distract me from the impending doom churning inside. Quite possibly, the mechanics which precede nearly every addictive tendency.

Suffice it to say, I created a secret place for myself where none were granted visitation, and where I made all rules and decisions. A fantasy land where I reigned.

Simply put, I became a highly-skilled control freak.

Diresk knew it and spoke openly of my inner sanctum, constantly alluding to its dangers. He was forever coaxing me away from this place with his charm and undeniable quest for overcoming life's challenges. He believed a life taken too seriously was a life given away, and unhappiness is in direct proportion to our unwillingness to accept reality. After years of self-tortuous travels, I finally concur.

But with all of his courage and stamina, I still find it difficult to accept he could simply disappear from my life so many years ago.

Why?

I whisper that word to myself whenever his memory washes through me like hot liquid electricity. *Why, Diresk?* And for God's sake, why haven't you called?

I received my first close look at Diresk while being pinned to the frozen dirt of my new school playground by a bully. It was the month of September and an early snowfall had found its way into my winter coat, chilling my neck and spine as I fought helplessly against my attacker's weight and the humiliating chants of the gathered crowd. Diresk's form appeared out of nowhere and through frosted tears I watched his hazy facial features stop no more than six inches from my own.

"You look like you might need some assistance here, son," the face told me. I remember refusing to nod as I did not trust anyone at my new school and was still invested in saving my frosted head.

"Get away, Diresk!" the bully barked. "This ain't none of your business. This is between the cry-baby and me. Ain't it…Cry Baby?"

"Now Larry, this is no way to act towards a new kid in our school," the new face continued. "Why don't you let him up and we can talk about this some. *Shit*, it's so cold down there and it don't look much to me like he wants to fight you anyways."

"I told him to get off my property, man. He was sitting next to the field, and that's my turf. I ain't gonna hurt him none. I'm just gonna scare him a bit and let him know what's what around here. Leave it be. I ain't got no beef with you!"

"Tell you what," Diresk said. "You let him up…and I won't embarrass you in front of your disciples. We'll just let things slide and pretend this didn't happen. This is my new buddy and I can't have him crying all over himself the first week of school. It won't look good for the girlies. Be a pal, now, and let the kid up before we all get busted by Fiala."

Larry didn't move.

"I'm serious, Larry," Diresk said. "Get off him before I kick your fat ass all over your turf!"

Larry, the school bully who was at least six inches taller than all of us (including Diresk who could nearly look him in the eye), silently pondered this proposition, spit in my face, and then removed his body from mine.

I immediately sat up to hide my tears from the scrutiny of the hungry crowd. The face pulled me to a standing position from under my arms and tossed me my stocking cap that had been dislodged during the scuffle.

It was his eyes I will recall most vividly that crisp morning. They appeared to reach directly into mine as if they could absorb all of my scorn and debasement. Rich, dusty eyes of deepest brown, framed by wisps of dark hair escaping from his own winter cap. One of them winked at me as he deftly spun around to deliver a crushing kick to the bully's genitals.

All of us standing there jumped to attention and nervously scanned the perimeter for adult witnesses. One had been spotted, jogging towards the battlefield, causing much of the crowd to slowly disperse towards ground cover of any kind.

I scraped away frozen saliva with my mitten and nervously waited for the man to converge upon myself, the vanquished villain, and my new hero and savior who flashed me an animated grin before issuing a warning to his fallen foe.

"That wasn't part of the deal, dipstick. You spit in his face again and I'll kick your frigging jaw through the top of your head! What are you looking at, Serfoss?" Diresk said.

Serfoss was a lieutenant in Larry's gang and quickly averted his attentions from the face's threatening stance.

"That's what I thought. Well…Mr. Dorton is going to pay us all a visit, it looks like. Nice of him to take time from his cigarettes to drop in, isn't it, Larry?" Diresk asked him.

The face leaned over to whisper instructions in Larry's exposed ear, and I was unable to make them out with my eyes still tracking the concerned looking faculty member who by now had broken into gallop. The face stood up and offered me a bare hand.

"Name's Diresk Webster, pal."

I blinked through frosted tears and continued to assess the trouble we were about to be in. I grabbed his hand with both of mine and pumped it feverishly.

"Thanks," I managed. "I'm Christopher. I didn't do anything, but when I tried to talk to him he threw me to the ground. I don't know how to fight very well. I don't know what I did to him to make him so mad at…"

He cut me off. "You didn't do anything wrong. Larry just thinks he's got to prove to everyone he's not retarded. Let me do the talking here, Slick. Mr. Dorton really likes me a lot."

This provoked some nervous laughter from the remaining members of the shifting mob who had decided to stay and brave the elements.

"Diresk! Why'd you kick him like that? For crying out loud! You could kill someone kicking them there! I want to know just what happened here and I want the truth!" the agitated math teacher said. (He was also the man who would later coach us in basketball.)

"Larry and I had a misunderstanding is all, Coach. I feel really bad about what I did. Not as bad as Larry, though," Diresk stated as he winked at his fans and was rewarded with hand-covered laughter.

"You get your ass up to Fiala's office RIGHT NOW!" Mr. Dorton said. "I'll be there in five minutes. Eggers? Go get the nurse and tell her to hurry up! The rest of you get inside and go to your next period. NOW! Why are you crying, kid? What did Diresk do to you?"

"He did nothing to me," I replied. I had considered enlightening Mr. Dorton on Larry's blatant disregard for my safety and disposition, as well as my new best friend's harrowing rescue from the bully's diabolical clutches, but caught the movement in Diresk's eyes asking me to remain silent.

So I did.

"See you later," Diresk threw over his shoulder to me as he started for the school. He stopped, spun around, and smiled at our fetal-positioned, fellow alumni. "Larry? I meant what I said, man, and I know you heard me."

"DIRESK!" the teacher said again. "Get your butt in that building and up to Fiala's office before I kick it all the way up the stairs, for crying out loud!"

I watched him saunter towards the building and found myself following with the crowd, leaving Larry to his painful reflections. Mr. Dorton hustled ahead of us and entered the building just behind my new best friend—on his way to get the belt from Mr. Fiala, our principal, no doubt. It had not been Diresk's first visit as such.

I looked for Diresk after school but could not find him. I later learned he had been expelled for the day and picked up by his father. I spotted him the very next morning and he was smiling like he had just thought up the funniest joke ever. He sauntered towards me as I sat near the bicycle rack, alone, waiting for the school bell to signal the beginning of another day at my new, scary school.

He approached me wearing the grin that would attain legendary status in our small town. His never combed, jet-black hair lounged atop a thick skull resting on a powerful neck and matching shoulders. Though slender, his body was a sculpted physique wound tightly with strong, fibrous chords of powerful muscles—muscles that had been stretched and fed by hours of cutting pine trees with his father in the ample forests surrounding Custer. He wore a neon orange winter jacket and sweat pants tucked into imitation green lizard cowboy boots. I thought he walked like a gunfighter, or maybe Steve McQueen. His twinkling eyes could suddenly burn through you like a laser straddled on an errant nose, broken twice as a child, which hung slightly to his left. The impressive work, (I would later learn), of Diresk's father who struck him with a back hand to his face for using questionable sentence structure and tone during a family meal.

Diresk's ears clung tightly to his head which served to maximize his aerodynamic appearance, unlike my own receptors that perpetually strained forward like catcher's mitts in order to capture optimal resonance. (Diresk once told me my head looked like a car driving with its doors open.) He would spend the next hour or so attempting to set me back on my wheels following my perilous plunge through an emotional guardrail.

I rolled several times and barely managed to escape with only a few inner scratches. As a child, my ears bothered me to the point of never jumping into a public pool, as my hair would no longer cover them. Later, it was Diresk who would finally drag me through the mud and murk of that irrational fear by cutting most of my hair off with a hunting knife in the fort we built behind his house.

I was not a happy camper, then, but by God, I learned to swim.

Diresk constantly licked his chapped lips, giving me something that never ran out of reason to tease or enlighten him. He looked and acted exactly as I would have wanted to be—the way I wanted to look and act when I lay adrift upon my imaginary raft, alone in my room. He was regarded as a movie star and acted like some kind of banished warrior, sentenced to roam the Earth fighting for the justice of those unable to attain it for themselves.

He had been, you can certainly surmise, a most welcomed addition to my meager intimate circle.

Unable to maintain my composure, I immediately pulled myself up and yelled his name. He acknowledged me with a slight nod of his head, and I could not avert my eyes from the burning cigarette pinched between his cold fingers.

(He smokes! Holy crap!)

Real cigarettes with real tobacco and everything! I silently prayed he would speak to me.

"Hey, Topher. One of these yours?" he asked, pointing towards the bikes. *Topher? He must have forgotten my name. That's okay...he's talking to me!*

"What? Um...no," I answered. "My step-dad won't allow me to ride to school on account it's so far. I only live right over that hill there."

"You've got to have wheels, Jerry. You've got to be mobile, man. Never know when you have to get up and split to some place quick!"

Jerry? Who's Jerry? Should I tell him what my name is? No...don't be weird. Be cool. Just be very cool, and don't upset him.

"You ride to school?" I asked, engrossed by his presence and still somewhat curious regarding who this Jerry person was.

"Green one down at the end there," he pointed out. "Five speed with the banana seat and oversized tires. Used to have this speedometer and light on it, but I tore them off. I live behind them trees over there. We should ride to school together, man. I could swing around and pick you up on my way."

"My dad won't let me..."

Don't tell him that, you idiot. Stall and change the topic!

"I mean..." I said, "he gets real worried for no reason, but I'll talk him into letting me... You think that guy is okay after yesterday?"

"Just ride it. What's he going to do, Slick? He's not going to kill you, is he? I'd have to mess him up for that."

Slick? Why's he calling me Slick? Let him call you whatever he wants, for heaven sake! Stay cool and don't say anything stupid! Let him know you are cool, too.

"What did you call me when you first came over here?" I asked.

"Dumbshit?" Diresk responded, lips pursed and brows stretching towards his feathery bangs. "What do you mean? I probably called you a couple things by now, man."

"Toe-something," I said. "Something like that. But it was cool."

"Topher. Your new name, man. Christopher sounds like something out of Winnie the Pooh. Topher's the best part of Christopher. Topher. I think I dig it."

I had been nicknamed for the first time in my young life and felt utterly blissful, mutated into something resembling a cool person.

Things were certainly looking up. The kid who had saved my life the previous day—quite possibly the most relevant and revered fifth grader of my generation—had just coined my new name, thusly proving he had devoted at least some of his time considering me! This gave birth to a possible friendship. My mind began to feed on a string of scenarios when I was snapped back to reality like an inner tube tied between saplings.

"Anyway, you can take her for a spin sometime, man. It's fast. Nobody can touch me on the flats."

"Thanks, man," I replied, using the phrase "man" proudly for the first time in my young life.

We sat there in silence for a while. He smoked his cigarette, and I simply basked in my enjoyment of being close to him.

"Smoke?" he asked, offering me his pack.

"I better not," I blurted out. "I'm still trying to defeat this cold I have had for more than a week now."

He nodded at me and put his pack inside of his coat pocket. Suddenly, he placed his hand on my shoulder and my throat slammed shut as he turned me to face him.

"Let's get something straight right now, man," he began. "You and I both know you haven't smoked a cigarette before in your life. I don't give a crap about the other day when Larry kicked your butt, or if you can't fight, or if you're cool or not." Diresk stepped back and his brows met in deep concern. I am certain I had begun to pucker up like a grape in a desert.

He continued. "You've got to relax, man. You look like I'm going to hit you, or something. I'm just going to say this one thing to you…so don't go whacko on me, okay?"

I feebly nodded.

"All I ask is you tell me the truth. You don't have to be anything but yourself around me, Topher. I mean it, man. I don't give two shits about what anybody thinks about you…or me! If you and I are going to be friends, you've got to do this one thing. Be yourself. Can you do that for me?"

I nodded.

"I'm not going to pretend to be something I'm not…so you don't either, man. All we have to do is just… Oh my God, I love her! Check it out, man! Billie Lee Sager." Direst pointed. "Sixth grader…but something went haywire in her hormones and she ends up being built like that. That's what you can get me for Christmas, Jethro!"

Jethro? Make up your mind.

I looked in the direction of Diresk's pointed finger and felt my eyes about to be sucked from my skull as they fixed on the coordinates of one of the most beautiful creatures I had ever seen. I then returned to why he had addressed me as Jethro. Then, back to Billie Lee Sager and the physical aroma that preceded and followed her like a mist. I tried to remember our discussion and what Diresk had said before his thought train jumped tracks suddenly. I attempted to silently draft a succinct, yet momentous overview of our previous discourse, but gave up to watch Billie Lee Sager saunter into the large, brick school building.

I can still see her. God, she looked like a woman. Diresk and I joined eyes in silent vigil, returned to see her disappear into the doorway, concurrently shook heads, and then leaned back against the iron bike rack.

Overwhelmed by the moment, I was forced to emit a rather dispassionate soliloquy under my recently restored breath.

Please let him like me. Help me not to be a nerd.

"I would eat mud just to be able to spend some time in her underwear drawer, man!" Diresk exclaimed, bringing me out of my brooding self-doubt. "Man, she is finely made!" he continued. "Where was I? Oh, yeah, you've got to learn to lighten up, man. I can tell by looking at you that you are going to die at forty from your heart exploding. I got my work cut out for me, Slim, but that's the way I like it to be. I'm gonna teach you how to coast through life, and you're going to teach me whatever it is you're supposed to teach me. We'll be a great team. I need someone to hang with…and you look like you could use some company real fast! How's all this setting with you, Cowboy? You look like you need a smoke, or something."

"I know I'm not very good at relaxing, but I'll try harder," I replied. After the lunacy of my words set in we both began to chuckle, and as Diresk slapped me on my back I realized I was no longer alone in Custer.

As the two of us stood there at the bike rack, I couldn't help but notice that Diresk knew nearly everyone in that school. They all waved to him, and in many ways, appeared to pay homage as they strolled past. I was so proud to be next to him. Safe. Secure. Something I could never have on my own.

We were nearly inseparable from that day on. I remain baffled regarding his inclination to befriend me the way he did, but he would dismiss such interrogations with sarcasm or silence. Somehow, he always let me know how much he appreciated my presence in his life—never directly, but it was clear it was deeply received.

I never did learn how to fight or defend myself physically. I not once had to as long as Diresk was around to attend to my bullies. He must have known I was not cut out for hand-to-hand combat, though I do not doubt he secretly believed a couple of bouts would have enhanced my self-confidence. I silently cursed myself whenever I would voice a fear in his presence, as it would invariably lead to being nudged upon trembling legs to the edge of said precipice to peer down into its molten belly. Then, Diresk quietly, yet sternly, urged me to jump. To this day it is as if I can feel his hot breath on the back of my neck as I continue to face the myriad of lies my fear tells me with its shiny tongue. I can hear him whisper, "Jump, Toph. Come on, man…jump right down its throat and tear its heart out!"

I have heard that voice whenever I needed to since the morning after the night he chose to take his life to another place. In death, as in life, he has only been but a breath away. There've been times I'm more angry with him than I have ever been at another human being. I spent so much time concentrating on the pain *I felt* I managed to look right past his own. He was, after all, Diresk. Bullet-proof and immortal.

I ask myself daily how in God's sweet name could I have missed something so profoundly blatant? I failed many times to look away from myself and my problems long enough to notice he was dying. I never noticed his pain or suffering. I just went about my life as if he was always going to be there.

My anger has long since slipped through a crack, I imagine. /But how I hated myself for such a long time to allow him to make that choice. Still, I somehow understood there was no rational path save forgiveness and understanding. For myself, as much as for him.

I believe the question I have wrestled with the most is *Why not me?* I was the weak one. I was the psychiatric patient and "Mr. Panic Attack". I always thought I was the elephant in the front room, until it took a crap right on my head. It should have been me…

But it wasn't.

"You've got to learn how to get past yourself, man," he would say. "Once you get past yourself, you've got nothing but open field ahead of you. You get to run anywhere you want…go anyplace you want to go. And most importantly, you'll get free to help those who can't help themselves. And that's a hell of a lot of folks, Jerry. People are freaking and dying on the side of the road and if you can't stop seeing *you*, you can't *start* seeing them." But I ignored his most deliberate lesson. He mentioned it in one form or another a couple hundred times and it never sunk in until now.

It took me many years to understand what he was desperately trying to tell me. Jerry. Cecil. Partner. Jethro. They were all part of Diresk's idiosyncratic salutations. He was showing me there were many different facets to myself. And also, life's all about giving to others. Helping others because you simply want to, not because you have to. It's the oldest spiritual truth on the books, I imagine. Diresk lived it. Every day of his life.

And I watched him. Giving to others filled him and he could soar like no one else I have ever seen. But he hadn't plugged all his holes, and he finally bled out. My teacher. My best friend. God, I miss him so much. He was the first person I ever loved.

Diresk left me a message on my machine the night he murdered his pain. The night he swallowed a bullet. It was short and sad and I replayed it over and over in my head after I could no longer tolerate to hear it on the answering machine.

He drifted away with an ancient wind like a kite would that has finally snapped its line. The same wind would burn and blind my eyes with dust as I helped carry his coffin to the hole someone's best friend had dug for mine.

Memories plagued my mind.

I last spoke with Diresk the day before he died. I had found him in his parents' tire swing, intoxicated. His dog had made a dispassionate attempt to bite me, but even she had given up. I screamed in her face and she retreated to the bushes.

Diresk raised his head and waved me over, smiling through crusted lips. His face looked as if it had shattered, and he did not speak as I approached him. He reminded me of a one-man ghost town.

I held a folder as I walked towards him. I had stopped to return some of his poetry he had wanted me to read and finish for him. As he tried to push off the swing with his legs, he dropped a near-empty bottle of wine as his hands shot to the rope to regain his balance.

I knelt to retrieve it, but was halted by his graveled voice.

"Leave it! About got her drained anyways."

I lit two cigarettes and handed him one as his eyes fought for focus and finally settled on the folder in my left hand.

"What do you think of them? Pretty goofy, huh?" he asked as his fingers inserted the cigarette into his cracked lips, but his eyes failed to meet mine.

"They're good, D.," I lied, having never read them. "I can't finish these, though. They're yours, man. Maybe they are finished. These are your words and I can't…do not feel right about trampling over them. You just have to spend some time with them revising."

"Like you did?" he asked with a strange look.

After I failed to respond, he took another deep drag of his cigarette and tossed it into the bushes near his dog.

I felt guilty about not reading any of his poems. Diresk had eagerly read every word I had ever lined up with another. He read every short story I wrote in grade school. Hell, he was responsible for my ever attempting to write anything at all! My very first poem was written about Diresk and his dog, Grover. I still have it somewhere, though I can't remember where.

He looked at me silently for the longest time and finally took the folder from my hand and dropped it beside him in the sand. I waited for him to say something. Anything. I looked down at the papers that had fallen from the folder upon impact and felt immediately sick to my stomach. He looked passed me and into the woods near the site of our childhood fort.

I continued to wait for him to speak.

There was nothing left. I had looked right past it. I never even got close. I merely saw in front of me my alcoholic best friend who was above concern and pity. I now understand it was always my own sense of inadequacy that distanced myself from him. It was the truth of the matter that hurt the most. The truth of who Diresk was as he really was inside.

He had given me so much, and I couldn't even read a few poems of his. He had even read the first draft of my first novel three months previously. He told me it was some of the best "stuff" he had ever read, though I know now he must have forced his way through it. Maybe if I had spent some time with his writings I would have heard his cry for help. Or, maybe not. I was so selfish then.

After his father gave the poems back to me a year or so after Diresk died I heard his cries for help constantly.

Diresk had told me this on many occasions, but I could never grasp the simple truth set before me. All he ever wished for me was for me to see myself at his level. Eye-to-eye. Man-to-man. He desired a peer.

But I wanted a parent.

I miss his anger more than anything. His passionate plight to redeem everything and everyone he came in contact with in town. He fought to free himself by liberating other prisoners. His war was against fear. Yours and mine. Inevitably, I guess, it was all about his own. I never pondered fear's existence as he rarely spoke of it. Unheard of behavior for an emotional exhibitionist such as myself.

I now believe he wanted us all to shine with the brilliance he so desperately sought for himself. I believe I am only beginning to see some of the colors he described to me. The dimensions of our life together on this planet, so hidden by our own admissions and admonishments.

I am beginning to see them now and that has made all the difference. A time-released gift from my Diresk. He loved and embraced me despite my flaws. Our love was too pure to touch with a hand. Too simple to grasp with the mind. So powerful and present I had no alternative but to avert my gaze from its blinding light.

I used to believe he was the lover I could never find in a woman, and God only knows I searched. I am now inclined to believe the partner I have combed this land to find is God. However, more data must be gathered and assessed.

That day visiting, the last thing I said to Diresk was, "I'll call you soon and we can get together and talk."

"I don't want to talk, Toph," he said. "I'm tired and I want to sleep."

Not knowing what else to say to him, I walked away and went on with my life.

Sweet dreams, my Diresk.

Chapter Two

THE PICKUP

"I'm not riding in your coffee can, Topher," Diresk yelled as he dashed inside his house to grab the cigarettes and some beers he had hidden in his room. His parents were away from the house, leaving the coast clear to remove our contraband. We were sixteen and the world was ours.

I turned to yell something back at him, but he was already inside. He always got inside before I could reach him. The "coffee can" he had so rudely referred to was my 1974 AMC Pacer. It wasn't pretty, but at least it was very slow. Instead, we would be taking the Ford again— Diresk's 1972 Ford F-100 pickup. Just about every important aspect of my life I ever learned was honed and polished while riding around in that beat-up truck. It was a place I could let my guard down and where I could be myself. Jerry Jeff Walker tapes were turned up to ten as we slid sideways on nearly every curve we took.

Diresk's dog, Grover, accompanied us wherever we went, and no matter how much time I spent around that hound, she always tried to bite me when Diresk wasn't looking. I must have given that dog half of everything I ever ate. I'm still not very fond of basset hounds.

This particular summer night we had planned to drive to Stockade Lake for a bit of campground thievery of coolers. Park rangers were getting upset as countless tourists had been hit by roaming bandits in the many local campgrounds surrounding Custer. This practice was frowned upon by local law enforcement due to the fact Custer thrived mainly on tourism, and the last thing the area merchants wanted to see was a bunch of disgruntled visitors who would pass their complaints to prospective consumers.

Raiding campgrounds was our absolute favorite summer pastime in our teen years. Sometimes I couldn't believe some of the stuff we got away with during these capers. All we ever hoped for was beer and snack food, but occasionally we would stumble across something exciting.

One night, we happened upon a cooler full of thousands of dollars of camera equipment. It was 1978, and we were so alive.

"You are not going to believe this, D.," I said as I opened the cooler at my feet. I held the flashlight in my teeth as we sped away with the truck lights turned off. "It's Nikon City! Bunch of film...lenses...car keys... Hey! There are three cameras in here, man! Nice ones, too. Check it out, D."

"I can't drink no cameras, Slim. We've got to go back and get us some beers," Diresk quietly said, slapping my back. "I believe I might just roll me one of them funny cigarettes, too. Join me?"

"We're not going back there. If we get caught with this stuff—"

All at once we found ourselves in a power slide as Diresk slammed on the brakes and I was thrown to the dashboard. It had not been our first such argument.

"Give me that shit, Larry!" Diresk ordered as he reached over and grabbed the cooler before we had even stopped moving. The truck slid to a stop and Diresk tossed the cooler with all the camera equipment into the ditch.

Before I could submit comment or protest, tires were throwing gravel and the big Ford's engine was roaring like a foghorn.

We rode in silence for a while, and just as I was about to ask him why he had thrown out the loot, he whispered to me, "Don't get attached to nothing, Zeke."

Without taking his eyes off of the black road, he continued. "As long as you can leave it all behind you without looking back at a moment's notice...you can't throw yourself in no jails. We don't need cameras. We need alcohol. You've got to figure out what you need...first...then the rest will just fall into your hands. Roll us a number, and I can barely hear that song."

I obediently turned up the stereo and began to awkwardly fumble with some marijuana and rolling papers as Diresk lit himself a cigarette and leaned out the window to view the starry night.

A few hours later we'd drink beer lifted from a campground at

Bismark Lake. But all my polluted mind could think about for the rest of the night was going back to get those cameras.

I have yet to master the art of not getting attached to stuff.

Chapter Three

"She's done just about everybody in the school, and I say you're next."

Diresk had been leaning out of the truck's window to get a better rear view of Rhonda. Rhonda was the school temptress. Actually, Rhonda would reportedly have sex with just about any male who asked as long as he was either a basketball player or in possession of illegal drugs. I closed my eyes as Diresk spun the big truck around in pursuit of Custer High School's porno queen, lost in her own carnal stroll.

The girl could walk. Dancing flesh. Mae West with a ginseng overdose.

"I'm *not* going to screw her, D.! I mean it! I'm not going to catch some disease, and end up peeing green urine the rest of my life!"

"It's my sworn duty as your guru to rid you of this virginity curse once and for all. Topher, you gotta get started with sex, man. It's truly the best thing God ever gave to us…and in this life, we gotta make the best happen as much as possible."

"What if I can't get an erection? If that went around school, I'd have to move to France. I'm nervous, man. I'm serious, D… I can't perform under these circumstances. Why don't we just…"

"Rhonda will coax the nervousness right out of your little weenie, Cecil. Practice makes professionals, and this lady has put in her hours. I've done the deed a dozen times with her. Don't worry, she knows how to treat us poor guys. Discussion is done and gone! Let me do the talking and save you from freaking out on your wedding night."

We pulled alongside Rhonda. She was on her way home from her summer job at Dairy Queen.

To me, she looked like a dangerous proposition. When she smiled at us, I nearly knocked myself out on the rear window as I swung back to hide.

"Easy on the glass, Slim!" Diresk said. "She's just a girl. Cool out and lay back for the ride." He swung around and faced Rhonda. "Rhonda? My buddy, Topher, is coming up on his sweet sixteenth and hasn't had any proper female instruction. I was wondering if I could trouble you to assist in the deflowering of this lost lad? If he don't get laid pretty soon, his brains are going to start pushing out his ears."

Rhonda leaned over to get a better look at me as I cowered in the corner.

"I happen to have some purple pot I got from Frankenstein that'll make you think you're a Martian...and some Colt 45s chilled to the frigging bone," Diresk said. "What say you, fair damsel?"

"You're really an asshole, Diresk," Rhonda noted. Her eyes looked like they were going to explode and they scared the hell out of me. But at that moment, *everything* scared the hell out of me.

"Darling, if I were less of a man that might've cut me deeply. Get in the truck before we have to smoke all this reefer by ourselves," Diresk ordered, as he reached across my shaking legs and opened the door. He knew I could never have opened it.

Rhonda flipped us off, ran around the truck, and I barely avoided a collision as I managed to slide over just before she jumped in. She smelled like ice cream. I felt like I was going to shit my pants.

"Hey, Christopher," she said.

"Hey, Rhonda," I managed, wishing I could have a massive coronary on the spot.

Just when I thought my heart was going to fall out of my chest, I felt her painted lips on my neck. "You'll be fine," she whispered. "I'll take real good care of you. I haven't lost a patient yet. What's your dog's name again, Diresk?"

"Topher is a little nervous, darling. He's been poisoned by biblical dogma to the point he's convinced he's got to have some kind of relationship with the first woman he bumps uglies with," Diresk said as he winked at the both of us and inserted a joint into his chapped lips.

"Don't underestimate the bite of this dope now, fellas. Frank got Slime and I so stoned on this the other day, we were entirely incapable of communication. Looks like Slime's going to have to relearn the English language all over again, man." He continued to look forward. "My beautiful baby's name is Grover. She don't approve of drugs or premarital sex, so keep your paws to yourself."

Slime should be mentioned here. His real name was Gary, and he was renowned throughout our school as having the worst breath on record. No matter what he did, or how many times he brushed his teeth, or how much gum he chewed, his breath always smelled like he had just swallowed a bucket of maggots.

Diresk flashed us his grin, and passed the smoking joint to me, pointing out the chilled malt liquor to Rhonda. Grover licked Rhonda's hand as she opened the sliding rear window and removed a Colt 45 from the cooler in the truck's box. Thirty minutes prior, the dog had offered to relieve me of my right hand during a similar maneuver.

I took my turn and passed the dope to Rhonda, who put the lit end into her mouth and inserted the other into mine, blowing a tremendous flume of smoke into my lungs. I soon found myself in a struggle to keep the elephant in my lungs from jumping out of my nose and clenched mouth. I made it without coughing, which must have impressed her, because she winked and nodded at Diresk before taking her own delicious pull.

We drove out of town, and the next thing I remember is being absolutely enthralled by the colors on a Pink Floyd tape case to the point of forgetting, entirely, my angst over the impending sex deed. My trance was soon shattered as the rear view mirror all but chipped my teeth.

Diresk never rolled to a stop as long as I knew him. It was always a barely controlled skid whenever we arrived someplace. Both of them had left the cab before I could utter a single plea to my captors. I sat there alone, caressing my tender teeth and gums, terrified and stoned beyond comprehension. Not an erection in sight. I swear to my God I wished for the end.

I finally managed to exit the vehicle and looked around. Since I could not locate either of them, I called out but heard nothing. I remember my eyes felt like the sun was barely six feet from Earth. I nearly fainted at the sound of Grover's bark. Paranoia kicked in, and I became convinced the dog was going to attack me. I ran back towards where I believed the main road to be, when I sped down an embankment, circled around some pine trees and ran smack into Diresk, who was leaning back against a tree with Rhonda's head affixed to his crotch. He had been struggling to light another joint with an impotent lighter.

I stood there watching them. This surreal scene from a movie I was somehow in. I could not believe the three of us were doing what we were doing. Rhonda's head was bobbing back and forth as her bottomless eyes fixed on me with a blank stare I could not bear to return. Diresk, still intent on igniting the dope but having no luck, stood there as if his shoes were being shined.

It was all too much for me, and I slowly wandered back to the truck to wait for them. Grover barked and snarled at me through the window as I leaned forward in the cab and held my chemically-confused brain in my hands. They returned to the truck a few minutes later, wearing painted smiles.

"I'm not doing it, Diresk. I want my first time to mean something to me and I don't care what anyone thinks about that. No offense intended, Rhonda," I offered.

"Don't worry about it, Baby," she replied.

I looked to Diresk for approval, and his gaze slowly met mine. "Topher, you break my heart sometimes, but good for you."

We rode back to town in utter silence.

Chapter Four

Diresk and I took some girls we knew from a small town called Hill City to the mall and a movie in Rapid City. They worked at Mount Rushmore that summer, after Diresk and I had just completed our junior year in high school. They were college girls—older women—and we felt as if we'd hit the jackpot.

We had the usual going—smoking pot, drinking Colt 45s, and pushing the stereo up as far as it would go. I remember the girl I was with wore golden sandals and I couldn't take my eyes off of her tanned legs. It was the first time I really noticed having an affinity for women's legs. I stared at them the entire night and was certain she would mention my eccentricity if I continued. But I was powerless to stop, I was so drawn to her.

We left Rapid City around midnight following a late supper, and somehow made it safely to their apartment in Hill City, despite having chemically assaulted all of our senses beyond measure.

The girls invited us inside, and Diresk and his date quickly disappeared into her bedroom. After a heated petting session, I bravely asked my date if I could lick her legs. She laughed and informed me I could lick whatever I wanted.

I awkwardly said her legs would do just fine. I think her name was Mona. She was nearly as tall as I was, and I found her somewhat attractive. Long blonde hair with the tan of a lifeguard. Other than that, all I can remember about her is she had red, polished toes. She watched with bemused amusement as I lapped at her legs like a child with a melting ice cream cone as she reclined on their living room couch.

As I did so, I could hear Diresk and his girl going at it in one of the two bedrooms, making noises like tortured animals. I remember thinking, *This must be so strange to this girl; I'm licking her legs while her roommate is having sex in the next room with my best friend.*

It was the first time I ever felt dirty with a girl. It was also the first time I ever climaxed without being touched. I do not know who was more surprised. Probably her, because she quickly withdrew her leg from my face and made some excuse about having to get up early for work.

She excused herself to her bedroom and soon returned, a protective afterthought I assumed, to retrieve her purse. She thanked me for the movie and meal, and vanished behind her closed door.

I knocked on her roommate's bedroom door and announced to Diresk I would wait for him in his truck.

"Come on in, Toph... It's okay," he said breathlessly.

I opened the door slightly and was shocked to see my best friend receiving oral sex from his date on her bed. Her panicked face spun around to confront me, and I quickly slammed the door and stepped back as if she had shot daggers from her blazing eyes.

"SHIT, OH SHIT!" she exclaimed through the door. "Get the hell out of here, you asshole. I mean it! RIGHT NOW!"

"Come on, (I forget her name)," Diresk pleaded as his laughter cracked through his voice. "I didn't think he'd open the friggin' door. Come here. I'm sorry... He didn't see anything anyways."

She began to cry, and I bolted for the front door of the apartment, closing it softly behind me as a gesture of respect. Grover's head raised above the box and she eyed me suspiciously as I approached the truck, pleading for her silence in a whisper. My heart slammed against my ribs I was so shaken. But it didn't deter Grover. She began to announce her territorial rights to neighbors and canine peers, eager to throw their support or protestations to the sleepy night's wind.

Ignored requests to silence the ballistic hound fell back down into my throat, and I opened the passenger door to wait out the ruckus within the muffled sounds of the cab. The night's events rolled before my closed eyes and I became vibrantly aware of the semen in my underwear and my still-tingling penis. I smiled to myself as I felt the wet stain through my jeans and rolled the sticky residue between my thumb and forefinger.

It was then I noticed the endless spray of stars through the windshield.

Absolutely charmed by their numbers, I leaned forward to rest my chin on the dashboard. *Unbelievable.* Billions of stars and planets in this universe, and I suddenly felt like some invisible speck of atomic dust.

Alone in the pickup, I was overcome by such a rush and dance of electric emotions I thought I would burst. Magic I could not define or attribute to any sort of chemical boost. I simply felt as if someone had crashed silent cymbals in front of my eyes. I leaned further against the glass to seek the source of such mirth, and gazed awestruck into the countless eyes of the universe.

The barking chorus of the neighborhood soon brought me back to the reality of the truck and the cigarettes lying beside me on the seat. I lit one, and recall thinking how strange it was that my seeds of life lay dying in the cotton fabric of my jeans. The power to give life.

I saluted my penis, then sat back to enjoy my cigarette and review the night's activities in my mind. I could still taste her skin on my lips. I tried to remember the smell of her. The rolling lines of her tan legs. I smiled and blew smoke into the windshield, drunk on my awakened fetish.

I let my mind wander back to the fellatio I had just seen. The girl between Diresk's legs, praying on her knees for his pleasure. So sexy from behind. The curve of her buttocks as her long hair spread its fingers like a hand across her shoulder and back. God, I loved to look at women from behind! I reached down to touch my erection as it shifted in its dreamy sleep with the flick of a switch in my mind.

Did I have time to masturbate? No, he would have to shut the dog up and soon. I'd have to wait for my bed. It was a date.

But something powerful happened to me in that pickup that I am still unable to grasp. I was absolutely floored by the feelings I experienced that bounced around off each other and finally rested to join hands in my heightened brain. The event can only be diminished in the tapping of these lettered keys so many years later.

That night, in the old pickup, I passed aimlessly through a curtain and into a corridor I had never before reached. A corridor lit by the billion points of light that had captivated and drawn me near. It had sent a hurricane through its winding walls and halls into my squinted vision.

What I shall remember most of that evening was the manner in which my shame and embarrassment shook hands with elation, hungry for exit. I was struck, famished for erotic delights from that night forth. I would spend years trying to replicate the explosion I had felt that night. Pornography and restless sexual encounters would throw water on my flames, but they would soon ignite again, demanding fuel. It was as if I had sampled the drug of sex.

Although it would be another two years before I would have intercourse with a girl, I had lost my innocence in Hill City that night. Women's legs would be my muse, and my eyes would follow them forever like twin stalkers. It felt strange to bear this buried file. It is as if I can feel something or someone glaring at me for releasing it.

Diresk finally returned to the truck, and after the usual locker room talk, we headed for home. I never told him about my experience that night or shared with him my affinity for legs, but I think he knew. His main concern had been my failure, again, to consummate "the deed". He surprised me by requesting I drive home, and I listened to him recount his evening's escapades as I watched the road and thought about Mona's legs repeatedly meeting my mouth.

I got a speeding ticket that night on the way back to Custer. My mind had drifted from the task at hand.

Chapter Five

On all of our adventures, we only wrecked the truck once. And it was my fault, really. I wasn't driving but I still feel responsible as I had distracted Diresk. I can still see the woman's eyes as she braced for the blow. She had a red coat on, and I believe she had been driving a Ford Fiesta or similar car. She came out okay, but did end up suing Diresk's father's insurance company for injuries to her neck and spine. We totaled her car. Crushed it like a paper cup.

The most amazing aspect of the tale is we had not been drinking a single drop of alcohol that day. When I think back on our high school and college days together, it only happened a couple of times. Also, we had left Grover with Diresk's parents and he had managed to miss the festivities. Another rare, yet timely, happening.

Diresk was delighted to jump through the subsequent sobriety hoops for the first officer on "our scene". He got a trifle out of hand during the dexterity section while mimicking ballet and gymnastics moves.

The investigating officer was not impressed, but could do nothing more than cite Diresk for failing to observe potentially hazardous driving conditions. Technically, he was inclined to point part of his finger towards the woman we hit, due to icy conditions and her own failure to observe proper precaution.

This all could have been avoided had I not dropped a burning roach into Diresk's lap before his fingers could receive the pass. Basic drug culture infringement on my part. Anyway, had I not forced him into his impromptu disco dance while maneuvering through a precarious situation I am certain he would have won the day.

The second most amazing aspect of the tale is we would later run into this woman, figuratively, further down the proverbial road. They say God works in mysterious ways? Check this out.

This accident had happened in the winter of 1981. Diresk and I attended separate universities (Due to my following a fine pair of legs across the state.) and returned to Custer for Christmas vacation. We drove to Rapid City to shop for gifts and catch up on collegiate gossip, and we inadvertently trashed this poor woman's car. Nothing like a car wreck to ruin a good buzz. Or, give you a great excuse to pursue another.

The woman was terribly upset by the accident and demanded the officer arrest us for *something*. Diresk apologized for his actions, yet held firm to his stance of equal blame on the matter. She swore vengeance after exchanging the necessary data and details, and continued to scream at us while being whisked away by an ambulance. We wished her well, retrieved Diresk's license and paperwork, and found a body shop to obtain an estimate of the damages.

We considered phoning the hospital to check on her progress, but decided against it. The pesky lawsuit ensued and was settled out of court. I have no recollection of further details of that particular matter. I do, however, recall Diresk's father being brutal with him in retaliation. Diresk returned for the spring semester with a new bumper and front quarter panel on his truck, and the remnants of a black eye.

One year later, almost to the day, we again returned to Custer for the holidays and were out gallivanting in Rapid City. Neither of us gave any thought to the previous year's mishap and tucked any signs of trepidations to bed with potent doses of marijuana, methamphetamines, and an assorted alcoholic bouillabaisse. And, if my shell-shocked memory serves me correctly, a smattering of chocolate mescaline. The Formula 44 bottle we nursed from was, I assure you, legitimately self-prescribed for cold symptoms. *Merry Christmas, man!*

We stopped at an apartment belonging to a girl Diresk knew from his university to, as Diresk put it, "spread some holiday cheer along with some holiday legs".

I waited in the living room while Diresk did just that, continuing to assault my senses with the arsenal we had brought with us as I watched cartoons with the girl's four-year-old daughter. I do not recall us hitting it off and I cannot imagine why.

All at once, there arose such a clatter (the door) and I sprang from my stupor to see what or who could possibly be the matter. My investigative hunch precluded the opening of the door after spotting an enraged man pounding on it and screaming the little girl's name.

"Daddy!" the little girl cried from behind me, and was soon between my parted thighs attempting to open the door.

"Princess? Let Daddy in, honey!" a heavy voice slipped through the door.

I removed the little girl's hand from the lock mechanism and hoisted her away and into the hallway leading to her mother's bedroom. A series of animated, kicking, scratching, screaming, and biting soon followed as I nervously rapped on the love nest's door to enlist reinforcements.

The angry man's voice and pounding picked up steam *and volume*, as did his daughter. I tried the knob but found it locked.

By this time, I had sustained a number of painful blows to several crucial body areas and was rapidly losing my chemical calm. Also, the prospect of facing a gun wielding, jilted husband was not on my list of things to do for the afternoon and I loudly beseeched Diresk's immediate attention and appearance.

"So you mind getting your ass out here before Paul Bunyan comes through that door and kills me?" I squeaked.

"I know, I know… I'm coming, man!" Diresk announced as I backed into the hall, my eyes still glued to the front door.

Seconds later, the bedroom door swung open. I was now side-by-side with my half-dressed compadre, who was smoking a cigarette and had a bowling pin in his right hand.

"It's her husband, man…and he don't like me much," Diresk hissed and reached out for the little girl with his free hand.

I delightfully complied.

"Come here, baby," Diresk chanted to the child as he plucked her from my aching arms and disappeared with her into the bedroom. A hushed conversation drifted from within and Diresk again emerged, followed by one panic-stricken mother.

"He'll kill us all!" she shouted, and I was pushed aside by her words.

"He's not going to kill anybody," the mighty Diresk inserted. "Get on the horn and call the cops. Toph… Come with me, man. We're going to see what we can do about all this noise."

I wanted to match my friend's courageous demeanor with my own, but was much too busy quelling a panic attack. However, there was nothing else I could do but follow my best friend into battle. I desperately searched the living room for suitable weaponry. My heart stopped with the opening of the front door.

I prayed she had called the police.

"Get out of my way, Diresk!" a very large, hairy man ordered, stepping into the living room. "You better put that away before I jam it up your ass!" He gestured to the bowling pin with his blazing eyes.

"Slow down and talk to me, man!" Diresk barked, stepping in front of the man's path leading to his cowering wife.

"Talk to you? Talk to you about what? Get out of the way, or I'll break you in half! I mean it... I ain't in the mood to play here!"

"She doesn't want to see you no more, Jeff!" Diresk held his ground. "You left her, remember? Jeff? Remember, man?"

A pause rang out through the room. Diresk and Jeff stood not more than six inches from each other, breathing like two bulls in a pen. Diresk took a step back and set the pin beside him, maintaining eye contact with Jeff. He tossed his cigarette out the opened front door.

It happened so fast I don't even know who hit who first. Before I knew what happened, several punches were thrown and Diresk and Jeff were on the carpet, upending furniture and flailing away.

My first reaction was to freeze. I soon tired of this, and quickly approached the battling bodies, circling them as if I were a referee.

Before long, Diresk gained the upper hand and pinned Jeff beneath him, face down, with Jeff's arm twisted painfully behind his back. Diresk bled from his nose and a cut on his forehead. His shirt was nearly torn off and a red trail led from the bottom of his chin down to the middle of his chest. They struggled in this position for a while, without noise or comment. I had no idea what to do, so I asked, "What do you want me to do, D.?"

"Just go out and wait for the cops. And thanks for all the help, Fuzzy!"

I did what I was told, feeling entirely worthless as a friend and fellow man. What should I have done? Should I have clobbered the guy with the bowling pin? What if I would have hit Diresk instead? Then what? I continued to quiz and berate myself in the parking lot of the complex. I was fairly certain I would have done something had Diresk failed to subdue his opponent.

More than likely I would have jumped on Jeff's back like some character in a Jerry Lewis movie. Still, I was happy Diresk had prevailed, and it had not been necessary for me to display my nonexistent fighting prowess. I thanked God for large favors.

By the time the police pulled into the lot and I led them to the apartment, Diresk had released his hold on Jeff. We found him comforting his defeated opponent as they sat facing each other on the floor, both bleeding from various lesions.

Not exactly the picture I had painted and presented law enforcement with during our hurried approach. I just shrugged as the officers looked at me, and proceeded to make myself as scarce as possible. There was no sign of mother or daughter at this point, either.

"What's going on here, guys?" one of the officers asked the resting warriors.

"Not much. Just beating the shit out of each other," Diresk quipped. "What you guys got going on today?"

"Whose apartment is this?" the other officer inquired.

"Used to be mine," Jeff stammered. "I'm separated from my wife right now and I ain't supposed to be here so go ahead and bust me. I just wanted to visit my little girl."

"Restraining order?" the first officer asked.

Jeff nodded his head.

The officers tracked down mother and daughter, spoke to each of them briefly, and started to escort Jeff to their patrol unit when Diresk felt the need to disrupt the balance of the situation.

"You don't have to bust him, do you? He was just freaked out and needed to blow off some steam." Diresk gestured with his hands as if he was signaling a base runner "safe".

"Thank you for your psychiatric assessment, but he broke the law, Sir," the second officer inserted. "He is not to approach the premises, his wife or his daughter, within two hundred yards... without permission from the court. What are you, his best friend all of a sudden? Maybe you ought to check your face in the mirror. It doesn't appear you two get along very well."

"That's none of your business." Diresk shot back. "I try not to look at myself in the mirror much because it takes me so damned long to peel myself away. Look at his profile, man. Friggin' Al Pacino."

"If you would like to continue with your current attitude and end up riding beside your buddy to the station, we can arrange it. Your call, Mr. Comedian." The first officer was not kidding as he stood glaring at Diresk, holding Jeff by his elbow at the front doorway.

Diresk lit a cigarette and glanced at me with smiling eyes. I discreetly shook my head and raised my eyebrows as if bracing for a cold splash of water. We were mere seconds away from emerging unscathed from a very heavy incident. I sat down at the kitchen table to await the inevitable.

"Do you know why the pervert crossed the road?" my friend asked the uniformed men, one of which had already started for him. "Because he had his pecker stuck in a chicken. How's that for comedy?"

Suffice it to say it was not a happy ending to our afternoon. Diresk put up a spirited fight, but pepper spray located and severed his Achilles' heel.

He departed, cuffed and temporarily blinded. "Do not blame these gentlemen for upholding the law! They know not what they do! Besides...it was my bright idea to call them in the first place. Don't blame yourselves, lad, but if you can swing bail I would dig you for eternity!"

I followed the police cruiser to the Pennington County Courthouse in Diresk's truck, flabbergasted and paranoid behind the wheel. The roads were sheer ice. I doubt I took more than eight breaths during my five minute glacial traverse, four of which due only to my lit cigarette.

Just when our story brightened again, we suffered a cathartic relapse.

Upon my hesitant entrance to police headquarters, I was delighted to learn Diresk would not be arrested and held, and would be released with a perfunctory slap on the wrist.

The demons had once again smiled upon us!

I thanked the officer for being a gracious host and for his department's benevolence and holiday gesture, promising to dig deep into my pockets to support any and all policeman's balls henceforth.

My unbridled zeal was slammed by his obvious failure to accept my joyous tidings, as well as his ensuing reply.

"On behalf of all Pennington County servants, I would like to thank you for your support and to invite you to immediately sit your skinny ass down in that chair over there before I find out what drugs you've been doing. He'll be joining you shortly, and if either one of you punks thinks you are driving away from here in your current condition...well, let's just say you're going to need to arrange alternate transportation."

The smug grin fell from my face and shattered on the concrete floor. I quietly limped to my quarantined area to await my fellow hoodlum who soon appeared, handcuffed and minus his smug grin, escorted by an unusually large, fire-spewing deputy. Diresk's face appeared to be smeared with catsup.

I elected to forgo attempts to engage the armed giant in conversation, and instead committed to memory every detail of my tennis shoes.

"You tell this one he's not driving?" the giant asked the officer I had failed to bond with there.

"Yep. Told him he better find another way home," he replied without glancing up from his paperwork.

"Could we please use a phone to call a cab?" Diresk inquired with startling humility.

"Pay phone next to the door in the lobby," the giant offered, releasing the cuffed hands of my broken best friend. "If I catch either of you driving today, I'll personally drag you back here behind my car. Clear?"

We felt it was a reasonable request under said circumstances and nodded solemnly to our three-hundred pound captor.

"Get the hell out of here," the big man added, "before you make me sick!"

We both felt this too was a reasonable request and darted out of the lobby doors. We continued, without comment, out of the building and to Diresk's truck.

"How in God's sweet name did you get out of that?" I asked, handing him the truck keys. "And why in God's name did you get us into that?"

"I don't know. Guess one of them cops thought I learned my lesson. Maybe they don't have room in the inn. Hell, I don't care why. Besides, I don't know why I had to mess with them cops. I guess I felt kind of sorry for Jeff for whipping his butt on his old turf. Let's get the hell out of here and go get some groceries."

It suddenly registered. He was about to start the truck.

"Wait!" I blurted. "What are we doing? We can't drive this truck! They'll kill us!"

"You think they're watching, man?" Diresk asked, raising a bruised eyelid.

"Of course they are. They're watching out a window right now and are going to bust us if we even move an inch."

"Shit!" Diresk said. "What do we do? I'm not walking in this cold, Jimmy. Let's call a cab and head to the mall. We'll run into someone we know, and can come back for the truck tomorrow. How much dough we got?"

We wandered back into the building, located a pay phone, and I called the only taxi company in Rapid City. Diresk located a restroom and washed the blood from his face, then borrowed some supplies and scotch-taped his shirt together.

We bought sodas from a machine and sat down in theatre chairs to await the arrival of our coach. Neither of us had touched our beverages when a red cab appeared near the back lot.

"That's us," Diresk stated and punched my shoulder. "I'm going to miss this place, man. Maybe when I get sober I can come back and it won't be so darn painful to be here."

I ignored his comments, thrilled to escape the halls and grip of justice, and bee-lined for the taxi. We asked the woman to drive us to the mall, and had barely exited the parking lot when her voice slammed us back into our seats.

"Do you know I will have pain in my neck and shoulders for the rest of my life?" she asked us.

I was cold-packing my forehead against the icy window and was stung. I spun around quick by her words. Diresk's brow furrowed and his ears popped up as his searching eyes met mine. His eyes drifted to the back of the woman's head, squinted, and returned, pie-eyed to mine. He remembered before I had.

"You're the lady we hit last year," Diresk exclaimed more than asked.

"One year and two days ago," our driver answered and spoke into her handset.

We both silently mouthed *Holy Shit!* to each other and quickly buckled our belts, poised for the worst.

"Your wonderful insurance company still hasn't paid me what we settled on—about ten thousand dollars less than what I'm going to need to pay for therapy. I had to quit my job because of the pain. Can you believe I'm driving a taxi cab so I can buy my daughter Christmas presents? I am actually *driving* a taxi cab. And then, as these wonders never cease, I get a call to pick up the two guys who helped destroy my life as I knew it...and I get to drive them so they aren't cold getting to their next destination," she baby-talked.

"That road was really slick and..." Diresk attempted, silenced by her sudden tears.

"I won't hear it! I won't! Do you hear me? I have seen it happen a thousand times in my mind." The woman turned around to face us with her tears. Her face was soft. I expected bitter rage to shoot with spit from her mouth and braced myself for such an attack. But her face was absolutely soft. She looked like a woman who had driven way too far down the road less traveled.

Something in her eyes snagged me like a fishing hook. At the time, I thought it may have been precarious sanity.

We silently watched her tears spill down her face, dragging a black mascara tail. I felt, more than saw, her anguish turn colors as she spoke during our ride.

"This one's on me, gentlemen," she said. "I hope you have a wonderful holiday season and a blissful year. From this day on, if either of you visits me in thought or physical presence I shall bless you and wish only what I would wish for myself. I forgive you both, and will carry this burden no longer. I have changed my latitude with an attitude of gratitude."

She dropped us off at the mall with not even a glance in the rearview mirror, delivering us like a couple of packages into the biting wind. Diresk stuffed his head in a stocking cap and leaned back on his heels with his eyes closed to the conversation only he could hear. I waited for him to speak.

"This all happened for a reason today, didn't it? I mean…every damn thing that happened. Every little detail. All part of some message or plan."

"Yeah, I think so," I nodded. "But I think it's like that every day of our lives… It's just that most days we aren't paying enough attention to connect the dots."

"Shit!" Diresk said. "You think she's really as messed up as she says?"

"Yep, but it doesn't matter," I replied and donned my own cap and gloves.

"What do you mean it doesn't matter? You and I were screwin' around and popped this chic and she may be in pain for the rest of her life. Christ, Topher…she's driving a friggin' cab and you know she's got smarts spilling out of her ears! *Shit.* She could probably be…"

"Doesn't matter, D."

"The hell it don't! It matters a lot, man! What if Dad's insurance company doesn't pay her? Shit! What do I do, man? How do I make this right with her? I don't have any money to give her."

"It's over, and she's got to do what she's got to do. People make mistakes and we made one. Period. She's forgiven us."

"What a frigging day. I feel like I just got electrocuted. I can't even think. I've got to get some medicine in me before I start turning into you, man! We got any of them pills left?"

"Two. Want one?"

"Shit, no! I love feeling like this, Cecil. Builds character and opens up the bowels. Now give me one before I knock your nose through the back of your head, you friggin' rocket scientist."

We swallowed the last of our stash, lit cigarettes, and calmly strolled into the mall like a couple of gunfighters into a saloon. It didn't take us long to find a ride back to Custer, and we barely spoke of the cab driver again.

Christmas came and went, and we both returned to school to wait for spring to wake up and relieve the previous shift. But I never forgot that woman or the gift she gave me that day. Forgiveness.

I tried to track her down a couple of years ago, but she had moved out of state. After making a few calls, I accepted I had done all I could to try to reach her and decided to turn it over to the Playmaker. One never knows what interesting bank shots that character will pull off!

Chapter Six

Diresk shared an upstairs apartment with a cousin of mine during a fall semester in Spearfish. They lived above this elderly woman who constantly called the police to complain about the "racket" upstairs.

One night during one of my frequent Spearfish visits, Diresk, cousin Mike, and yours truly decided to even up the score a bit.

This particular afternoon we had purchased a couple ounces of marijuana and were busy bagging up "quarters" to sell and pay for our own supply when we heard loud music coming up through the floor from the old woman's apartment.

"Shhhh. Listen to that, man," Diresk alerted us.

"Is Grandma rocking down there?" Mike asked, his mouth a perfect circle.

"She's got a stereo, man! I'll be dipped in goose shit," Diresk said in his best southern dialect. "We can't have loud music like that in this neighborhood, Toph. Next thing you know we'll have senior citizens thinking they can just move in wherever they want. You ever been hit by a golf cart? It ain't a party, Reggie. Those people have loud card parties and shit and they can't hear a damn thing, so they gotta yell at each other. We'll never sleep!"

"Rash action is called for," I half-heartedly said.

"I must thwart this diabolical pimple before it bursts and we are paddling around in pus. Topher...the phone, lad. Law enforcement is our only hope."

I shook my stoned head, handed Diresk the Donald Duck phone, and continued to weigh and sort buds into baggies— (the official contraband container for the Association of United Drug Addicts of America).

"Yes, thank you. You can help me, Lois. I would like to report a disturbance," Diresk announced into the receiver. "Yes, my neighbor is playing a stereo a bit too loud and has repeatedly ignored my requests to turn it down."

Diresk gave the dispatcher the address of the house, thanked her for her time and cooperation, and hung the phone up.

That would teach her.

We high-fived and loaded a water bong for a celebratory toast before finishing the crucial task at hand. Not a cloud in the sky, hundreds of buds to smoke and sell, chilled beer in the fridge, and a zinger on the way for our geriatric nemesis. Life was indeed grand!

We finished bagging the dope and Diresk stashed most of it in his special hiding place. Then, the three of us bellied up to the dinner table for a smoke-feast. Only God knew how many times the water bong circled that table before a knock was heard at the front door.

"It's open!" Diresk yelled to whichever lucky friend was about to be treated to a cerebral festival. He lit and inhaled ferociously.

I sensed it was not a good thing that two police officers had entered the apartment. As nerve impulses slowly passed like maple syrup from one reaction unit cell to another, I gathered and sorted enough appropriate data to determine we were very, very screwed!

My compatriots silently concurred as faces whitened and sphincters slammed shut with almost perceptible velocities.

"Oh…wow!" Diresk managed, holding the bong as traitorous smoke escaped from his nose.

"You better dunk your head in the sink because it appears your brain's on fire," the tallest police officer joked from behind pale blue eyes. "Who called about the noise?"

"We did," Diresk mumbled, as the smoke continued to dance around his troubled expression. Overwhelmed by the sheer weight of the moment, he gave up his struggle and blew a large cloud of smoke into the air above his head. "Guess I wasn't specific about which apartment, huh?"

"I guess not," the other officer replied. This guy looked very nice, and I desperately searched my mind for an appropriate greeting to sway his affections.

"We called the cops on ourselves, man," Diresk matter-of-factly stated to himself. "I can't believe I did this."

I looked at Mike, who had begun to make a strange gurgling sound from his throat. I considered my options of escape. There were none.

My mind kicked into overdrive as I waited for the officer's next move.

Diresk continued his private conference.

"We called the cops...on ourselves. I called the police...and invited them into the apartment. I really got the old bag, didn't I? Put her right in her place. *Jesus!* Do you guys understand what I did? I mean...I know you do...but...do you really dig the fact I just called the cops to my own apartment?"

I did. Mike did. The cops did. The only one in the building who was not hip to our misstep was the old woman who was still listening to her stereo.

"Looks like you boys have got quite a pile of marijuana," the tall officer pointed out.

"Is that what this is?" Diresk asked with a horrified expression. "Marijuana? That guy brought drugs into our home? No wonder I'm flunking algebra, guys. This is dope!"

Diresk gave it the old college try, but I could tell he was as freaked out as I was. He was simply better at holding his beasts at bay in combat situations. I, on the other hand, with my imagination was going to jail for the rest of my life where I would be placed in a tiny cell with a Hell's Angel who would daily sodomize and beat me. I would become a sex toy to be tossed from gorilla to gorilla as barter for cigarettes, cocaine, and potato chips.

My mother was going to kill me!

My digression from the law would be in all the local papers, thereby destroying any chance of obtaining gainful employment should I ever be released from whatever federal penitentiary the judge would throw me in. It would be soup kitchens and army cots for the rest of my life. I'd be a convicted felon. I would be forced to buy fake leather jackets with thrift store vouchers to encase my hypothermic limbs as I curled up in a cardboard cabin and sucked cheap wine through my bleeding, toothless gums.

Psychosis would soon follow, and I would be forced to end my days begging for spare pennies during brief reprieves from hallucinations and hypovolemic shock, brought on by the inevitable bleeding ulcers one would expect from a catastrophe such as this.

Snapped back to the harsh reality of the apartment and the several bags of pot before me on the table, I gathered all available courage and lifted my head to face the officers.

I pled for clemency with murky pupils and desperate posturing. My efforts were met by uncontrollable laughter from the officers, which I interpreted to be a good omen with the three percent of my essence not about to piss my pants.

"I don't think I've ever seen someone call the police on themselves before," the taller officer beamed. "You, Phil?"

"This breaks my cherry," Phil replied, shaking his head. "Looks like we got almost an ounce. Bong…pipes…scale? Looks like these boys take their pot pretty seriously, Ron. What's the scale for boys?"

"We were splitting it up even between us," Diresk offered, holding his breath.

It might have been mere imagination, but I could have sworn the old woman's music got louder downstairs. The noise in Mike's throat descended into his stomach and I feared he might vomit on the evidence.

Officer Phil continued his interrogations.

"If I didn't know better, I'd say you guys had intent to distribute. That's a whole different bag of apples, boys. You boys are looking at two felonies right here. This is no game."

"You boys are sitting on some serious shit," Officer Ron chimed in. "Don't smell too good, does it?"

We sat in abundant silence as the jury deliberated, sneaking glances at each other as if one of us would save the day. I considered grabbing the pot and making a mad dash for the toilet, but Officer Phil looked pretty fast and one could not forget they had guns.

Finally, Officer Ron, the obvious leader of the dastardly duo, approached the table and hovered over us like a thunderhead. Mike's face looked like a raisin dipped in chalk as his eyes rose to meet the towering lawman. It looked as if he would speak, but no sound escaped his moving lips.

Officer Phil began further search of the premises as Officer Ron's deep voice filled the crime scene.

"Tell you what we're gonna do. I'm going to flush this shit down the toilet and confiscate these toys. I'm going to take your licenses away and you can come down and get them on Monday. By then, I'll have thought something up for you boys to do to serve your community. I'm giving you a break and…"

"THANK YOU!" Mike exploded all over the table. "We promise we won't…"

"Keep your mouth closed, young man!" Officer Ron ordered. "As I was saying… I don't know why I'm giving you this break, but I guess

I'm going to. Must be in a good mood today, Phil."

Officer Phil failed to reply as he disappeared into the back bedrooms.

"I don't want to see your lives go into the shitter because of one stupid mistake. Felony charges don't just go away, boys. Understand?"

Boy, did we ever!

"Cough up them licenses and if they're clean, which I am certain they will be considering what fine, upstanding young men you are, we'll be on our way. I expect to see your asses down at the station early Monday morning."

I was positive our collective sighs were heard by the old woman when that front door finally closed behind the exiting officers.

It took us awhile, but we managed to drum up quite a chuckle about the whole mess. We gratefully watched them flush our pot down the toilet and confiscate our pipes, scale, and bong. We, of course, had been tickled Diresk had hidden most of our stash before calling the police to our kitchen of iniquity.

We stopped at the station the following Monday to serve our sentences. It never went through the courts, never appeared on paper or our records. A simple agreement between gentlemen that we would each dedicate one hundred hours of community service to an organization of our choice.

Diresk and I chose the local fish hatchery. Mike picked up trash in Spearfish Park and along interstate 90. We had agreed to remain chemically celibate during our penance as a gesture of respect for the non-arresting officers.

Diresk and I made it three hours. To my knowledge, Mike never smoked pot again. I could never understand how some people could just stop like that. Just say to themselves, "Hey…this is causing me a lot of trouble in my life. I think I had better quit."

For me, the wake up calls would continue to ring, ignored until finally they would lose all patience and join together to trigger an enormous explosion in my brain that would resonate for several months. At that point I would hear or feel nothing else, as they took turns slapping me awake in a treatment center.

Diresk must have had some really good ear plugs.

Chapter Seven

FISHING

"You can't reel so fast, Junior. You've got to let them get a good look at the goods," Diresk whispered and blew cigarette smoke into my ear.

This particular morning we were at our favorite spot near Blue Bell Lodge, using spinners for Speckled Brown Trout. It was the summer following high school graduation and we went fishing every chance we could. The lakes surrounding Custer were our churches. I can still smell the mossy water and pine sap. I can see Diresk, cigarette pinched between his creviced lips, bouncing to the beat of his words. One eye was driven closed by wisps of tobacco smoke as he seduced his prey with cold calculation. To Diresk, fishing was the ultimate male sport.

"Fishing is like screwing, Bobby. You've got to know when to take it real slow, and when to reel in like a son of a bitch!" he added, gyrating his hips for emphasis.

"Problem is," he continued, "you don't believe you are ever going to catch anything. Life is nothing but picturing shit happening and then putting yourself in the right places. You've got to believe you can do everything you try to do. It pains me to see you struggle through life like you do, son." Diresk tossed his cigarette at my feet and set his pole beside him in the sweating weeds.

I stomped out his cigarette but continued to listen.

"Remember that day I hooked that big bastard of a fish which nearly broke my pole? I knew I was going to catch that fish on the way up to the dam. I knew it!"

"You always think you are going to catch some gigantic trout every time we fish," I offered.

"People are psychic, man, but the moment you have a doubt about what you feel inside, it runs away and it don't come back. I win because I know when to play. You always sit on the bench and do nothing perfectly. You can't win like that, Toph!"

"Just because we do things differently doesn't make my way wrong! I don't have the confidence that you do. Okay? Announce it to the entire world if you have to, but it isn't going to change anything until I learn to look at things differently. That takes time."

"That's just the thing I'm talking about here. It's not going to change until you change it! You have to want all the aces and just know beyond a friggin' shadow of a doubt, you're going to get them. I'm not saying I can teach that to you…"

"Thank you, oh great one of the lake," I said. "So where do I go to learn this mystical new way of life, then? Huh? Is there some class I can take, or a book I can read? Like I haven't read a million friggin' books already?"

"I didn't mean to piss you off, man. There's only one place that has these answers and it's inside you. It's the only place this shit comes together and makes sense. I been hearing this from my old man since I was born. I know he's right, but I can't prove it with words. I've got to…"

I shrugged. "You've got to let me live my life and take my shots! I'm not exactly dying here. I do some things right, you know. Lots of things I do right."

"I know you do. But we've got to figure out a way to get inside your mind and redecorate. I see you struggle every day, Toph. I see you freak out about everything in sight. Man…you think I like watching that shit? Don't you think friends are supposed to try to help friends when they see them stepping in the same holes over and over again? Toss me them matches."

"Why is it every time we get together you automatically think my life stinks and it is your job to fix it?" I asked. "Just because I don't get laid every night and run around thinking I'm some big shot doesn't mean that I lead a miserable existence." I was angry and as usual, he caught all the fish that day. I tossed him my matches. The defense was not ready to rest.

"You don't know what it's like to feel what I do," I said. "You don't get scared and freak out and wonder if you are ever going to feel okay.

You have no concept of what I deal with all the time, D! You don't, man."

"Maybe not." Diresk paused and looked down at his tennis shoes, then into the sky as he released a deep breath. "I don't know what your shit feels like, but my pain hurts, okay? It does. I don't get scared like you do, and I don't know why that is. I'll be honest with you though. I'm glad I don't! Really friggin' glad!"

"You should be!" I said.

I got angrier and angrier and wanted to find a way to shut him down or make it better. I decided to quit trying and sat down in the weeds.

Diresk lit a cigarette and shook his head, then sat down and rested his heels. "I don't run around acting like some big shot, maggot brain. I run around sucking the juice out of life and spitting out the poison. You live in fear and I live in Technicolor. I live there, because I won't have it any other way."

I lit a cigarette and waited for him to continue with my lesson.

"You know, you're the only human I can talk to on a regular basis. I'm not trying to drive you down here. I wear the same uniform you do and we play in the same friggin' game. I just want you to get in and score some points, too. Mostly because you always got matches and you think I'm the coolest dude around."

"Shit." I smiled and shook my head.

"You know you do, so don't even try to say you don't! I know what you think of me. I appreciate it, I really do. You don't know how much you help me by being around, man. I'm never going to get good at telling you, either, so you have to just know it. I also know what's true and what isn't about me. You got everything I got inside of you. All the good stuff. You just got to take some shots, man. You're always going to miss a bunch of them. Some asshole is always going to come over and throw one down your throat. But it's better to jump in the game, man. No matter how you feel. Who gives a shit how you feel. It only matters what you do."

We smoked in silence, watching trout rise for early morning insects.

Grover soon returned from an excursion and cooled off in the translucent water, emerging with an invigorating shake that sprayed Diresk's back and sent him diving forward with a yell. He spun away and picked up his hound, only to toss her into the lake. As usual, he never lost an ash.

His words penetrated my hurt and continued to tunnel through my thoughts like moles. We sat and watched the lake water, and the reflections of the birds as they hovered and dove for breakfast before returning to the swaying trees. I watched him from the corner of my eye and wondered if we would be friends forever.

Partners forever.

I saw no other way for me back then. No other options, but to stick close to him and hope he could guide me through the thorns and mine fields. I pushed any thought away that might hint otherwise. Diresk removed his shorts and tennis shoes and dove into the lake, surfacing supine with an extinguished cigarette pinched between clenched teeth that shined within his dark tan. Grover soon joined the swim, and I ignored Diresk's demands to join them. I watched as he kicked and lazily backstroked around the lake, with Grover trailing obediently behind like a hairy ball. He soon emerged a greased warrior, his muscles shining and underlined by sunlit shadows and the chilled skin stretched taught across his heaving chest.

He was stunning, and I shook my head as I tossed him a towel. His jaw vibrated and chattered as he drew deep, heavy breaths of the sweet and refreshing forest air. He turned towards me, and his gaze burned through all foreboding thoughts of fear and doubt, as his skin dried in the sun, as did whatever else had spilled in me earlier.

After a time, I could take it no longer and leaned over to hug my very best friend.

Chapter Eight

We used to drive out to this rancher's stock dam and fish for bass every so often. Diresk knew the guy because he had worked for him a few times; tossing hay or doing other odd jobs. We would throw this old wooden boat in the truck with the dog and drive up there before the sun came up. I could never understand why it never bothered Diresk to get up so early in the morning. It almost killed me. It still does. And Grover always chewed on the boat during the drive, and made teeth marks all over the damn thing.

I remember the afternoon we purchased the rotting travesty for eight dollars at a rummage sale. Diresk talked the woman down two bucks and was thrilled when we took it to his home to begin repairs. Extensive repairs.

It looked like it had been used in the Civil War. First time we took it out to Legion Lake, it sprung only a couple of leaks and we managed to fix them as well—and, we had ourselves a vessel. We always took Grover with us in the boat and even taught her not to bark while we were fishing. Well, Diresk did, anyway.

We went up to the stock dam on Diresk's birthday and stayed there the entire day on July 27, 1979, the summer before our senior year. Diresk's mom had planned a party for him and was not pleased after we failed to show.

"My mom is going to kill me," Diresk said as he finessed his lure near some shadowed reeds.

"How come?" I asked, monitoring him peripherally for any fishing tactics I could possibly benefit from.

"She's having this friggin' party for me, and my aunt and uncle are driving up from Wyoming for it."

"What time does it start?" I asked.

"A couple hours ago. Do you think they'll know we're not there?" He laughed and tossed his cigarette with a flick of his finger. It spun helplessly and fell into formation with the many tossed before it. He reeled in the last of his line and expertly sent it out to the exact same place he had previously tried.

"Shit, D. We better get there!" I placed my pole in the boat and went to pull up our anchor, which was a cinder block tied to a logging chain.

"Keep it down, Fuzz Face!" Diresk ordered me. "I'm not going to no boring party to sit there and field a million questions about what I'm going to do with the rest of my life. 'Where you going to college? What are you going to major in? You should go to law school, young man. How about being a dentist?' I would rather roll around in Grover's crap than put up with that bunch tonight. I am doing what I love to do on my birthday, and I'm not going to blow it on a bunch of wet brains!" His tongue rolled over his lips and left a wax-like sheen before being sucked back into its cave.

"But, D., they are your family, and your mom, she gets so excited about…"

"DROP IT TOPHER! I mean it, man. I unpacked my guilt trip bags a long time ago and I'm not going to feel bad about not going, and that's the end of it! I want to get stoned and drunk and fish. It's my party and I'll fish if I want to! Besides, I've got a little surprise for us, Billy. We're going space trucking tonight, and I don't think Mommy would approve of her offspring crashing his party in such a state."

Diresk set down his pole and reached inside of his sock. He always hid contraband inside of his sock like some spy. It was also where he kept his condoms and money. He removed a wrapped piece of tinfoil and waved his tongue at me like a serpent.

"ALL ABOARD!" he yelled at the top of his lungs and began to unwrap the foil with the precision of a neurosurgeon, periodically glancing up to wink at me. I felt my bowels tense and knew I was about to try some new drug that would probably leave me intellectually impotent for the rest of my adult life. Diresk was fearless when it came to drugs. *Hell*, he was that way when it came to just about anything.

I always crossed my fingers and held my breath when it came to living life.

"What is it, D.? I want to know exactly what it is, what it will do to me, and if there are harmful side effects. I mean it, man. I'm not sticking a needle in my vein and I'm not going to spend the next fifteen hours fighting for my sanity. What is it, and don't lie to me! Birthday or no birthday! I'm supposed to be your friend, remember?"

Diresk stopped unwrapping for a moment and gave me this strange look.. Then he closed his eyes and raised them to the darkening sky, shaking his head slowly like a fish tail in a slow current.

"When are you going to stop living life as if it's some kind of friggin' hassle for you? *Jesus*, Topher. It's cocaine, okay? I just thought we could try it tonight. Shit, we have only talked about wanting to do it a hundred million times. I got it from Max for my birthday. I'll do it myself, and you can just walk home to the party if you are so damned concerned about my family and their feelings!"

Again, we sat there in one of our reflective standoffs. Periods of agony for me because I always feared the severing of our friendship. No matter how many times we argued, I thought the next one would finish us as friends. I did not know what I would do without Diresk in my life. The thought terrified me.

I can still feel that foreboding stranger pacing my insides, strumming the muscles of my stomach like a banjo.

After an average length of silence for us passed, I broke down and tried to mend things with him.

"I'm sorry, D. We can do whatever you want on your birthday. I just always hate it when people get mad or get their feelings hurt. I know your mom gets excited about throwing you a party and she's going to be disappointed if we don't show up. I also know this is none of my business."

He stared at me. "No, it's not."

"You're right. I don't know how to relax. You think I like being this way, man? I drive myself nuts over tiny details that nobody else gives two shits about! I sit and watch you let things roll off your back like you're some kind of metal man and it pisses me off! I don't exactly enjoy worrying about every damn thing in the world. It's not my fault I'm like this, D. I'm trying to learn to be more like you, but it's not as easy as you might think. Shit... I hate being me, man! I would give anything to be more like you, but I can't just snap my fingers and be something I don't know *how* to be! You should try being me for a couple days, and then let's see how calm and confident you are. You might just find out... HEY! YOU GOT ONE!"

We both stared blankly at his pole as it danced and jerked around on the bottom of the boat. Diresk shrugged his brown shoulders and flashed me the grin I could never say no to. He looked down at the foil still resting in his palm and beckoned me with his waving eyebrows. I slowly nodded and forced the trepidation from my face with a labored smile.

"Give me some green," Diresk ordered as he opened the foil.

I leaned sideways and fished a ten dollar bill from my tight shorts. He snatched it from my hands, rolled it into a tight straw, and soon we were snorting our first lines of cocaine off the top of a tackle box.

The fish miraculously stayed on the line. It turned out to only be a midget bass. Grover played with it in the bottom of the boat until it eventually died. We finished the cocaine by flashlight, and as our hearts raced and our brains peeled open like the petals of a spring flower, I was suddenly drunk on a delicious rush of tepid adrenaline that blew a gale force through my very soul. I braced myself against the rowing hooks of the boat and felt myself orgasm over and over inside my head.

"Can you get sperm inside of your brain?" I asked, attempting to slow my breathing as I monitored my carotid pulse and felt my blood pound like a hammer.

"Don't know. Let me cum in your ear and let's see," Diresk answered with blazing eyes and almost palpable omniscience.

We shared laughter and lit cigarettes under a million blinking stars. Diresk closed his eyes and leaned back in the boat. I tried to see what was flashing across the inside of his eyelids. I imagined it to be the two of us—together forever! We listened to the frog and cricket orchestra playing that night. Maybe an hour went by before he finally spoke.

"Topher?" Diresk asked as he spread the last of the powder across his teeth and gums.

"What?" I smiled, drifting with my thoughts as they went down blood red rapids.

"You want the good news or the bad news?"

"Good," I said.

"I think I may have found my direct line to God, Fuzzy!"

I lay there, almost lifeless in the boat. "I feel like I'm having a cerebral orgasm, but I'm not sure if it's God or Satan here right now, man. What's the bad news?"

"You owe me fifteen bucks for the blow, man." Diresk licked my ten dollar bill and put it in his pocket.

Chapter Nine

"I can't see him... Where is he? There! Don't let him get tangled in those weeds. Pull him up... Shit! There you go, don't let him under the boat. *Topher!* Just...get him over here and I'll net him. Come to Papa, you big son of a bitch. Oh, shit, he's a biggie... Keep his head up."

"He's going to snap the line, man!" I screamed.

I had finally hooked a monster!

"Let me get the line," Diresk said. "There. I can't friggin' believe you caught this, man. *Holy shit!* Another foot over towards me, and I got him! There he is! Hold him up."

"I caught a trophy," I sang, and steadied myself in the swaying boat.

"Watch it, man. Yeah, just like that. Keep his head up or he'll snap it!"

"I am! I am! Use the net, man."

"Just hold him," Diresk said. "I got him! Man! That is one big fish, Jethro! Get him closer to the boat. Up...no, over to this side. Closer. Just a little closer. Come here, you big sumbitch! He's the biggest we've seen all summer, Toph! You caught the biggest fish of the..."

"And I'm going to lose the biggest fish if you don't net him!" I yelled.

"I can't friggin' believe you got him and I didn't. Unbelievable! Judas Priest! He's the one we've been searching for our whole bloody lives! The shark that's been eating up the tourists, lad. We got him and we're gonna cut him up good and proper," Diresk chanted in his always horrible Scottish accent he would only attempt at while we were fishing.

"Come on, D. Don't screw around, man. Please just get the net. I'll bring him up to you." I was really beginning to wonder if the line was going to hold. The fish kept going under the boat and there were tons of weeds for it to get snagged on. I could not lose this fish. My entire existence depended on landing it at this point.

"Fear not, my young angler a' Scotland. I'll be bringing this one in and don't you worry, lad!"

"DIRESK! GET THE GOD DAMNED NET NOW!"

"Okay, settle down, man. Keep tension on him. Don't jerk him like that, Toph... Let me do the lifting. I'll grab his gills, if you can get him up and over. Do it now, man. On three..."

"No! Don't count. It'll be too fast and he may not come up if I jerk it! JUST FRIGGIN' GRAB HIM, D.! I put him right up there a couple times and all you have to do is grab his gills. If you'd just use the net, we wouldn't have to..."

"Couple more inches is all I need, Jerry! If I can...just...get my finger...under his..."

"Please use the net, man!" I begged through excitement I rarely let myself experience. I was laughing by this point and having an incredibly wonderful time underneath my anguished concern for my partner's proficiency.

"Don't need it. I got him. You just keep that line tight and don't try to lift him. Let him come up and see what we look like. He'll get tired. *There!* He's on his way up. Keep *with* him. Oh, man he's huge! I got you, you... Shit!"

I sat there in the boat with my heart pumping through my chest, blinking helplessly at the snapped line as it waved to me with the rhythm of the breeze. I dropped my pole and closed my eyes to the sound of Diresk's hearty laughter. It was the biggest bass we had seen that summer, and I had it right up to the boat before it was gone.

I tore open my eyes and searched for some way to make it all better, or to make the fish come back. Diresk was bent over backwards, hysterically laughing and pounding his muscled chest.

Suddenly, I wished I could hurt him. A rage welled inside of me and I was swollen with a hateful pressure I couldn't repress. I dove at him with my fists flailing at his face, neck, and chest.

"YOU LOST HIM ON PURPOSE, YOU SON OF A BITCH! I'M GONNA KILL YOU! YOU ALWAYS HAVE TO WIN! DON'T YOU? YOU CAN'T LET ME WIN JUST THIS ONCE!"

Diresk bled from his nose and lip as I struck him with glancing blows before he could position himself to protect or retaliate.

Within seconds, the boat was overturned and both of us, including the dog and our fishing gear were tossed around in the lake in a splashing fit of swinging arms and legs.

Immediately, Diresk got the upper hand and I found myself under the surface of the water with his hands pushing down on my shoulders. I desperately searched for the bottom with my kicking legs and took a large amount of water into my lungs.

I felt a panic overtake me like nothing I had ever experienced before or since. I could sense a darkness overtaking my mind. I could not tell if my eyes were open or closed as my body quit fighting and my bladder released a warm stream of urine into my jeans.

Suddenly, I felt my body being tugged upward towards the surface. My mind snapped to attention as I felt my head break through the water. I could no longer feel Diresk's hand on my body. I felt my stomach contract and expel a rush of water out of my mouth. I spit and coughed as I blindly sought a hand hold.

I felt his hand grasp the back of my T-shirt and pull me toward the shore not more than fifty feet away. We swam in silence and I allowed myself to drift with his guidance. My mind, a blank canvas.

My feet felt the sandy bottom skim underneath them and I gathered my footing and felt his grasp release. I stood there, panting as the air scraped my inner-flesh as it entered and exited my mouth. I held my face in my hands as tears began to sting my eyes and my body expelled another wave from my stomach.

I watched through my fingered mask as Diresk pushed his legs through the water and onto the shore, towards his truck parked nearby. My next thought concerned the dog and I turned towards the floating debris and spotted her shaking water from her coat on the opposite shore.

The dog. Why would I think of that dog? I was puzzled by my sudden concern for an animal that had given me no truck. My anger returned to me as if the thoughts had been pushed aside by all others on their way from the back of some room in my mind. The entire scene played again as I made my way to the grassy sand.

I sat for an eternity there, softly crying and digging with a stick in wet earth as Diresk retrieved the boat and nearly all our gear.

"I'm leaving," he yelled at me from the truck after he had loaded everything by himself.

I wanted to stay there forever. I saw myself seated at a table under a slow ceiling fan. Shadows concealed much of my face as I drank from a dusty bottle. A cigarette turned to ash in dried catsup on a dirty plate in front of me. Sinatra crooned in the background as hungry flies lit on my lined face to feed on the salt of my sweat and tears. I wore a white silk suit with a porkpie hat pulled low over glistening brows. A wicker chair supported me in my melancholy bliss as the ocean lapped the sanded edges of my hidden cove. I would drink and await the end of my life in the humid breath of my tiny, infected room, mourning the big one that got away.

Self-pity at it's very finest.

I heard the truck start and pull away from the lake. I listened as the parking lot's gravel was crushed beneath the tires and the stereo suddenly filled the silence surrounding the beautiful quiet of the lake. I listened as Diresk shifted gears and the sound of the truck drifted away. I was finally smiling.

Chapter Ten

The very last time we fished together, I nearly had to carry Diresk back to his truck. I could still keep up with his cigarette smoking, but I had given up booze and drugs by then, and sipped on Diet Cokes while I watched my friend inebriate himself. I do not recall if we even caught a fish.

We took the boat out on Iron Creek Lake near Spearfish one weekend afternoon, and I do remember harboring a crushing sadness the entire time. My sobriety had driven a wedge between us, and though Diresk supported me as best as he was able, I could sense his frustration lingering within our midst.

At the time, I thought he must have viewed my divergence as an act of treason. I ached for the fun times of our "old days", but not as much as for my friend, Diresk. It took me a very long time to realize that looking back for those seemingly magical times would only provide me with a sore neck.

As our boat sliced through the clear waters and hushed reflections filled conversation spaces once savored like treasure, our eyes refused to meet. Instead, we danced like fireflies in and around the lake. We circled and smelled each other like hounds meeting on a path. It hurt me deeply and I longed for the intimacy buried beneath our fears and forced smiles.

I loved him with my entire heart. I had signed my name in blood back in grade school that I'd be his friend always, and he was as much a part of me as my own pride. Pride that kept me from him that day. Pride that keeps me from myself today.

"Ain't it wild how they built all them cabins around this puddle?" Diresk asked, breaking the uncomfortable silence.

"I wonder if this will all be covered in concrete someday," I nodded. "I can't even drive by those surface mines in Lead anymore without wanting to drive into a tree. Then, of course, what do I do? Throw cigarette butts in the lake. Nothing worse than a sanctimonious smoker, man. Except maybe a surface miner."

"Speaking of smoking, I believe I'll have one of them illegal non-filters now. Hand me that pack under the net."

I tossed him his backpack and our eyes met for an instant, then darted away just as quickly like startled trout. Diresk licked his lips as if he could taste his impending anxiousness. I saved him the trouble.

"It doesn't bother me if you smoke in front of me, D."

"If it does, you can swim back to Spearfish," he chided. His words poked me in the stomach, though he had tried to cover the strike with a good-natured grin. He must have sensed my reaction because it stopped him fast.

"I'm sorry, Toph. Look, I'm not going to lie to you about any of this shit. I hate it that you don't smoke or drink anymore, man. I know you got your reasons, and you got real sick and everything. I'm smart enough to know that. I just…"

Our eyes met for a moment before I looked away. The sadness in my chest inflated and the words I so wanted to speak could not gain momentum and rise through my pinched throat.

I wanted to tell Diresk how I really felt about him. That he had always been the one guy I could respect and look up to. *I know it's changing my life and our friendship, but if I didn't quit I would've died! We can work this out. I want you to be sober, too! I want to scream across the many dimensions like rockets in the sky and then throw ourselves at the feet of God and await the very command of the One who lit the sun! You are my most treasured friend. I will walk through fire and crawl through icy snow to meet you on the other side!*

My lips parted as unspoken words began to ricochet somewhere in the back of my mind. I could no longer lift to meet his gaze and my eyes dropped to the patched bottom of the boat.

Still not leaking, I thought to myself with detached pride. Diresk's stare raked through my hair and I spoke to his feet. "This is really weird, isn't it? I feel like I'm a stranger or something. Has so much changed between us that we don't even… Oh, God, I don't understand this life at all, man. Never did!"

"I'm not going to do this, Toph. I'm not going to dig into this shit today. I'm going to get stoned and catch some fish. I wish you could get fried right alongside of me, but you're not going to, and that's that. Gotta accept what I can't change, right?"

"Don't you feel what I feel inside though, D.? Do we have to tip-toe around the truth? *Jesus.* This is big stuff, man! Look what has happened in my life the past couple months. I can't pretend it never happened and..."

"I can, okay?" Diresk said. "I can pretend nothing happened because I'm the same guy. You're the one who's changed! I don't have to do nothing different or look at nothing that ain't mine."

"But I'm new inside, D. Brand new inside, and I don't know what to make of any of it yet. You are still living your life and going down the same trail you..."

"You don't know nothing about my trail, Slick. All you ever see is what you want to see. While you've been socked away in your little treatment centers and psych wards, I've been digging friggin' trenches and ducking bombs and bullets like I ain't ever seen before. You know life hasn't exactly been a birthday party for me, either!"

"I know," I whispered low.

"So you're sober now. Yay for you. But all the dope and booze in the world don't make me who or what I am, Slick. I drink because I love it! Okay? I smoke dope because it makes everything quiet inside for a while and I get to laugh at things all around me that make everybody else cry. I love drugs and I don't see one reason why I can't live happily ever after. It's all part of my mix, man. I got doors opening to rooms inside me that you can't even dream of!"

I looked at him. "Then tell me about them! That's what I'm talking about here. You don't tell me about..."

"I tell you all the time but I don't use your words," he interrupted me. "You think I'm still on the same trail? Don't go trying to corner no market on life's a bitch, Slim! I do what I do. You do the same and that's all there is to all this. But remember one thing, man. I haven't been the one crawling around on all fours begging the shrinks to fix my brain."

He went right for my buttons. Every time. He meant to put me down so I couldn't come back at him. And I heard him. Loud and clear. I listened to every word and I knew he was telling me some kind of truth. I also knew we were never going to have what we both wanted. The tight friendship we once shared, and this awareness drove into me like a sharp spear.

I cursed out God under my breath. *Why?* Was it not enough I had to give up nearly everything I had come to know? I was not going to give up on him, too! Non-negotiable. Throw whatever you will at me, but Diresk was my best friend. And best friends try to never let each other down.

Diresk rolled a joint and began to smoke it. I watched him inhale its sweet incense. Watched his eyes and face shift gears as the butterflies took flight from that place in the brain where all chemical interactions find their wings.

I began to shake with stuttered movements and thoughts. I wanted it so bad—the joint. I inhaled along with him. Clutched the humid soot deep within my breast and held on for the ride. Expelled the smoke as it left its magic crystals hanging on my lungs like ornaments.

I opened my eyes to a strange expression on Diresk's face.

"You're getting high with me. Taking it in and holding it, and shit. Man, that was weird watching you. I'm sorry, Toph. I said some shitty stuff and I don't mean none of it. You know it."

I nodded self-consciously as if I was caught in some lie.

"Let's just fish and forget all this shit for now," he said. "We can talk about what happened later. I know this is hard for you. I'm not making it any easier by waving this dope in front of you. It's just what I do, man. You know that. You know me, and you know I'm going to get high. I have to!"

His words stunned me.

"I have to!" he repeated.

He had finished the joint and now licked his lips and reached for a cigarette in his shirt pocket. He pet Grover, asleep at his feet.

I reached for his hand and then covered my move by grabbing for my pole. He missed it. Thankfully. I loved the guy, but wasn't "in love" with him. This was all getting too big for either of us and we no longer acted as a team.

I remember that day when as two best friends we sat miles apart from each other in a tiny wooden boat, still holding on with our hearts.

Chapter Eleven

BASKETBALL

There's nothing quite like being part of a team. I feel sorry for kids who never play sports. Kids who never know how it feels to sweat yourself out with teammates to the point you can taste and smell each other. Kids who never insert their hand with those of their team into the pre-game shake and victory chant. Who never get to taste cool water following a practice drill you swore would kill you.

Nothing tastes like that.

I played in my first organized basketball game in fifth grade. I scored four baskets and made five foul shots. I counted the points like coins in my head from that day forward. No matter *what* anyone ever tells you, they want the ball, so they can drop it through those strings and hear the crowd. Feel the rush inside of them as they see a play develop in a split second, then make it happen with a deft move off of a planted foot or a barely-controlled flick of a wrist.

Or the first time you steal a pass and end it with a lay-up.

Or the first come-from-behind win.

The hush of the crowd that follows a whistle. The first time you touch the net. Or when the cheerleaders drone on like a sound track as your father's comments pierce the muffled orchestra of buzzers, heated voices, and shoe squeaks echoing together off bannered walls.

Showing off in warm-ups for some imagined talent scout for the Los Angeles Lakers who might be in town. Practicing moves in front of a mirror until you think you can fake your shadow.

The last thing a basketball player ever sees before drifting off to play in sleep is a poster of a professional hero thumb-tacked to the wall.

My personal goodnight ritual starred a life-sized Julius Erving. Diresk held a shrine for Pete Maravich. Oscar Robertson was always our close second.

Diresk and I started every game from fifth grade through senior high. I was the point guard, he was the power forward or center. We won a lot more than we lost in those years and miles of sprinting down tile and wood floors, but losing one game would overshadow us winning ten. Losing gracefully was an admirable concept as long as it was the other guys who shuffled like senior citizens back to their locker room carrying the final buzzer on their slouching shoulders. We didn't want it.

Revenge! It was all a guy had to hold on to. I remember, we lost a big game to Mother Butler School of Rapid City in sixth grade. We managed to botch a fifteen point lead with careless turnovers and poor fourth quarter shooting. Diresk squared off with some mindless giant in the second half and was ejected from the game. The giant, however, was allowed to remain in the game and burned us for over twenty points, and God only knew how many rebounds. Without Diresk in the middle to muscle their big man, we were forced to rely on outside shooting and a zone defense we knew nothing about. So, trying to get a bunch of kids to implement and hold together a 2-3 zone when they can barely remember to pee before the game was something else entirely.

We lost by three points. I had no power to stop the tears from humiliating me almost as much as losing did. Diresk chose to emote in his own creative manner.

He grabbed the giant on the team by his ears and pulled him to the floor. Soon after, my tears were benched by dumbfounded amusement as I watched my best friend grapple with Mr. Pituitary, as coaches and officials pried them apart.

In my opinion, Diresk won in a split-decision. Had the fight not been stopped when it was, he would surely have knocked the large lad out no later than the second round. Diresk was the kind of power forward/ center who took the coaching phrase "Now go out there and kick some butt!" literally. I found myself restraining my best friend on a regular basis as we progressed through the years of Custer Wildcat Basketball. We were chewed out after the game for losing our composure (as if you have anything resembling composure in sixth grade), losing the game, and for losing our tempers and embarrassing the school. (Locker rooms are great for coaches who cannot quite cut it in theatre or evangelism.)

My brave teammate raised his hand in question and waved it around like a parade beauty queen until he was finally acknowledged by a disgruntled Coach Dorton.

"Oh, for Christ's sake, what now, Diresk?" Coach asked.

"On behalf of the team, we're real sorry about losing the game. We played like a bunch of sissies. I lost my temper again, and these guys didn't have nothing to do with it, so if anyone's going to run extra jayhawks, it's going to be me."

Jayhawks. That word could strike terror in a basketball player's heart more than any other, possibly excluding the word "pregnant". Every coach I ever played for used this universally accepted penalty to purge his players of any number of ethical, technical, behavioral, or spiritual transgressions. Diresk ran more of them than any human on record. His cross to bear for serving as team captain. He was our leader, fearless and full of free-floating bravado.

"If you're so concerned about jayhawks, why don't you go out and run some right now?" Coach inquired.

"On their court? In front of the enemy?" Diresk hissed.

"Why not? In fact, why don't we all go out there and do about ten for the winning team?"

Shocked, we begged for a last second stay that never arrived. One by one, we retied our sneakers and donned sweaty uniforms for another lesson in basketball dogma. As we filed into the gymnasium as if in a police lineup, I couldn't help but glare at my best friend. He was gloating for our cheerleaders, who were waiting for us to shower and dress for the ride home.

"You're an asshole, man," I whispered to Diresk as we waited for the appearance of our coach and the attention of every person in the gym.

"He's not going to do it, man," Diresk boldly announced to his teammates. "He's just bluffing to teach me a lesson. Don't think for a second he'd embarrass us like this. School board would freak out if any parents found out. And got pissed. Anybody want to lay some cash on it?"

None of us had the wherewithal to discuss, let alone wager on, the tremulous situation befalling us. Diresk leaned against the wall, whistling and rolling his eyes up with impressive abandon. As he snapped to attention, our collective stares swung from him to our approaching coach, clipboard and ever-present coffee in hand.

"You girls going to get showered and dressed, or are you going to move to Rapid City? Better get moving ladies; bus leaves in fifteen minutes," Coach Dorton spouted as he continued out towards the lobby and trophy area.

"Any questions or other problems I can help you with today?" Diresk offered our stunned teammates. "You guys have to start learning to trust your old buddy Diresk. It's a cold, cruel world, lads. Listen, watch... and learn."

Chapter Twelve

We won three games in the ninth grade. I think we beat Edgemont and Holy Rosary. Maybe Hill City. We got destroyed by Hot Springs all four games we played them that year. Hot Springs was our most hated, challenging rival and we would have tried anything to beat them. We played our final game against them that year in a tournament on our home floor.

I remember my mother drove me to the gym early that Saturday morning and we barely made it through the deep snow. It was so cold the butterflies in my stomach had frozen like lumps of coal as I held my purple Converse tennis shoes to my chest as my mother cursed and fought to control our Buick in the winter storm. I remember hoping Hot Springs wouldn't be able to make the thirty mile drive. But no such luck.

We won our first game against Edgemont and we were bound and determined to get those Hot Springs Bison. A couple of them had hit me so hard during the previous football season I had been unable to focus my eyes as I staggered off the field. My replacement at quarterback finished the game because I refused to re-enter the battle, pretending to have blurred vision. Everyone must have believed me because nothing was ever mentioned. I never told another soul until now. Diresk would have killed me.

Hot Springs, as expected, handily defeated Hill City and was matched against us in the tournament final to be played that evening. I silently prayed for the game to be cancelled due to the snow that continued to paint layer upon layer on our streets the entire day. Alas, as tip-off time approached it was decided the game would continue as scheduled. I was once again forced to weather another bout of fears.

I could never understand why my teammates would never react the way I would. Every game I would be followed and surrounded by the same pack of fears that haunted me throughout nearly three decades of existence. My nerves tortured me and I was utterly powerless against their arrival or departure. Every speech, test, athletic contest, date, important event or change of any kind was preceded by often paralyzing, gut-seizing terrorizing anxiety. No matter what I did or did not do, I would be overtaken and held hostage by my own mind.

Diresk told me I was more than likely dropped on my head at birth, or was quite possibly raped in a previous life. He could never understand my fears. To him, fear was just another one of life's bummers he had no time for. The worst thing anyone can say to a person having anxiety attacks is, "Hey, it's only in your head."

Geez, is that the same head that can cure cancer or cause it? You're right, what am I thinking? It's silly of me to throw up before every game, and rather childish the way I haven't slept in two days or been able to hold food down. Mind over matter. I'll simply change the mind that wants to kill me with the mind that wants to kill me!

Great idea! Why didn't my mind think of that?

Before we were to play Hot Springs, our coach launched into a moving soliloquy, eulogizing and laying to rest our previous losses to the mighty Bison. He delivered a tidy analysis of their offense and outlined our strategy to shut down their titan in the middle. Williams was his name. Six feet, six inches tall, he could dunk the basketball with one hand.

To a ninth grader in 1977, it was scary shit!

Coach Dorton summed up his sermon and released us to opening warm-ups where my fears would finally evaporate and leave me with a sense of relief. All of our eyes found their grinning giant as we jogged onto the court, forced to accept the gripping reality he had not, in fact, died in his sleep the previous night.

"Topher, come here. We have a little problem." Diresk told me in the team huddle before the opening tip that he had plans for "Mr. Jumping Jacks". "Those guys are really good and they know we're really shitty. Our parents know we're really shitty. Our coach knows we're really shitty. Our deceased relatives know we…"

"DIRESK? Would you like to sit this game out so you can have more time to develop your communication skills?" Coach Dorton hated Diresk, but he was our tallest player. Without him, we would have been humiliated as opposed to disappointed.

Diresk feigned deep consideration before responding, "I believe I can help the team better in a playing capacity, sir."

"Then shut your mouth and listen to me, because these guys are going to tear those cute little smiles off of your cute little faces unless you came here to play. I don't want to see Williams camping out in the paint, okay? Keep him off the boards and deny him the basketball. Diresk, if he goes to the bathroom, I want you to go with him! Understand?"

"Yes, sir," Diresk responded with a salute to his breast. "I'll stick myself to him like a piece of duct tape, boss...uh, sir."

Coach Dorton, I believe, had considered benching Diresk at this point. After a considerable glare down and strategic silence, Dorton reconsidered and offered his hand for the team hand touch and simultaneous chant of "Defense!"

As our starters proceeded into battle and a most certain demise, Diresk pulled me aside again to whisper into my ear. "How many basketball players does it take to piss off a Hot Springs' crowd?"

"Don't do anything stupid, D.," I begged, grabbing him below his elbow.

"*Moi?* Answer me, Topher. How many?"

I was afraid to. Who knew what Diresk would do. Not even Diresk I suspected knew.

We lined up and shook hands with our worthy opponents. They were Amazons next to me. Williams and Diresk squared off to jump center. I was playing the position of point guard and lined up back in their court, near the top of the key. We all wore our hair the same way, feathered back with spray, and chewed gum. We pulled our socks as high as they would go. It was also customary to untuck the back of our jerseys as the game progressed.

I could feel Diresk's smiling eyes beckoning me for a final diabolical gesture as the officials assumed their positions and prepared to start the game.

The referee tossed up the ball and every player crouched and readied himself to shift to a necessary position for quick movement to the ball.

I never saw it happen.

I was watching the ball and getting ready to retrieve or defend when I saw Williams glide effortlessly above the ground and tap the ball back towards his teammate, then quickly disappear from vision as both whistles stopped us all in our tracks.

A crowd hush quickly sucked the sounds out of the gymnasium and a crushing silence surrounded Williams, the fallen titan, who lay crunched in a fetal position at center court, clutching his privates. The referee called a flagrant foul. "Number 10, white!"

Diresk's number.

Diresk had already wandered over to the Hot Springs' bench to incite further reaction as the disapproving shouts overtook the gymnasium. I watched with dropped jaw as our coach made his way to retrieve Diresk from enemy territory.

An opposing player suddenly exploded from the bench and threw a roundhouse punch at my friend, who was performing some peculiar dance for the Hot Springs crowd. Then Diresk's nose appeared to detonate as darkened blood sprayed from the right side of his face as both team benches emptied and poured into each other like spilled beverages. Within seconds, brawling players were joined on the court by enraged spectators for a good, old-fashioned free-for-all!

Though I was terrified at the outset, it was the most fun I ever had during a sanctioned sporting event. I swung blindly at anyone wearing a blue jersey as blows glanced off of my back and shoulders, and bodies fell together on the tile resembling passionate lovers.

Passionate, bleeding lovers.

Even the cheerleaders squared off. It was a good fight.

Although we later lost the game after control was finally restored by police officers and frantic school officials, I know in my heart of hearts, Custer defeated Hot Springs in the wildest town fight in South Dakota High School Athletic Activities Association history.

Diresk was ejected from the game, as was the Hot Springs player who fired the first punch. Williams managed to regain his composure and score thirty points against our wounded defense. The final score was 78-69. The closest we had come all season to beating them. By far, it was our best game of the year.

In the dressing room after the game, my banished friend sauntered up to me grinning from ear to ear and holding a single digit in my face.

"It takes one player to piss off a Hot Springs crowd," he stated. "Only one, Larry!"

Chapter Thirteen

We played Little Wound Kyle for the District 30 Basketball Championship in Rapid City in 1978, our sophomore year in high school. Little Wound had this Native American player named Austin Richards. Austin was one of the most magical high school basketball players I had ever watched or played against. He was built solid and moved like a deer. Long brown hair flowed and framed him like a headdress as he drifted effortlessly up and down the court. I admired his grace on the court and I think of him still.

Defending him had been difficult, like trying to harness smoke. Unfortunately, his reservation swallowed him whole and he never played college basketball, though he received many gracious offers.

We had a very physical team that year and what we lacked in height across our front line was effectively remedied by quickness and heart. We ran the ball down most team's throats. It also helped to have Doug Herrmann, who later would help win a national college football championship at Nebraska and be drafted by the Washington Redskins. Not a bad guy to have around when we needed a couple rebounds and inside offensive muscle.

This was a fantastic and exciting game, and at the end I found myself standing on the foul line with two free throws to make to tie the game, and possibly send it into overtime. Seven clicks remained on the clock. We were down by two points—79-77. I had just been fouled in the act of shooting and after both teams called time-outs, I found myself with the entire season resting on my shaky shoulders.

Diresk, as usual, took his sweet time to get from the huddle to line up for foul shots. He sauntered towards me, picking his teeth and got right in my face as the referee waited to hand me the ball.

I glared at him. *Don't mess with me, Diresk. I really need to make these free throws!*

"Look at it this way, Zeke. If you miss one shot, we lose and the season is over. All that friggin' work to get to state and it'll all go down the tubes like a turd.

Ignore him! Just concentrate. I can do this. No problem, man.

"Just relax and do your best, Larry. We're all behind you and we'll still love you if you screw it up."

"Let's go," the referee barked. "Line up, number ten!"

Diresk gave me his famous wink, turned, and assumed his position on the lane. As an afterthought, he turned to me and inserted one final blow just prior to my beginning the crucial foul shot regimen.

"Oh, one more thing. I got fifty bucks bet with Hathaway you're sinking both these meatballs, so don't let me down. Do not leave me hanging, son."

Thanks, D. Thanks a lot!

Anyone who has played basketball is aware of the importance of the afore-mentioned foul shot routine. It is a player's means of preparation to shoot with precise regularity. While providing comfort and familiarity for the shooter, it also is a means of discharging stress from the shooter's body as well as providing a meditative focus which serves to bypass the mind and go directly into muscle memory.

I still remember mine.

My first step was always to take a deep breath, holding the ball firmly with both hands just above the knees, and measure the basket with my eyes and senses. Next, I would bend to deliver five rapid two-handed bounces of the ball, pause, and rise up while taking another deep breath, measuring the basket. At this point, I could go one of two ways: I could either spin-bounce the ball to myself two times by placing backspin on it; or, hold the ball with my left hand to execute a one-handed practice shot with my right. The next step was to gain proper alignment and seam placement with my fingertips until the optimal grip was achieved. Finally, the drawing of two measured breaths while bending my knees slightly as the ball rested softly against my tensed stomach muscles, then up and through with the ball using a deft flick of my right wrist; my eyes guiding the leather orb towards its whisk through the braided white strings.

When completed, my right arm resembled an embarrassed swan as the crowd's roar erupted and the score board added points to the team's total.

I don't know why Diresk did it, but it relaxed me. I made them both, tied the game and sent us into overtime. We won the game after Doug Herrmann was fouled while sinking a shot with ten seconds left in overtime. He made both free throws and the final score was 88-84. We won our regional championship and went to the state tournament in Sioux Falls, placing fourth out of eight teams.

Diresk made the All-Conference team that year and was honorable mention for the All-State Tournament Team. I also made the All-conference squad and led the team in assists, steals, and free throw percentage. Doug Herrmann won just about every award in three sports.

Our biggest mistake that year was to smoke pot before the semi-final game of the State tournament. After upsetting Wessington Springs the night before, we were set to challenge Eureka for the chance to play for the state championship.

Well, we got stoned and missed the start of it. Coach Luitjens banished the both of us to the bench for the entire first half after we were overtaken by a laughing fit during the pre-game warm-ups. Diresk taped a banana inside of his trunks and the sight of him running around the court like that with most of the state watching on television was too much for either of us to handle.

The cheerleaders loved it.

A befitting end that still triggers laughter when it crosses my mind. I miss being part of a team.

Chapter Fourteen

During our senior year of basketball, we were picked to win the conference championship and to seriously contend for the state title as well. Before the Christmas break, we had lost only one game, had won twelve, and were ranked third in our state class. The only game we had lost was to Newell and I had been forced to play with a severely sprained ankle and could not run our offense with the precision I was accustomed to doing.

We traveled east to Desmet after the holiday break to play the team ranked second in the state on their home court. We were excited to have an opportunity to test our potency against such a powerhouse team.

I'd had an incredible year up to this point, leading the team in scoring, assists, free throw percentage, and was team captain. I was quite capable of leading our balanced team to the state finals. All we had to do was get past Desmet and ride the winning wave through the rest of the season and into the tournaments.

The game was closely fought and the lead changed hands several times. I remember playing the game and feeling apart from it in some way. I played well, not missing a single shot the entire game while managing to shut down their leading scorer; but something felt wrong inside. Almost as if an engine had been turned off. It was an odd feeling.

I felt myself pull back and pass up shots I would have normally taken without question. I desperately wanted to win the game and the crowd was feverish with excitement, but some part of me simply quit playing. I was powerless to do anything about it.

Coach Luitjens sensed it and called me out of the game.

"What in the hell are you doing? You had three shots to take and you passed them all up. I need to have you in there leading this team, Chris. We're running out of time. Are you feeling okay?"

"Yeah, Coach, I feel fine," I responded. "Let me get back in there and let's get these guys."

He gave me this strange look, then sent me to the scorer's table to check back into the game. I perfectly recall wondering myself what was wrong with me and why I was pulling back. I had no answer.

Diresk gave me a hint during the next dead ball when I was called back into the game.

"Topher, you're pissing me off, man. What the hell are you doing?"

"What do you mean?" I replied, guilt filling me.

"You know exactly what I'm talking about! You can score on that guy fifty times in a row if you want to!"

I nodded and knew he was right.

"I can't get open with three friggin' monkeys on my back, Jack!" he said. "You're the man here, Topher! We need you, man!"

"I know, I know. I'm sorry. I don't know why I'm holding back."

"I know exactly what's happening here. You can't handle us winning! You can't handle being so good, can you? Well, you are, so start playing like it, dammit! Keep your friggin' head in the game and play with your guts, man. Do it, Topher. We need YOU in this game NOW!"

We were down by two baskets when I re-entered the game with just under two minutes left. I proceeded to make two lay-ups to tie the game. I had four personal fouls by this time and Desmet had the ball.

We stopped them, and Rick Woods grabbed their missed shot off the rim, threw it to me as I was breaking down the left side of the court and we were off. I never even looked at Diresk or Chip Hathaway who were both streaking down the court on either side of me as I drove the ball down the center of the court.

I was going to the rim and was not about to be stopped. I pump-faked to Diresk, took a long step with my right foot and sailed passed a confused defender, planted my left foot and launched myself towards the hoop and laid the ball in effortlessly as my right hand brushed the upper edge of the rim.

It was a great move. I never even saw the Desmet defender slide underneath me until I fell on top of him, spraining my ankle. The referee blew the whistle and I knew I was out of the game. My final foul. No basket.

I limped to the bench, replaced by Doug Knutson. We were tied with less than one minute left on the game clock. Plenty of time for anything to happen.

To this day, I know it was a terrible call. The Desmet guy was not even close to set when he slid under me. I knew it. Coach Luitjens knew it. Hell, even the other official talked to me after the game and told me his partner had blown a couple calls and I should never have received as many offensive fouls. It probably would not have mattered, but it still makes me sick to my stomach when I think about that game. Something inside me had kept us from winning. Kept *me* from winning.

Now I realize it was fear of success.

My next foolish move continues to haunt me to this day. Just before I reached my team's bench, I felt the necessity to provide the referee with some constructive feedback.

"How long you been refereeing basketball, three days?" I asked.

"Sit down, son. He had plenty of time to get position on you and I was right there to make that call," the official replied, pointing me to a seat next to my disappointed and red-faced coach.

"You better read up on the rules a little more before you put that uniform on again," I heatedly issued and sat down.

His patience thinned, he blew the whistle and issued a technical foul.

I was stunned. Mortified at what I had done. Coach Luitjens glared at me. All I could do was shake my head, wordlessly. The pain in my ankle was no longer apparent as the opposing crowd issued taunts to me and to my teammates who stood helplessly on the court.

The Desmet player made the foul shot and they got the ball back. I held my head between my hands and prayed for a miracle. But the tide had turned and Desmet's momentum was too much for us as we allowed them to score again, then turned the ball over against their pressing defense.

I don't remember anything else about that game other than we lost. We lost and we kept on losing the rest of the year. My game all but disappeared on me, and we were upset in our district tournament and didn't go on to state. We did manage to tie with Spearfish for the conference title, but it meant nothing to us. I finished the year averaging ten points a game. I had been averaging twenty before the Desmet game. I fell apart. I simply fell apart.

One day after the season was over, Diresk and I were hanging around downtown and a local business owner came out of his store to talk to us. He greeted us both and asked us if we were going to college and the usual jazz. Then, he looked down at his feet and said something I will never forget.

"Chris, I've been watching basketball in this town for over twenty years and you were the most exciting player I ever saw in a Custer uniform. I never saw anyone handle the ball like you could. Too bad you could never see it. You break my heart, son."

He excused himself and went back into his store, leaving me with a pain in my stomach and a taste in my mouth I get from time to time. After a time, Diresk spoke. "I knew the minute you quit playing that game at Desmet. I saw it happen and I couldn't do a friggin' thing to stop it or get you going again. You are going to break a lot of hearts, Topher. You're not going to change though…until you break your own bad enough. Let's go, man. I need some medicine."

Chapter Fifteen

I rummaged through a cardboard box a few days ago and was struck breathless by the sight of a basketball. I had not seen it in four of five years and was surprised to find it fully inflated. Our basketball.

Diresk and I used the same Wilson Jet leather basketball whenever we shot hoops. I received it as a Christmas gift from my step-father in 1977 and Diresk kept it at his house because he knew it drove me crazy. It was beautiful when it was brand new. I used to smell it and lick the dirty spots off. I managed to keep it in pristine order until Diresk finally talked me into playing outdoors with it on the asphalt courts at Custer's grade school.

Consecrated ground for a round baller in Custer. I shall never forget the games we played there on steamy summer afternoons when everyone got a chance to play like a pro. The rims were only eight feet above the jagged ground which tore layers upon layers of skin from our knees and elbows whenever we fell. Nearly every player could dunk, and attempted to, every time the ball was touched. We customized the rims with red, white and blue nets and on some afternoons had cheerleaders. It was quite simply the place to be if the sun was shining and the fish weren't biting.

Diresk and I played on the same team. I don't recall losing many games, but you know how far pride can fly unchecked. Unquestionable facts regarding "mini-rim" basketball may be shared.

Passing was not part of the game. Defense would be played only to prevent one's opponent from executing a dunk. Rebounding was crucial because God only knew when anyone would get to touch the ball again.

Another interesting aspect of playground pickup games was the "defense calls their own fouls" rule. It was an honor among thieves set-up that resulted in a tremendous number of fistfights and injurious misunderstandings among fierce competitors, all vying for the attentions and affections of a handful of aloof, dreamy-eyed maidens.

As I write these memories down, I'm able to recall specific games and joyous moments, one decade in passing. My favorite will always be the day Diresk signed my ball. Sophomore summer.

We had just conquered a spirited bunch of upperclassmen who had sauntered onto our turf to treat us to a nasty thwarting, and were basking in their demise with a round of Dr. Peppers and cigarettes. Our humbled foes demanded a rematch.

Diresk thanked them for their offer but failed to acquiesce without first scheduling an emergency team meeting.

"No way, man!" Kenna Venekamp spoke first in our huddle. "We beat the seniors and they're gonna be out for blood this time. We won... now let's split."

"We can take these assholes again. No problemo," Diresk countered.

"We got lucky, man!" I interjected, nursing a scraped knee with a chilled soda bottle. The "referees" had been unkind to us in the contest and all of us were battle-scarred. "I do not feel the need to subject myself to torture again. Look at them. They're pissed! The next game won't be a picnic, I can..."

"This is our turf!" Diresk said.

"I'm not sure you are aware of the full extent of this situation," I attempted. "These guys can make our lives hell if they want to, D. They're not going to practice good basketball fundamentals to beat us this time. They'll hurt us and hurt us bad. And if we manage to somehow win again, they'll kill us. Violently!"

"Vote!" Diresk piped into the mix.

Four hands went up to retire healthy and fight another day. Diresk shook his head, crushed his cigarette beneath a Converse, and strolled over to deliver the poll results.

"Chicken shit assholes," he shot back to us.

Our decision had not been received graciously to say the least. Before any of us knew what happened, Diresk switched to boxing and squared off against a horizontally and vertically gifted senior behemoth answering to the name of Don Burdeen.

"Oh shit. They're going to kill us," I whispered to Kenna Venekamp, who was eyeing the exit.

Diresk fought valiantly, but was no match for Burdeen, who outweighed him by at least thirty pounds. My friend landed more punches early in the fight, exciting and terrifying his teammates simultaneously, but was finally caught by a staggering right hook that snapped his head back and brought him to his scraped knees.

Always a trooper, Diresk gave himself an eight count and staggered to his feet to reengage. Just as Burdeen was to deliver the "lights out" blow, a miracle happened in the sound of an automobile horn.

All heads turned to locate the source of the metallic howl and unconsciously shifted positions as local highway patrolman, Dean Fix, emerged from his cruiser and glared towards the ring with flexing nostrils that often appeared to smoke like a recently fired double barreled shotgun.

In short, we were collectively chastised by a tongue lashing we wouldn't soon forget and the seniors were ordered to evacuate the premises. The seniors swore further revenge as they drifted through the chain link gate, taunting our bloodied hero, Diresk, who by this time had managed to recoup his faculties, poise, and equilibrium to bark counteroffensives. The cheerleaders and fans had long since vanished. And our team was asked to stay after the game by our gun-toting savior.

Patrolman Fix was a voracious basketball fan and would occasionally take a break from his highway duties to catch a game or two at the playground. He never missed a high school basketball game and received an honorary seat in the gym's front row. His timing had reached beyond impeccable that afternoon, as had his closing remarks.

"You guys play them horses?" Patrolman Fix asked from behind his ever-present toothpick.

We nodded in unison. Five kittens watching a yo-yo.

"Beat them?" His eyebrows and toothpick pointed up towards the cloudless sky.

Again, we nodded.

"Let's see the nose," he snorted and Diresk approached, head bent back.

"It's not broke," Diresk proudly announced as Fix palmed his head with both hands, concurring.

"Get the hell out of here," Fix ordered, tucking his thumbs in his gun belt and stretching his back and shoulders.

We all filed towards the gate eyeing each other nervously, wearing our bittersweet grins.

"Diresk!" Fix shouted, halting our hearts and steps. We turned to face him as the sun reflected off no less than ten parts of his body.

"Yeah?" Diresk answered.

"You were doing good, but next time don't forget to duck."

Diresk broke into a smile that infected the four of us for the rest of the day. He was our hero and we told him as much. That was when he signed my ball after absorbing our adulation.

"To Topher," he said as he wrote the words in permanent black marker. "Don't forget to duck! Love, D."

I'm going to sleep with that ball tonight.

Chapter Sixteen

THE GAS STATION

My first real job was working for my next door neighbor at his service station. I temporarily worked as a bus boy at the Trade Winds Restaurant when I was twelve, but it only lasted a few weeks because I was too nervous to work. Here again, fear kicked at my insides and all I could do was lie there and bleed inside.

I ran away from that restaurant one day and I never went back. It was the first time I ever seriously considered killing myself. I sat up on the hill behind my house after leaving my shift and begged God to take my life. I wanted so desperately to be brave. Strong. Peaceful. Just like Diresk. But nothing happened.

I began working at the gas station a couple years later for a friend of our family, Dar Heuer. This time, I did not freak out and fell in love with my job. Gasoline was fifty cents a gallon.

And, I was good at fixing tires! The best. I could work that tire machine faster than anyone would believe. Fixing flats became somewhat of a meditative experience for me. One move flowed into the next and customers would enjoy watching me. I could locate a leak, patch it, and slam it back on a vehicle before a song would end on the radio that blared constantly in the shop.

My mother would tell me how handsome I looked in my uniform and I believed her. I never wore a dirty one. That from a kid who could conceivably don the same pair of jeans for weeks at a time.

I also excelled at making side money from pop machines and neglecting to ring up cash sales. Of course, I treated myself to a free tank of gas now and then, and my car burned the best that money did not have to buy. Premium. Ironically, I have not used it since.

Diresk would talk me through my periodic guilt episodes, insisting my actions were nothing more that "creative financing". I worked hard. I deserved a little fringe with my salary. This was also the source of our booze and drug money. My paycheck, at Mother's urging, went straight into the old college fund. She'd not see me pilfering my savings account to secure illicit recreational substances.

I was a good son.

I became so dependable and efficient, my boss would leave for hours at a time and let me run the place. I was proud of his trust in me and gained much confidence. I loved conversing with tourists and went out of my way to charm tips and chuckles from them.

Custer was and is a tourist town, crammed full with travelers the whole summer long. I enjoyed the customer rushes and when I worked alone, I was fast. That is, when I was not bothered by Diresk who rarely, if ever, worked.

One hot day I was at the station alone when Diresk brought me some lunch and a much-needed joint to alter my weary senses. He had an idea. He said it was a really good one.

"I do not know why I waste my precious summertime to hang around with your sorry ass," Diresk said, his cigarette bouncing around his chapped lips. "You work too much, Larry. You got the rest of your life to do this shit. Do you have any idea how many bikinis are probably out at the lake today? Do you want me to tell you how many I think are out at the lake today?"

I didn't wish for him to tell me, so I wolfed down the sandwiches he had brought me. I was a working man and couldn't be bothered, nor tempted, by such slothful nonsense. I chewed as Diresk rambled on.

"I shall tell you how many beautiful bikini-clad maidens I think are scorching their finely tuned chassis at the lake today. More than both of us could shake a pecker at!"

"Wonderful," I said. "So go out there then."

"Got a better idea, Slim. Why don't you call Darwin and tell him you've been puking your guts out and you have to split before it goes terminal?"

"I can't, man. He's…"

"'Can't' is just a word you can't afford to use, Virgil. We don't get days like this too much around here and you need to get some sun on your skin because you're starting to look like a friggin' oyster."

"Dar went to Rapid today. He won't be back until late tonight," I informed my friend. "I'm stuck here, so why don't you take your complaining ass out of here and go to the lake yourself. Leave me some smoke. I have to work till close because Wayne can't come in tonight. His back is all messed up again and he can't even get out of bed."

"That's fascinating stuff, Larry. Hold it. I'm getting something! Yes! A thought has just arrived to save the day, Ivory Face. Where'd it go? It was just here and it felt like a great idea. Hmmm. Yes! I have it! What say we do a bit of adjusting to the power supply? No power, no work."

"No!" I yelled. "Absolutely not. I mean it."

"Where's the box for this joint, Slim? Got me some work to do. We'll be up to our eyeballs in babes in one hour." Diresk always checked his arm for a watch when discussing time, though I never saw him wear one.

Before I could begin to cross-examine him, he dashed out of the office and grabbed his cigarettes from his truck. Grover was in the cab wearing the swimming trunks Diresk designed for her. She could never jump down from the truck by herself and waited whenever Diresk opened the door until it was time for her to get out. Then she'd rush to the edge of the seat to be plucked from the vehicle.

I helplessly watched as my best friend slammed Grover's face in the door for the millionth time and jogged into the office to make his way into the back of the station. I always flinched whenever Diresk would slam the door behind him.

I boldly stepped in front of him, shifting the sandwich mass in my mouth to my cheek for verbal protest. "NO! I mean it, D. You are NOT going near the box and you are NOT going to screw up the power here. Do you want to get me fired or killed? I need this job. I don't get money from my mamma like some of us do around here and I need to have an income! Do you understand what I am saying to you? Wipe that smile off your face because I'm not listening to you. I mean it, D! Let me spell it out for you. I WILL NOT DO IT AND NEITHER WILL YOU! I have next Saturday off and we can go to the…"

"Screw Saturday! We may not be alive that long, Topher. Where's the box, and wipe your face off. You look like you been eating out of

Grover's dish. Come on…where's the box? Give, give, give. Screw it. I'll find it myself."

Distracted by the mustard streak on the back of my hand, I was unable to stop Diresk from dashing past me into the service area to locate the breaker box. My terrified self trailed behind him.

"Don't go in there, D.! Dar will know we did something to mess it up and I am not going down again because of another one of your great ideas. Just go to the lake and chase your girls without me. Party your brains out. Maybe I can get another day off."

"Hello there, Mr. Fuse Box," Diresk proudly announced. "I'm going to need some tools, Larry. What the hell am I saying? We're in a friggin' gas station. I need a screwdriver and some electric tape. And maybe a hammer. Oh, and get me one of those wire cutters and a soldering iron. Toph? You going to just stand there shitting your pants, or are you going to help me? Get moving!"

"Oh, Jesus Christ! I'm so dead. I'm fired and going to prison. Diresk, I will kill you if you do anything to that box. I mean it!"

"How much power you think this thing's got running through it? If I'm wearing rubber soles it can't fry me, right?" Diresk sized up the fuse box with his hands on his hips. I needed about ten cigarettes to calm my nerves.

"I'll kill you if you do anything, D.! I swear I will kill you, and I'll call the police if you…"

"Better not call the cops if you kill me, Jerry. I'd just take my truck and get the hell gone. You know, I think if I short this wire out with this part right here it'll knock the whole shebang out of business."

"Dammit, Diresk! I'm not kidding, man. This is my job and this is serious. You screw up the power and it'll cost Dar a fortune to…"

Diresk spun on me mid-sentence and pinned my shoulders against the wall of the shop. He had a smile on his face. I knew he wasn't going to hurt me. I knew he was going to change my mind.

"Most young men would be honored to have a guardian angel the likes of me, and you just bitch, bitch, bitch." Diresk kissed me hard on the cheek. I was rapidly losing ground.

"Topher? How long are you going to act like a sissy? This is *our* town. We rule this place and there ain't nothing or nobody going to stop us! What's Dar going to do?"

"Fire me, cut off my scrotum, and have me thrown in prison."

"Oh, DAMN! Your friggin' life would be over! Who cares if you lose your job? And you're not going to lose your job because nobody's going to question the fact the fuse box is old and just messed up. It happens, Cecil. Shit breaks down and that's why everybody's got jobs. It's Sunday and he won't be able to get it worked on anyway, so he's got no choice but to close down for the day. No big deal. Just one day."

He let this soak in before continuing. I was starting to drown.

"Dar trusts you with his business and he's not going to think you have the balls or brains to do something like this. That's where I come in, Pal. I got plenty of both! Plenty to go around for all you misguided and troubled souls. We have gotten along pretty well up to this point and have pulled more shit in this town than anyone ever thought of trying. Right? Am I lying? Topher? Am I?"

I looked down at my shoes and dejectedly shook my head. He had me. Nothing short of divine intervention could have helped me at this point. He could always waltz through my boundaries like they were tissue paper. I felt like a prisoner helping my executioner weave his rope for my afternoon hanging.

"If I'm lying, I'm crying. You and I both know I'll never do that. You've got to have faith in your best buddy, Buford," he continued with a better than usual grin.

"What are you going to do?" I asked him, completely defeated. There was nothing left for me to do but stand back and watch my life be destroyed. My best friend had already selected a few tools from the work bench. He lit a fresh cigarette to prepare for his hostile takeover of my life.

The station bell rang and I nearly jumped out of my uniform. A car pulled into the full service island and I was forced to leave Diresk to his dirty deed while I attended to it. I meekly approached the car and could not, for the life of me, recall how I usually greeted a customer.

I filled the car with gasoline, washed the windows and checked the oil. My heart slammed against my chest. Somehow, I managed to give the man his change and send him off. I dashed back inside the garage to check on my friend's diabolical progress. I barely reached the lobby when I felt and heard the power go. Everything was dead. I made my deliberate trek to the utility room, dark by now, and peered through the doorway.

"Diresk? What did you do? I can't believe you really did this to me! Diresk? Don't play games with me, you asshole! I'm going to kill you."

My throat slammed shut with my breath as my foot touched his body on the ground. I immediately fell to my knees and, gripped with fear, ordered Diresk to cease his sick, little game.

"I know you are okay and I'm not falling for any of this shit. Diresk?"

I shook him. I tickled him. I hit him in the stomach. Nothing.

"DIRESK? You son of a bitch! Oh God, what do I do now? Diresk… if you are messing with me, this isn't funny anymore. I'm calling an ambulance and you are in deep shit when they get here!"

Nothing.

I felt for a pulse. I was positive I felt one, but was not certain if it was his or mine beating fast in my disoriented state. I gave him one more chance.

"I'm calling them now. If you are messing with me you better come clean!"

I ran to the lobby phone and dialed 9-1-1 as loudly as I could, quietly disconnected the call, and pretended to firmly speak to the dispatcher.

"I'm at Dar's Mobil station and I need an ambulance right away. My friend just got electrocuted or something, and I think he may be dead. Please hurry!"

I slammed down the receiver and loudly announced "I called them, Diresk! They are on their way! You better come clean in a hurry because I'm telling them the truth when they get here!"

Again nothing.

I freaked!

I ran to the doorway, then back to the phone.

"Oh, Jesus! I'm sorry. I'll call them. Don't die, D.! I can't make it without you in this world! Shit!"

I frantically dialed 9-1-1, heard the first ring, then felt a hand on my shoulder. I have no idea why my heart did not split in half.

"Got ya!" Diresk announced and fell to his knees in laughter.

I stood there blinking until I heard a faraway voice on the phone. I quickly hung up and stared at the phone. I could not figure out what in God's name had just happened. Had I talked to the dispatcher? Were they on their way? Was my boss going to still fire me? I was confused, pissed off, and scared beyond belief.

"You son of a bitch!" I said as I kicked him.

He continued to laugh hysterically on the lobby floor. "'I thought you were dead!' That is really funny, man! You are so cool."

I stood there with my eyes closed and listened to his hysterics. I could not disappear off the face of the Earth fast enough. I really wanted to.

"I suppose you ruined the box, too," I muttered. "Not only did you make a fool out of me, I'm still going to get fired. Nice friend. My best buddy. Thanks a lot!"

I considered kicking him in the face as hard as I could, decided against it, and shuffled around the counter. I sat down behind the cash register to think. I had to clear my head before I made my next move.

Suddenly, electric devices sprang to life as power surged through the station, startling me. I dejectedly waited for his next assault.

"Just hit the main," Diresk proudly announced as he turned the corner from the garage. "You're not going to hold this against me for the rest of our lives, are you? I still get to be your son's godfather and everything? Topher? Come on, man. You have got to admit that was friggin' great. One of my greatest moments." He shrugged. "One of your worst. Hey, I'm sorry. Look at me, man." He moved towards me.

"Get out!" The words that escaped my mouth surprised me.

"You have just received an important lesson, free of charge, from the universe. Well, *don't* thank me or anything. You just burn in anger over there and I'll do the talking, okay? Cool."

"Get out!"

"The lesson is that you can't take yourself or life so friggin' seriously, Jack. Laugh at yourself, and who cares if the world laughs with you or not? Not me, man. Hey, you got a customer. I better split if I'm going to bag me a lake babe. Give me a hug."

"GET OUT!"

"I'm going, Jerry," Diresk said. "Tone it down before you get hemorrhoids. I must get my finely tuned chassis to the lake anyway. Call me tonight."

Diresk started for the door, turned, grabbed a stick of beef jerky from the counter, and said, "For Grover." He shoved the door open and raised his brows for a final pearl of petulance. "Toph? The fake ambulance call was a nice touch, really. You're getting better at this stuff, man. One thing though. You should've seen your face when I snuck up on you. Priceless."

With that he was gone. I watched him back out of the lot and disappear around the corner before I could bring myself to forgive him and share in his laughter. The one thing I couldn't figure out was why he didn't get up when I pretended to call 9-1-1 the first time. I thought he must have had balls of ice for that one. Did he know I would fake it once just to see if he would react? Did he know me that well?

90

Later, he would insist he knew what I was going to do and had planned the whole thing to go exactly as it had. I was so amazed by his ability to read me. Although he made a fool out of me, I looked up to him even more. It would be a couple months before he could take it no longer and had to 'fess up.

"I listened on the phone…in the back, you dipstick!"

Chapter Seventeen

I remember the time Diresk talked me into dropping acid before going in to work. I told him there was no way I was going to go to work tripping, but he had a way of putting things so they didn't sound so bad. We met for breakfast that morning. He was on his way to Bismarck Lake to go fishing and I, of course, was on my way to fill gas tanks and fix flats.

"My main man," Diresk said, "I have a little something special for you to help make your employment an adventure today. All you must do is suck on this tiny piece of paper, and fairly soon, you will find yourself starring in your own movie. Purple microdot or something like that. Jimmy Hendrix shit. Vietnam and Woodstock."

"Yeah, right," I said in a sarcastic tone. "I'm going to drop acid and go work where I have to deal with tourists and my boss all day with purple people flying at me. Excellent idea! While I am at it, why don't I just try to take an engine apart and see if I can get it back together again. I don't think work is an appropriate environment to experiment with hallucinogenics, D."

"Work is the perfect place to experiment with acid, Jerry. Where else can you get paid to do drugs? I'm not going to give you too much. You'll just get a little goofy and have a ton of energy. Just like with those mushrooms we took last summer. I'll drop one too and we can meet back tonight and share our adventures. Come on, Topher, live a little."

"What if I wig out and have to leave or something? Dar would friggin' kill me if I screwed something up."

"What in the hell are you going to screw up?" Diresk asked. "Put a tire on inside out? You're not exactly the main man around there. 'Oh,

I'm sorry, sir. I put gasoline in your radiator. What in God's name was I thinking. Must be the acid.' Come now and partake of this cerebral feast."

Diresk handed me a tiny piece of paper across our breakfast table, placing another on his tongue and wagging it at me like a dog's tail. I obediently inserted mine and silently cursed myself for being such a submissive dolt.

"Atta boy. Just a little tab'll do you. I must split. I'll come by the station later if I haven't completely lost my mind by then. Good luck trying to make change today, Virgil. Grab the check and we'll call it even on the dope. Later days."

Diresk grabbed some toast off the table, tipped his hat to an older tourist couple next to us, and left the restaurant, leaving me to my impending sense of doom and flickering paranoia. I had fifteen minutes to get to work, and by the time I arrived to open the station for the day, I had convinced myself I would be okay. It might actually be a fun day. I didn't know what to expect, but I *assumed* it would be something like taking mushrooms. It would be a serious miscalculation.

I was alone that morning as I worked with Dar, who would usually show up around lunchtime, unless I got really busy and called him in. A giddy feeling had begun to overtake me as I performed my opening duties and prepared for the morning traffic. It was kind of like the feeling when you haven't slept for a long time and everything starts to seem really funny.

My first customer pulled into the full service island and I strutted out to make the first sale of the day.

I remember engaging this gentleman in small talk about the weather and how beautiful the area was. Everything was going smoothly until he followed me to the lobby to pay for his gasoline. I think I told him a joke. Maybe he told me one.

I started to laugh. I would not stop for several hours. The customer had this strange look on his face. I'm sure he did not fully appreciate the humor of the moment the way I did. His eyes told of his deep concern for my sanity and well-being as he backed out of the building and jogged to his car.

If you have never laughed for six hours straight, you probably have no conception of what I endured that day. It sounds better than it was. I was laughing, but I was not happy or full of glee. I was freaked out of my mind. Things were happening around me that only I could see.

Thank God business was slow that morning. I managed to make it through a couple tire repairs and the gasoline trade. Dar came in around lunchtime but immediately knew something was up with me.

"Christopher, what the hell is wrong with your eyes? You look like you've seen a ghost."

Actually, I had probably witnessed colors shooting from Dar's head or traces of his words as they bolted from his mouth. Falling into hysterical guffaws had not helped my situation any and proved to be an untimely maneuver as my boss circled me as if I was a live grenade. I fought desperately for control of my cascading emotions and visual mirages, but to no avail. I completely lost it!

I escaped to the restroom as his questions came at me from behind, laughing and terrified as I slammed the door and locked it behind me. Slowly, I forced myself to the mirror to have a serious talk with myself. Distracted by the image of the left side of my face melting, I closed one eye and gave myself a much inspired, yet doleful pep talk that bounced uselessly off the reflective glass and fell into an ignored heap to the floor, next to my facial features.

It's difficult to change tires amidst a fit of hysterics when one's face is dripping like wax off of one's skull. Still, I held tight to the hope I could regain my composure with ancient deep breathing techniques such as those used by fakirs who could stop their hearts and exist without oxygen. I collapsed on the toilet to implement my meditative blueprint when suddenly someone pounded on the metal door, jolting me into a giggling, terror-induced hiccupping frenzy.

Nothing like spasmodic inhalations and the closing of vocal chords, laced with intermittent laughing gasps to send a hallucinating gas jockey on a dry-heaving, puking jag. A trilogy of terror one should avoid, if at all possible.

This act merely serves to heighten both awareness and potency of such a drug experience. It's somewhat like consuming twelve cups of coffee, then injecting an amphetamine derivative directly into your brain. Diresk called it, "The ultimate brain blow job".

I couldn't imagine what Dar was thinking. I hoped he thought I was drunk. I entertained the notion of making a break for my car, but my keys were in Dar's office and I was in no shape for another confrontation with my employer. I was forced to wait it out, hoping for a lapse in the drug's hold on me and a vomit reprieve. I slid to the floor and closed my eyes, trying for calm. Though, I continued to laugh like a tickled hyena.

Diresk, I would later learn, did not go fishing that morning, and instead had parked across the street to monitor said fiasco from a Laundromat window with some pals of ours. Smoking cigarettes and joints as thick as pencils, they fought over a pair of binoculars and mirthfully watched my scenario unfold like a diseased blanket.

I don't know how long I stayed in the bathroom, but I knew I had to eventually leave it. I gathered myself up, took a deep breath, and reentered the work force. I was a bit surprised, to say the very least, to see my mother waiting for me in the office with Dar, who was waiting on a customer.

At first, I thought maybe I was hallucinating and she wasn't really there. When she grabbed my arm and ushered me to the back room, I understood this was not to be the case.

"Christopher, what have you done to yourself?" Mom cried. She had been operating under a current prevarication her little angel was drug-free.

I would later be briefed Diresk had requested a moment of prayer for me when they had seen my mother pulling into the station lot. This was immediately followed by a hand slapping session. My buddies!

"MOM!" I said. "Hi. Um…I haven't done anything to myself. I'm not feeling well. I think I must have eaten something bad at the Skyway this morning. I feel really weird and dizzy and stuff."

My delivery would have been greatly enhanced had I been able to complete even a fragment of my recitation without chortling myself to tears. My mother looked as if she would collapse if even a bumblebee burped on her. I hurt for her concern and her abashment, deeply. But Mom probably couldn't tell from my seemingly jovial demeanor.

At this point, Dar entered the office. He was not a happy man.

"Dar, do you want me to take my lunch now? I can hurry back if you get busy," I offered.

"I think you better go home for the day. We can talk about this tonight when I get home. I'm going to call Wayne in to finish your shift. You can't be around here like this, Chris. What is wrong with you, for Christ's sake? Mrs. Thomas called me at home this morning and was worried about you after she came in for gas. She said you were dancing around while you were filling up her car and you kissed her forehead when she paid. Who else did you offend this morning? What am I supposed to tell my customers when my employee does that? You can't go around kissing people on the forehead. Jesus H. Christ!"

I froze up. I couldn't believe what was happening. I honestly could not remember kissing Mrs. Thomas or dancing around the pumps. All I could do was turn around and walk to my car, leaving my mother in tears and my boss glaring at me. I couldn't stop laughing, and to make things worse, I had to go back inside to get my car keys after trying to start my car without them. Neither Mom or Dar wanted me to drive but I dashed to my car before losing an argument.

I drove out of town. I guess the adrenaline kicked the acid into another gear because I was totally fried, and couldn't make heads or tails out of anything. I pulled into the golf course parking lot and laid down to die, giggling like some panic-struck firing squad target. I was afraid to open my eyes for fear of what I'd see next.

My heart raced. I could not slow down. I had to move. Had to get out of the car and walk. Somewhere.

It was then Diresk's truck slid to a halt beside me, followed by a cloud of dust that stung my eyes. He ordered me to shut off my engine and get in with him. I was ecstatic to see him and quickly complied. Then, I remembered whose goading had led me to my current status. Fighting through my concrete smile, I threw open the door, jumped out of the truck, took an awkward swing at a barking Grover, and launched into a chastising.

I told him I would never talk to him again and our friendship was over. I meant it, too, until he flew out and around the truck and tackled me. We laughed so hard we threw up together. Nearly in each other's arms.

Those were good times.

We drove his truck up Needles Highway and sat by the tunnel to watch our brains make things up for our eyes. We stayed there until the kaleidoscopic sun nodded and disappeared under rubber rocks and trees. I still felt I could run a hundred miles if I needed to. We must have smoked about five packs of cigarettes and consumed a case of beer, but neither of us felt remotely intoxicated. Just omniscient. I think we split a Seconal or something, and that helped us slow down some. I know we smoked a ton of dope after the darkness surrounded us, providing respite from the non-stop visual circus.

I suddenly remembered my mother tucking me in at night as a child and holding my puppy in my arms as I tried to make things better with my prayers. Hating God for allowing the dog to be hit by a car as its blood spilled into my lap. Even believing I could bring it back to life if I just believed. *If I just believed.*

I remembered Christmas and my grandfather's voice singing carols in my ear as we watched cars drive past the picture window, making bets on what color the next car would be. Hours of tape rolled past my eyes, and the sights and senses and sounds of my life returned to me, all within seconds.

Then the fear. Sneaking up from behind the truck to pounce upon my chest and stomach.

I remember crying. Like some artery in my soul was bleeding and it wouldn't ever stop. I will never forget asking Diresk a question that shook my very foundation.

"D.?" I said. "I don't think I'm supposed to do drugs. Do you think you can lose your soul?"

"Oh, Topher. Don't go wacky on me now, man. Let's just sit back and buzz out."

"Be my friend, please? Do you think you can lose your soul?"

He glanced over at me. "No. I don't think you can lose or sell your soul. I think God's got all the angles covered and he's not going to let us go down that way, no matter what. Drugs are not your problem, Slim. You *are* your problem and the only problem you'll ever have. Same as me."

I shook my head. "You don't even know what..."

"Same as me! I'm just better at not listening to the wrong voices. This is all part of life, man. It's no friggin' miracle you're having problems and doubting yourself. Everybody's got a place inside they have to get to sometime in their lives. It's way down deep. You probably don't ever know you're going there until you get there. People can go to shrinks their whole life and it won't do a friggin' bit of good until they get down to this place and just face what's there in front of them."

"How the hell am I supposed to do that?" I asked. "Huh? Face something I can't even see or don't even know where it is? Cripes, D. I'm dying, man! I feel like I'm getting sucked out from the inside, and I'm scared!"

"And you're going to be scared till you go down there and beat it. My place is like a cave. Black and cold. Like putting your hand in mud just about froze up. Whole point of life is to get down to that place and kick some ass, man! You've got to go down there and kick some ass."

He wasn't listening. "I'm tired of feeling scared all the time.

Sometimes, when I get high too much, I feel like I'm leaving some part of me farther and farther behind. I'm not like you. You don't..."

"Who gives a shit about that? You're not me. You're not like me, and you won't ever be. Don't you see? You don't *have* to be like anyone, man. Who gives a damn about what the rest of the world's like?"

"What I'm trying to say is, you don't feel like I do so you're not going to understand. Something horrible is going to happen to me if I don't change. It's like I can't even tell where I am anymore and I don't recognize feelings inside or..."

"You're tripping, Toph. Manage your buzz, man. Cool out and relax a little. Don't get wigged on me because I don't feel like babysitting insanity right now. Paranoia is in there. It's where it comes from—that place. That's where all the fear comes from. You can call it demons or the devil or whatever you want to... It's just some friggin' test we all have to pass before we get to move on, man. There's nothing real about it. You've got to get to where you can see that, Toph."

"It feels so real and big, though. I try to bear it every day, but it keeps coming back no matter how many times I face it. I can't take it anymore. It's too strong."

"It's all just dust and feathers, man. Screw fear! Chase it down to the deepest part of your guts and piss all over it! Kill it! I don't give a shit what you've got to do or how you get it done...just don't quit and don't surrender. Just keep walking through it and don't ever give up. It can't kill you, so what can it really do? Huh? What, man?" He nudged me in the shoulder.

I pulled away. "I can't explain it to you. It's just bigger than me is all. I don't know how else to explain it. It's just got me down and I can't get it off my chest. If there is some magical place inside of me where I can go to beat it...then God is going to have to show me where it is because I don't..."

Diresk interrupted me. "You can go there anytime you want to, man. All you've got to do is decide to call it out, then get as mad as you can get with it. That's how I beat mine. I get so pissed off I could snap steel with my bare hands and I tell the bastard to leave me alone! You've got to fight it with everything you have. One day, it's going to know you're not quitting no matter what and then it'll just leave. I fight mine, too.

"You're not alone here, okay? Just relax, man. It's all going to be okay. I'm not going to let nothing happen to you...ever. Okay?"

I wanted to tell him I understood. That I was going to rise up to defeat this monster and send it cowering away into the darkest places. All I could do was feel the physical humming of the drugs in my body and hear the doubt, rising up like flames within my chest. I didn't know how to be that angry.

Diresk opened beers for both of us, handed me one, and urinated on the iron guardrail next to the truck, howling and calling his demons out for a fight.

"Toph?" he said. "I feel like I could screw for about three hours straight right now! I feel like a caveman. You want to quit drugs? Quit them. Not me, man. I'm not trading in feeling this way for nothing. Drugs are the only..."

Diresk was quiet a moment. He pierced my eyes with his for a split second, then turned his back to me. He opened the truck's door, and all at once the stereo went dead. I could hear the wind rolling through the trees as if swept by a gigantic broom. It seemed as if I was chewing pine needles, and for a moment, I was no longer afraid.

But moments are designed that way. They change and point us somewhere else. I shall remember, my entire life, the momentum of the fear that struck me hard—like five tons of an iron train—as I sat alone on the hood of that truck. That beautiful summer night with electric trees and a breeze that was our very own. A sky so crisp I could not look at it without closing my eyes and inhaling deeply. Sweet smells colored green. Luminous rocks wearing jagged crowns glared down upon us like giant shadowed gods as my heart hammered and pounded me further and further away from myself. From Diresk.

And then, such sadness and doubt of everything.

I gasped as if something had reached up from inside my body and pulled an alarm in my brain. A bad trip? Pretentious slang tossed around drug culture. For me? It was the beginning of a crucial shattering that would echo and reverberate for years to come. My soul had begun to scream, and though I would ignore its pleas with all the vigor I could muster, I heard it. It had finally gotten through.

And it would be back.

I reached a point during this horrid vacation when I understood I was to make a decision. To either go crazy and never come back, or to somehow fight my way back to reality. It was so strange and clear. I knew I could lose my mind if I didn't fight for it. If I would have given up, I really believe I would have gone insane. Diresk, who invariably tolerated dope better than I, talked and walked me through it. I wandered through my mind's maze, pounding on corridor walls as my feet continued to sink deeper into the endless trails before me.

I laughed and cried and threw up, only to repeat the cycle again. I thought I was going to die. Knew I was going to die. I was a prophet. Not Christ, but with sufficient training and care? I smelled and tasted the blistering breath of demons and monsters as their mouths opened inches from my face and dripped their pungent, boiling sputum on my hands and feet. Slaw-like skinned reptiles crawled upon my back and I could never quite brush them off. Never quite catch them, as they scurried to safety through an opening in my spine.

I understood the seasons and the changes of darkness to light. As I wrapped myself in a blanket and raced through the carved tunnel, removing my clothes to anoint myself with the true night, I lost my footing and fell headlong into the graveled asphalt, my hands still attached to my tennis shoe. I laughed as blood filled my mouth and I felt Diresk's hands halt my fall.

I cried again. Mixed my tears with blood at my chin, as the planets spun and danced around us. I lived *years* that night. Screamed and dreamed my mind to sleep, though my eyes refused to rest or trust.

Maybe Diresk was right after all. Maybe we all have such a place inside us and everything is about going there and returning with its treasures. But what of those who never return? What then? What happens to them?

I made it. By the time Diresk and I ended up at a party at a friend's house after driving back from the Needles, I began to sense a light at the end of the strange tunnel I spent hours wandering.

I know Diresk had been concerned about me, but he covered it with jokes and anecdotes as he stayed with me through my hours of torment. He talked me through the field of land mines I had made for myself. I do not know what would have happened had he not been there to keep my consciousness pointing back to the trail I had left that morning. God only knows where I may have wandered off to then.

I didn't go home that night, but instead sat in Diresk's truck until the sun came up. I didn't sleep at all and spent the whole night considering either suicide or quitting dope for good. Diresk gave me a ride to my car in the morning and when he dropped me off, I didn't even look at him when I closed the door. Grover growled at me which sounded like an airplane taking off between my ears, it was so loud. I felt I had lost twenty pounds.

"I didn't mean to harm you any yesterday, man," Diresk offered. "I just wanted you to have some fun. I hope everything is cool with your mom. If you need a place to crash you can come over. Don't worry about Dar. All you've got to do is work your ass off for a few days and he'll forgive and forget everything. Dar is cool. He knows what it's like to be young."

I remember looking at Diresk. Somehow he looked haggard, older. I felt sorry for him, even though it was me who was in trouble. I got in my car without saying anything to him and he pulled away, spraying gravel all over the side of my car. It was at least a half an hour before I could bring myself to start the car and drive home to face my mother. I knew my step-father was at work, or I wouldn't have even considered going home to face that explosion. I should have never taken the acid. I should have went home and talked to Dar the previous night. I should have called my mom to tell her I was okay.

I started my car and listened to the engine purr for several minutes before I caught my eye in the rearview mirror. I wanted out. I wanted something I was not sure even existed and had no idea how to find. So much of me had leaked from my pores. I tried to pray. I couldn't get a word to form in my mouth. What would I say to God? I'm sorry?

I stared into my eyes in the mirror and something worked its way past the fog and my anxiousness, pushing to the front as if to catch me before I looked away. I cannot name it. Ego? Evil? Addiction? Simple words to paint below pictures we can never understand or label. It was an old friend who had stopped over to console me. With a wink of my eye, a slight smile came over the corners of my lips.

"You will never take acid again, you dumb son of a bitch! You knew better than to try that shit. You and I are going to stick with what we know and what we trust. You're going to have to quit someday. Just not today."

I prepared and smoked a pinch-hit of dope, turned up Jerry Jeff as loud as he could sing, and somehow found the courage to return home to a terrified mother in tears and a house full of luggage, packed for my guilt trip.

Chapter Eighteen

I can't recall a time when I felt closer to Diresk than the afternoon he showed up at the station, crying. I was absolutely floored by his overt display of emotion. Something I had never directly experienced or seen before.

I had just finished a service job and was ringing up the bill for a gentleman who was from out of town when I saw my friend's truck pull up beside the station, and park. He waited in his truck until the gentleman left, and that's when I realized something was wrong.

Diresk entered the lobby wearing dark glasses, and I could sense he had been crying. I could not force the words forming in my mind to escape from my mouth. Diresk broke the silence for both of us.

"I need some smokes, man. I'm losing it, Topher. I can't believe my dad! He hit my mom in the face this morning and I want to kill him! I swear if I had a gun, I'd shoot him!"

"Oh, man. I'm sorry, D.," I said. "Is she okay?"

"All she did was ask him about some checks he forgot to write down or something. He's not like this, man. I mean…he gets drunk and pissed off at me sometimes…but you know him. Right?"

"I guess so."

"He slaps me once in a while when I get smart with him. He's never hit my mom. Jesus Christ, man. I got right in his face and told him if he wanted to hit somebody he could hit me! I've never seen him like that, man. He freaked out. Mom was lying on the floor and everything went black."

"Jesus. I don't know what to say, man. Jesus."

Diresk shook his head. "He had tears in his eyes and he shoved me down on the couch and just took off. Mom was bleeding from her nose and I had to get out of there. I couldn't even help her, Toph. I couldn't even say nothing to her! I friggin' left. I've got to sit down, man. Got them smokes?"

I reached behind the counter and tossed him his favorites. Lucky Strikes. I found some matches and handed them to him. I wanted to put my hand on his shoulder to comfort him but I was too afraid. All I could manage to do was stand there. Waiting for him to guide me to my next move.

"Oh, man, I got a headache. Got any aspirin?" he asked.

I dashed back to find Dar's bottle in his office. I looked around for something else to help him. *Anything.* It was my chance to be there for my friend and I wanted to do it right.

But I couldn't concentrate. It was like Napoleon had come to ask a foot soldier for support and guidance.

I glanced around the office again for anything that would make him feel better. The safe was locked or I would have given him a bunch of money. I hurried back to the lobby with the aspirin.

I turned the corner to say something to him and saw him staring into his shaking hands. I felt like I was trespassing on sacred ground. I quickly slipped back around the corner and stood with my back against the wall. Listening. Waiting. Hoping nobody would show up. I felt helpless. My heart raced inside my chest. My best friend needed my help and I was impotent. I pounded my head against the wall, gathered my thoughts together, spun around, and walked into the lobby.

I removed a couple of Cokes from the cooler, opened his and handed it to him with the bottle of aspirin. I opened mine and pulled a chair from behind the counter and placed it directly in front of his, our knees nearly touching.

"No whiskey?" Diresk joked through tears. "Thanks." He swallowed a handful of pills, set his Coke down between his boots and rested his face in his hands.

We sat in silence until a customer pulled into the full service island.

"Shit!" I said to the top of his head. "I have to take care of this. If you want, you can go back into Dar's office and relax on the couch. I'll get rid of this guy as soon as I can."

This guy turned into about five or six others, and it was nearly a half hour before I could get back to the office to check on my best friend. I found him smoking a cigarette on the couch, watching cartoons on the office television.

"Sorry about that, D. Got kind of busy there for a while. You need anything? I mean, I know you are okay and everything—"

"No, I am *not* okay and everything! Jesus, Topher. Why do you always think I can handle everything? Don't you think I get all messed up, too?"

"I didn't mean it like that," I said. "It's just...I'm not used to seeing you upset like—"

"I get upset all the friggin' time! Do you think you are the only human being who has a tough time? I hurt all the time! I feel like I'm going to lose my mind just about every day. *Every day,* Topher. I don't run around wearing it like a friggin' badge like you and everybody else does."

"I didn't mean to make you mad or anything, D."

He shrugged. "I can't let this shit beat me down. I keep swinging and the shit just keeps coming at me like a bunch of birds. It comes at me and I swing as hard as I can. Over and over, man. They keep coming and I keep swinging! I'm going to break their skulls! I'm losing my mind, man. I can't do this shit. I can't feel like this all the time!"

Diresk cried harder and pounded his fists against the leather cushions.

"I'm not going down, man! DO YOU HEAR ME? GOD. I AIN'T GONNA QUIT SO YOU CAN THROW WHATEVER YOU WANT AT ME. GOD DAMMIT!" Diresk screamed at the office ceiling, then threw his cigarette through the door into the shop, and stood up blazing.

I held my breath and waited for him to speak as his words continued to bounce off the office walls. What did he mean by cussing God like that? He was always telling me how God was nothing but love and everything. I wanted to ask him what he meant. Did God really do that? Did God *want us* to cave in under His pressure? I started to ask him when he lashed out at me again.

"That's the difference between you and me, Toph," Diresk said. His eyes struggled against the office's fluorescent lighting. "I keep swinging and you keep ducking!"

I dropped my head and stared at the polished tiles, fighting back my own tears. I had not meant to upset him. I wanted to help him in any way I could. I didn't know what he was talking about until later. I felt I had blown it and I wasn't sure why.

"Topher?" Diresk finally spoke and I fought to raise my head to meet his piercing eyes. "Look. I don't want to lay any trip on you, okay? I'm just pissed and upset and I hate doing this shit. I can't remember the last time I cried. I know I haven't cried like this since I was a kid. I'm okay, Toph. Guess I just had to clean some shit out of me. If you tell anyone I blubbered, I'll cut your friggin' tongue out."

He smiled at me and removed another cigarette from the pack I gave him. I smiled too, but I was the one who felt about to cry.

"All I'm trying to tell you is you need to see yourself like I see you. I know what you are capable of. I've seen how strong and brave you can be, man."

"Shit. I wish."

"See? That's what I mean, man. Until you see this yourself, you and me are going to have this thing between us. You'll put me up above you and you won't meet me eye to eye. That's where I need you. I need you right here. With me. You can't see me, because you need me to be some superman or something."

Diresk stood up and tossed his Coke can in the trash. He messed up my hair as he walked past Dar's desk and out the door. I couldn't let him get away this time. I had to get something out. I hurried to catch him before he left the lobby.

"D.? Wait up." I caught the lobby door as it was closing and rushed out behind him. The sun hit my eyes and I saw him turn around like a shadow boxer. Grover barked and jumped in the back of the truck, excited to see him. Diresk silenced him with a wave of his smoking hand.

"I love you, man," I said. "I'll try to be better at that stuff. I don't want to be like this forever. I just don't know how to change yet. I'm sorry about your mom."

"I know. Thanks. It's okay." He smiled half-heartedly. "It's all going to be okay, man."

"If you want to hang out after I get off, call me later. Okay? You mean the world to me, man, and I don't care what you think about me saying this. I just…want to be there for you like you are here for me all the time."

"All you've got to do is get rid of the shit that isn't you, brother," Diresk said. "You don't have to build anything fancy or anything. Just let go of the shit that is keeping you small. Call me tonight when you get off and maybe we can chase some girlies. I've got to get home and see how Ma's doing."

I watched him get into his truck and then flinched as the big engine took off like a gun shot and eased to an idle as Diresk lit another cigarette and dropped it into reverse. He pulled away from the parking lot and I heard Jimmy Buffet begin to sing about Florida. I started back for the lobby when I heard the brakes lock up and the music die just as quickly.

The same anticipatory jitters shot through my body as I turned to face him, squinting into the burning sun.

"Thanks for the smoke and the soda, Slick," Diresk yelled with a faint wave of his head. He sat there and looked at the steering wheel. I waited for him to say more. He rocked forward in his seat and spoke softly. "You know what we are, man? You and I?"

I shook my head, walking closer to the truck.

"We're mechanics of some weird kind. Like them guys who work in the pits at race tracks. We're supposed to help people get back on the road. Like giving them back their wings."

I stared at him. "I don't quite know what you mean, D."

"It's like we're all butterflies inside, but sometimes all we see is the cocoon or whatever. Like you. All you ever see is your cocoon, and all I see is the butterfly. But you're like me. We're different than a lot of people. We have a gift to help people see who they are and not what this friggin' world wants them to see. Our job is to get people out of their cocoons so they can be butterflies. Cocoon mechanics or something. Yeah, that's it. We work on butterflies, man. The butterfly pit crew."

He glanced back at me, turned the stereo up, and nodded at me with eyes connected to something deeper than I had ever seen.

The big truck spun out of the lot and disappeared around the corner towards the grade school. I walked back into the lobby and grabbed another Coke from the cooler, then sat down and lit a cigarette. The butterfly pit crew. I loved the sound of it, though its true concept would escape me for several years.

Chapter Nineteen

"Van Halen was at the station and we missed it?" Diresk had nearly bitten his cigarette in half after hearing my exciting news. He and Grover had stopped to visit me at work on their way home. We had hung out at the lake the previous day and camped out that night. I had left the campsite early in the morning to report for work. Diresk and the dog got to sleep in.

"Wayne told me they were all driving around the Hills in this white van, and they were kicking back and seeing the sights," I answered. "I can't believe they were here on my day off. Man!"

Wayne had worked my shift and had written the name of their band on a piece of paper for me. He had never heard of Van Halen, but he had an idea I would be interested because of all the attention they got from some local kids who had spotted the band from the Dairy Queen and rushed over to meet them. Wayne also told me one of the band members put a hundred dollar bill in a jar we had on the counter to raise money for this friend of mine who was real sick. Diresk and I played basketball with him but he was in Denver now with what they thought was an inoperable brain tumor.

That is a story in itself.

Diresk and I went to visit Doug in Denver, Colorado at the hospital where he was staying that same summer and I didn't think he was going to make it. I'll never forget that day. We were in the room with Doug and his parents. His mom and dad were both crying, and I could tell Doug didn't have much hope left. Diresk tried to get everyone to laugh. I felt terrible and wanted to leave immediately after we had arrived.

All of a sudden, this guy walked in the room and introduced himself to everyone—Doug first. I can't remember this guy's name, but I will never forget what he looked like. He came in that room like God. He was the most confident and together person I had ever seen.

Even Diresk told me later he wished he could be like this guy. Anyway, this guy asks Doug if it would be okay if he looked at Doug's chart and x-rays. Turns out he was this world-renowned neurosurgeon who happened to be in Denver to present some paper at a conference. He had discussed Doug's case with Doug's surgeon, who had requested a consultation.

Doug and his family just nodded and this guy shifts through Doug's chart for a few minutes while we hold our breaths in stunned silence. Then, this guy puts Doug's chart back and politely excuses himself from the hospital room.

We all waited and nobody said a word. A few minutes later, he returns with Doug's doctor and a nurse on his heels. This new guy holds some x-rays up to a light beside Doug's bed and points out some discrepancies to Doug's doctor who nods accordingly.

What happened next was one of the most incredible things I have ever witnessed.

This guy turns to Doug and says, "Why don't we go in and fix you up, Doug? This isn't a tumor. I am positive we are dealing with what we refer to as an abscess growth. Pus surrounded by inflamed tissue. I can go in with a laser and drain this in no time. You will be fine, son. I promise that."

We all dropped our jaws like anchors and Doug began to cry, asking if the surgeon was serious.

"Entirely!" the new guy answered. "Can we get a room to do this quickly, because I have to get on a plane this afternoon?" he asked Doug's doctor who quickly nodded and disappeared with the nurse.

The new guy shook Doug's hand, hugged his parents, shook my hand and Diresk's, and before disappearing out of the room asked us to join him in prayer. I remember being freaked out that this guy believed in God. He was God.

Two hours later, this surgeon had delivered exactly what he said he would.

Unbelievable! Still gives me goose bumps when I think of it. We never saw the surgeon after the procedure. He simply flew away to perform another miracle. And Doug is doing fine.

"I'll bet it was Eddie," Diresk said. "Eddie would be the one to give money to a stranger, man. Van-Friggin'-Halen was here and we were at the lake. Makes me want to get a job, Slick. I will kill myself if I ever hear Farrah Fawcett Majors is in Custer and I miss her! Van Halen. In Custer. I believe we should blow a number in their honor, Gerald."

And we did just that. Several, to be precise.

Chapter Twenty

HOSPITALS

I was hospitalized for depression for the first time in the spring of 1982. I was in there for a month. When it happens, you question most everything you have ever done or believed in. Nervous breakdown. Funny phrase. Unless you have had one. The worst part, for me, had always been the unreachable anger and crushing fear that "it" is never going away. I know why people take their lives. Part of me still wonders why I have not gone through with the act myself.

You wake up and you're in a psychiatric hospital, still unable to grasp the powerlessness and lack of control you have in your life. *Locked up.* Paper slippers and a striped blue robe. I recall being glad I was tan. I'm sure I looked absolutely smashing and dashing to those able to forgive the fact I had lost thirty-five pounds and spent the previous three weeks curled up in a fetal position chain smoking cigarettes and sipping vodka.

Diresk later told me I looked like Iggy Pop, which had been somehow comforting to me. The rock star was still alive in me, but he couldn't leave the building without a doctor's order.

Diresk had learned of what my mother referred to as my "problems" and had driven across the state to check on me and spring me if necessary. I had been attending college at Vermillion's University of South Dakota Business School while Diresk was pursuing studies in Creative Pharmacology with a minor in Coed Debauchery.

I still cannot believe we attended separate institutions. I followed a girl straight into hell. Believe me, nothing short of a desperate addiction to a girl would have pried me from Diresk. God, I went back there to the memories just then. I could nearly smell it. Sioux Falls, McKenna Hospital's Psychiatric Unit.

"Give me Librium, or give me Meth!" Diresk entered the lobby as I was playing cards with my roommate, David. His voice caused an eruption of both panic and hope deep inside me. I could tell he was somewhat nervous.

"I didn't know you were coming, D.," I managed. "This is David. David, this is my friend, Diresk." They shook hands and David excused himself to wash his hands for the thousandth time that day.

"Dave looks a bit frazzled, Bubba," Diresk stated.

After we stared at each other for a few minutes, he continued, "Your mom called me yesterday and told me you were here. You know what I think about shrinks and all this...shit and everything (pointing around us). This isn't easy for me to say, but I've got to tell you the truth."

He took a deep breath and paused.

"I love you like a brother, Topher, but you are the most self-centered son of a bitch I have ever met in my life! You got here because you can't get out of yourself long enough to see any light on the friggin' road! You think the whole world revolves around you, man. Topher's world."

"Look," Diresk said, "I know you're a great human and all that happy horseshit, but you've got to learn to quit sinking your own ship."

Anger welled up inside me and I gathered myself to stand him down. "Do you know how much pain I have been in for the past—"

"WE ALL HAVE PAIN!" Diresk looked around the room at the many faces staring at him. "I can tell you are beat to shit, man. I know it's not easy getting past these demons. I love you, you know that. Right, man?"

I nodded. Tears trickled down my face. Diresk sank to his knees and I could smell the cigarettes on his breath as his face met mine.

"Can I smoke here?" he asked. I nodded and he said, "Thank God!"

He handed me one and we lit up together. After a few drags, he patted my knees, stood up, and took David's chair.

"Just don't die, Topher. We got a whole lifetime to figure this shit out, okay? Don't cash in your chips because you can't see past this. I didn't come down here to beat up on you. I came here because my best friend is in trouble, and there isn't anything more important to me in this world than you being well."

I broke down and melted into his awkward embrace. I could feel his muscles tighten in his strong arms, but he let me hold on to him.

By this time, David had returned from our room and was pacing in a circle, moaning like the wounded warrior he was. Dave couldn't stand the sight or sound of another human crying. Or, the thought of germs on his body or possessions. Seeing me cry with Diresk nonchalantly fingering the playing cards was too much for Dave to take.

"Christopher is getting better today because I am helping him," David said. "You are in my place today. I am helping him today and we are getting out of this hospital before too long, huh? Diresk is in my place today, but he's going to leave again. Diresk is Christopher's friend, huh? He can sit in my place for a little while, huh, Christopher? It won't bother me today, will it? Not today. Are you going to help Christopher get better today, Diresk?" Dave shifted from heel to toe and back again, wringing pain from his fingers.

Diresk glanced at me and I nodded that it would be okay. I wiped my tears on my sleeve and attempted a smile for David.

"I got a good doctor and so does Christopher, huh?" David continued. His voice picked up volume and speed with every sentence.

"Christopher is getting better today because we are going to help him, huh, Diresk? Crying is okay, right Christopher? Right. I can cry later because my mother wants me to get better. I'm going to so I can help her with the dishes and the plants and the puppy at home. I'm not going to stay here forever am I, Christopher? Nope, I'm not. I need to wash these cups again because I need to wash them before visiting hours are over. Then, we go to recreation after visiting hours are over, huh, Christopher? Yep. Mother is coming Tuesday, Diresk, and she's bringing more pictures for our room huh, Christopher? Yep, and Christopher's going to help me put them on the wall again with my pictures of the puppy. We can always play cards. Can't we, Christopher? We can finish our game some other time. I don't have to worry about finishing this game because there will be a bunch of games we will play, huh? Yes, and everything is okay and we aren't going to worry about it anymore!"

"David...settle down," I said. "It's okay. I'm right here and we don't have to get excited today about anything because we're safe right where we are. We don't have to get scared. No way, Jose," I attempted with as calm a voice as I could muster.

"No way, Jose," he repeated. "I'm going to need some help today because I'm feeling it again and I'm going to need some HELP TODAY! You can hear me fine because you are right in front of me, so I don't have to yell like that anymore. I feel it again. I don't want it here! I DON'T WANT IT HERE TODAY! I need some HELP TODAY! HELP TODAAAAAAAAY!"

"Hey, David, it's okay, man," Diresk said. "You can sit in your chair and I can get another chair." Diresk stood up and backed away.

"I NEED SOME HELP NOW!" David yelled. "NOW! I CAN'T SEE! I CAN'T SEE NO MORE OF IT! I NEED STAFF TODAY. TIME OUT! I NEED TIME OUT TODAY! I NEED—"

Dave was surrounded immediately by three male staff members who escorted him to a quiet room where he would remain until someone or something could help him settle down. Diresk had started to speak to Dave as he was taken away, but no words escaped from his open mouth.

I wiped my eyes and stood up as if there was some place I could go, sat back down and took another drag from my cigarette.

Diresk checked his watch and parted his hair. I waited for his words.

"Jesus Christ, Topher," Diresk muttered. "I can't stay here much longer, man. I'll come back tonight for a while. Need anything from the store?"

"No, I don't need anything. Thanks, D.," I answered. "Just please come back tonight. It's so great to see you! I need to know I'm not crazy. I don't think I am, but I'm not sure how much room I have left. These last couple months almost killed me, man. I lost it. I just lost it and I couldn't climb out no matter what I did." I took another drag from my cigarette and waited for him to meet my eyes. "When do you have to get back?"

"Tomorrow. I've got to get a paper done for Tuesday. Dave's mom is coming on Tuesday." We both smiled. "What's wrong with Dave, man?" Diresk asked.

I shrugged. "Dave's actually a brilliant guy," I said. "He was going to go to medical school, but something happened to him a couple years ago and he lost it. He's usually not like that and pretty calm...but he worries about everything. He goes around washing everything about a million times a day. We both have the same shrink."

"His brain probably doesn't have anything better to do than to try to kill him, if he's that smart. He's got some of the same shit you got, man. Ingrown self. They don't do that lobotomy shit in here, do they?"

I smiled. They did not.

"Tell Dave to hang on, man. I'll be back tonight to see if we can figure some of this shit out. I need to get some medicine into my system before I crawl in here beside you."

We slapped hands and he tossed me a half-filled pack of Kool Filter Kings. He took a few steps towards the doorway before turning and taking in the entire room a final time.

"Toph, I know you think I'm stronger than you. I'm not. I just know to let the air out of my balloon before it pops. If you're all freaked about what people are going to think and everything…that's your problem. Life isn't meant to be taken seriously, Jerry. If it was God wouldn't have given us hallucinogenics and porno movies. You let me worry about what all the friggin' people in the world think about you. You just help Dave get those cups washed and see if you can find somebody in here to give some hope to. Man, you look like Iggy Pop. You better get some groceries in you."

I watched as he made his way to the elevator and flirted with a nurse as he waited for the doors to open. I wondered to myself how he always kept himself so strong. So full of life and hope.

I went to my room to pray for David. Hell, for all of us.

Chapter Twenty-One

My next stint in a hospital was a chemical dependency unit in Rapid City. December of 1986, four years later. I had crawled back to South Dakota from California after nearly killing myself with drugs and alcohol while living there. I had begun to suffer from anxiety attacks. They got so bad, I could barely leave my grandfather's apartment where I was staying. My grandparents were wintering in Arizona at the time and I had moved in to their Spearfish apartment to basically die. One thing led to another, and a couple friends intervened and got me into the treatment center.

That saved my life—what was left of it.

It had never before occurred to me my chemical use may have accelerated my depressive tendencies. In fact, during my first hospitalization in Sioux Falls, my therapist, Dr. Richey, spent a great deal of time expounding on the virtues of casual pot smoking, and basically blamed my "nervous breakthrough" on the horrific job my parents had done with raising me.

I could dig that, man.

It wasn't until two weeks into treatment that I began to see a connection between the problems I was having and my self-medication regime. I had no idea that sobriety would only be the beginning of an arduous adventure. If I had known what I was in for, I may not have been able to stop using sedatives.

The first week of treatment we weren't allowed visitation or phone contact with friends or family members under any circumstances. Any such contact was handled by facility staff and would be passed on to patients should such contact be deemed appropriate by the treatment team. The only visit I was allowed to receive during that first week was from a priest. Clergy were allowed to visit patients as the spiritual foundation of treatment was considered a vital asset for success. I had been reading in my room when a staff member had softly knocked on my door and asked me if I felt up to receiving a visitor.

"I didn't think we got to have visitors," I responded in my best victim dictum.

"Your priest from Custer would like to visit with you in the greeting room," said Robert, the male staff member. "I told him you could have one hour, if you felt up to it."

"My priest from Custer?" I asked. "Pastor Chuck?"

"No. This gentleman said his name was Father Diresk. You are not Catholic?" he asked.

I nearly bit my tongue, somehow avoiding a smile. "Father Diresk is here? Of course I'll see him."

I quickly swung out of bed and followed the man down the hallway towards the greeting room—the only place we were allowed to smoke and play cards. My heart was beating wildly in my chest at the possibility of seeing my friend. I couldn't imagine what was going to happen to me if we got busted. What was I to do?

I ran out of time for a decision as we turned the corner and I was greeted with a hug from the dashing young priest from Custer, decked out with white collar and slicked back hair.

I cannot believe, to this day, neither of us cracked a smile. How we held it together the way we did was unbelievable.

"Christopher, my son. It is so good to see you here. I have prayed for this day to come for you," Diresk stated as he awkwardly hugged me.

"Thank you very kindly, Robert," Diresk said, turning to the staff member. "We shouldn't require the entire hour. I must return to Custer to meet with a young couple who desires to wed."

Robert shrugged his shoulders and told us we had an hour anyway, and closed the door behind him.

"Don't smile or laugh," Diresk ordered with clenched jaw. "Let's wander back to those tables and see if we can't strike us up some ole' time religious magic. How they hanging, Larry?"

"I can't believe you did this," I whispered, fighting back a smile with every ounce of energy at my disposal. "I could get kicked out of here for this."

"And that would be a...bad thing?" Diresk whispered back.

We sat at a table near the ping pong/pool table area. I casually glanced at the staff viewing window at Robert, who had lost himself in a magazine. The coast looked unbelievably clear, though my pulse increased with every passing second.

I lit a cigarette, begging him with my eyes not to follow suit.

"Didn't they ask you for some identification or something?" I asked. "I can't believe you just waltzed in here like this. You would think this place is a CIA installation, the way they talk around here. Where did you get that collar?" The unavoidable lightheartedness was now in my voice.

"Ask and the Lord shall provide, dear brother. I got it from Hal. He swiped it from the church. Hal is a good Christian boy, Topher, but he has this problem with not being able to say no to drugs and we cut a deal. If I'm not mistaken, Hal could probably use a stay in a place like this, but I'm not one to gossip."

"Keep your voice down, man," I begged him. Begging is what I was always reduced to in Diresk's presence. "You couldn't wait until next weekend to come and see me?"

"And let my best student go through the entire week without his medicine? Do you consider me a fuddy duddy? I thought I might just stop in and lay some happy pills in your sweaty palms. Give you something to help you relax so you can absorb all of this important and necessary information. Must be like being in school again. I admire the folks who can jump on the wagon, man. Me? I am thankful if I can make it a couple hours without my medicine. But hey, I'm a seriously disturbed camper, Sidney. Shall we get on our knees and pray for the locals?"

Before I could insert an objection Diresk knelt beside me. All I could do was join him. Both complete humiliation and confusion I endured in that moment. I knew I was about to receive drugs from my best friend, who was posing as a Catholic priest, in the chemical dependency treatment center I had begged my way into due to the fact my life had gone way past falling to pieces.

I closed my eyes and did, in fact, begin to pray in silent desperation. My reflections were derailed by the sound of Father Diresk's voice, beaming in prayer.

"Father?" he said, "we come before you sinners in the worst way, shape, and form. We ask that you bless Topher and prevent him from being tossed out of this holy place because of my little fib here. Or the bounty he is about to humbly receive. I ask you, Lord…to keep

Topher in your—"

"This isn't funny anymore," I interrupted him. "I believe in God and I don't think we should kneel and make fun of Him, just so you can get off on one of your sick, little schemes. I need God, okay? Maybe you don't, but I most certainly do. The last thing I need is God getting pissed at me and—"

My words were interrupted—no—pinned to the ground, by Diresk's grip on my left hand. He immediately released the pressure when he sensed I had been silenced. I turned to look at him, and his eyes were still closed as if in prayer.

"You just don't get it, do you, Topher? You fear God like he's some kind of screwed up teenager. God made the entire universe, man. The whole, entire bucket of chicken! Think about it. God made everything in the universe and we don't even know how friggin' big it is. Flowers, trees, love, books, drugs, sex, guns, sunsets, music, eyeballs, vaginas, hurricanes…"

"Keep it down" I attempted.

"…colors, apples, snow, air, ice cream, magic tricks, blow jobs, Frisbees, and rock music. The whole thing! God's bigger than you or even I can ever imagine, man, so don't you think He gets a big kick out of all of this? All of us humans running around the planet like rats pretending to know where we're going and what we're doing. And there isn't one of us who has a friggin' clue about the big picture. He just wants us to have fun and help each other, man. God invented humor just like everything else."

"I know, I know," I said. "But this is a treatment center. It's a sacred place for those of us trying to get well. I know you hate me to say that, but it's my life and what I must do. You can't just waltz in here carrying dope and…"

"I didn't bring any dope in here, man. Just wanted to brighten your day a bit. If you want to get sober, then I'm behind you all the way. I don't have to like it and I'm not going to. But it's not my call to make. Don't think for a second I don't believe in God!"

"Do you pray?" I stared at him.

"Talk to Him all the time. He's the only one that'll listen to all my shit, man. I don't need to talk about Him because we got a deal worked out between us, and that's all you or I have to know. I know you've been dying. Shit, I can't stand watching it. I don't ever know what to do for you. Do you know what it's like? Watching your brother go down in flames again and again, and you can't do anything to stop it?"

"I know. I'm sorry." I looked away, ashamed.

"Don't be! I just wish I could trade places with you and take my shot at it for a while. Whatever it is you been fighting. Least I'd have something to work on instead of just stand around with my dick in my hands like I've been doing."

"You have no idea how you help me, man. I can't begin to tell you how much you mean to me; how much hope I get just knowing you are out there somewhere." I squeezed his hand and he pretended to wipe the germs off on his pants, smiling at me with tears in his eyes.

"I'm no genius like you, but I think you better get yourself a new God. Mine's like Mark Twain. Yours always sounds to me like your old man or something. God's going to take care of you whether you know about Him or not. I know that for a fact, Jack. You better decide what kind of God you want to believe in who can save your ass because we're all down here swimming in the same pickle barrel, and I think the key is to take things as easy as possible. An angry God isn't going to do you much good as hard as you are on yourself." He grinned to soften his words, then went on. "Life don't hit you as hard as you think it does. You do. You best be learning how to start kissing yourself. Here, let me show you what it feels like."

Diresk kissed me on the forehead, and for a split second I knew it was for real. I felt it seep down inside me. I guess...it was love.

We knelt in silence a little longer before another patient wandered in to smoke. We both got to our feet and Diresk greeted him. I introduced them to each other, calling my friend Father Diresk. The patient was an older man named Roger. He had drunk up several businesses and had also ruined a couple of marriages. He had been a millionaire several times over in his late thirties. When I met him in the treatment center, he had been sleeping in a car his brother had given him. He was seventy-two years old and homeless.

"Nice to meet you, Father Diresk," Roger stated as he lit his cigarette and watched as Diresk made his way to the door to leave. "If you're a Catholic priest, I'm an astronaut. Christopher, tell that damn nurse to get her ass in here with some aspirin, would you, son?"

Roger was quickly bribed with a pack of cigarettes to keep his assessment of the situation to himself.

Chapter Twenty-Two

I celebrated my twenty-sixth birthday locked up in a state hospital. 1988. I had been free from chemicals for nearly two years, but I couldn't keep the wheels on the road and I crashed again—due in part to my sudden dive into fire and brimstone religiosity, and another ill-fated romance with a woman I believed could save me. I had been looking for God as if there were only three seconds left on the clock.

Pain does that to a person.

I had spent the previous two weeks sparring with overwhelming anxiety and was left prostrate on my bedroom carpet, full bottle of Stelazine in hand. I had uncapped and dumped the pills in my hand when the phone rang and forced me to toss them back into the bottle like some child caught stealing. Why my Narcotics Anonymous sponsor Steve E. let it ring for several minutes continues to escape me. After finally relenting and spilling my current state, I agreed to wait for him to drive to my basement apartment and not to harm myself. Together, we called my psychiatrist and he ordered me to check into a psychiatric unit in Rapid City immediately. I could still taste the red pills in my mouth as I packed a simple bag for yet another humiliating admission. I grabbed some school books, nearly shook the smirk from my face, and tossed them into a closet.

I was again signed up for college in Spearfish with Diresk but had not attended a class in weeks. Diresk had not stopped over to check on me for a few days. His way of coping with his best friend's disintegration.

My roommate, Paul, showed up and began to cry when I told him where I was going. I begged him not to divulge my whereabouts to anyone, especially Diresk. Paul assured me of his confidentiality and hugged me tight, in a way like I always wanted my father to embrace me.

Steve and I smoked in silence as we drove to the unit. I could not believe I had lost control again after laboring so diligently on my recovery program. I felt utterly betrayed by this God I believed in and had bet all my marbles on.

For the next few months, my prayers would usually begin with: "If this is what you have in store for me, you can kiss my ass!" Not exactly your run-of-the-mill Savior salutation. I was still praying because I had nothing left but ragged faith peeking from beneath the anger and fear that literally kills in its wake.

We arrived at the unit and I pushed the intercom to announce my arrival, somewhat relieved and anxious to be alone in a safe place.

I was initially admitted to a posh little facility, but due to lack of insurance, was shipped away to the state holding tank in Yankton. I don't remember the van ride thanks to the Xanax and Ativan, but I do remember the sores I had on my wrists from the handcuffs I wore during the nine-hour trip.

We stopped in Sioux Falls on the way to deposit prisoners in the penitentiary like dirty, greasy envelopes. Envelopes with no stamps or return addresses.

We arrived. Here I was checked for lice, showered like an animal, clothed in a thin gown, and escorted to a locked unit filled to the brim by persistently mentally ill patients, psychotic down the line.

My psychiatrist was a tiny Vietnamese woman who spoke broken English at best and displayed a strange facial tic when struggling for proper enunciation. She promptly started me on a medication regime that would have floored a rhinoceros.

I did not complain.

I remember a tiny woman with blood red eyes who sat crouched on a bench and hissed at whoever approached her the entire six days I was a guest. A few hours after arriving and tiring of endless pacing and problem solving, I risked a conversation with her.

"Do you want a cigarette?" I asked her, nervously approaching as if she would leap from her perch and affix herself to my throat at any second. The other patients, I had noted, gave her a wide berth.

She looked through me with those eyes, and I waited for maybe ten seconds for a response that would never come. I silently offered her a cigarette and nearly soiled myself as she quickly snatched it from my hand, hissing like an air hose. I turned and approached a table full of peers and the thick haze of cigarette smoke surrounding them like a lazy cloud. Playing some card game, each were immersed in deep converse with unseen specters hiding in subconscious alleys.

It was akin to listening to seven albums simultaneously.

I remember being struck with a sudden awareness I could never take my own life. I could not go crazy, and I could not kill myself. I was stuck with life on life's terms. I had no choice but to continue smoking and wandering, waiting for someone or something to take the pain away.

I walked to my room and sat on the bed, completely defeated and more alone than I had ever been in my life. I could not imagine my life ever emerging from the rotted cauldron it had fallen into here. Where was my hope and faith? My girlfriend? My God?

I wanted to pray, but to whom or what? I needed help STAT!

The feelings of anxious panic and disorientation bubbled within me as my tiny room closed in like a vise. For the first time in my life, I decided to give Satan a shot. God had received my very best of efforts and had abandoned me. I hated Him! I hated me. I was ready for another remedy. Fast-acting, thank you very friggin' much!

I leaned back to rest my pounding head against the cool concrete wall and closed my eyes to the cognitive chill of echoes tangled in my brain. I stepped through foreboding feelings of what I was about to do, and began to speak from some place behind myself.

"I don't know what I am doing here, but I have done everything I was told to do. I have prayed and gone to meetings. I have worked the 12-steps to the best of my ability. I have stayed away from drugs and alcohol and I have read books. If this is God's world, then He can kiss my ass! I mean it! If you have a better deal, then let me see it. Do you hear me? I said, let me see it! I can't take this shit any longer. I can't walk around with this pain in my soul another day. I want out and I want out right now! I can't face anyone like this anymore. I can't fail one more time! I can't kill myself or I would have a long time ago. If you are real, then let me see you and what you have to offer. I'm done, man! DONE!"

A strange feeling pulsed through me like some supernatural breeze. A fearful, yet enticing sense that I had breached a forbidden plane. I felt terrified but elated. Horrified and released at the same time. Possibly the sense of relief claimed by those who finally commit to kill themselves.

Finally, it is at an end. Finally!

I remember with razor clarity my very next thought. I was not playing some game. I understood I had a choice to make. The most crucial choice I had ever, possibly would ever, make. Who was I? What was I? Was I going to quit, or believe against the gale? Period. There was no middle ground in that room. No place on a fence to test my feet on both sides as I kicked the planks and viewed the accompanying terrain. There simply was no fence. Just a line drawn in the blood that pumps within all sentience. I was to give up and quite possibly murder my soul, *or* I could keep walking, breathing, and wishing like a forsaken child. No matter the degree of pain and suffering, would I trust this God and do whatever was placed before me? Would I accept the velvet hand of a demon to fly effortlessly into a darkened abyss?

I knew it was up to me. For the first time in my life, it was *finally* up to me.

It was during this instant in a state hospital I embraced the concept we are all alone on this planet, yet never alone in our hearts. It was simply a matter of which side to listen to. I did not doubt the existence of evil on that day. Neither did I doubt the existence of a vast God beyond any understanding or limit. I felt them both. Tasted them both. I would swallow only one.

I immediately sprang from the bed and bowed on my knees in prayer.

"Please forgive me for what I just did, Father. I can't carry this burden any longer. I have been hating you and trying to do this by myself. I can't! I'm going to choose to believe in You. I'm going to trust You no matter how I feel inside or how much pain I get hit with every day. There is nothing left for me to do. Please show me You are listening. I need to know I'm going to be okay. I just know that if you're not there I am fucked! Amen."

I knelt on the floor for what must have been fifteen minutes. I had made my decision.

I started to do push-ups. I was going to believe. I was going to eat and exercise again; I was going to pray and tell God the truth. My truth, no matter how sparse or conflicting. God must be big enough to scream at. To cry to, and demand to be held. I would turn away from any biblical or religious precepts and begin to search for God on my own terms. Terms that walked hand-in-hand with my inner voice. Terms resonating with consoling covenant. Pleasing entrees of a splendid meal.

I was going to trust my process and try not to think about it or figure things out. Not an easy proposition for an obsessively compulsive addict harboring a dependency character disorder. But I was on my way.

"Chris? Are you okay?"

I was startled from my solace by a voice and greeted it with a gaze fraught with hopeful tears. A staff person. A woman. She looked like an angel and I considered embracing her leg.

"You have a phone call in the social area from a friend of yours. A Diresk or something like that. Do you want to take it? You know you don't have to talk to anyone until you feel ready?"

"Yeah," I managed. "Where?"

"Come with me. You can use the staff phone," she answered. "You're going to make it, you know. I can tell. I can feel it in you. You can't see yourself like I can, Chris. I was a patient here five years ago. I didn't think I had any hope left. I made it…and so can you. If you want to talk after supper I'll probably have some time available, okay? My name is Marcia."

"Thanks, Marcia. I would really like that. I better find that phone," I added.

Marcia led me to the nurse's station and handed me the phone from behind the glassed counter.

"Hello?" I said into the phone. I was amazed he had found me.

"I hate it when you go schizo and don't call me, you know that?"

I laughed. "Diresk! Oh, God it's good to hear your voice. How did you find out I was here?"

"From Paul. That dude can keep a secret, man. I had to nearly grab him by the throat! How's the food and the nurses?"

"I haven't eaten anything for a couple of days. I don't even know what a girl looks like anymore. I have been dying, man. This one is ten times worse than anything I have ever went through. Don't drive down here, D. It's too far and I don't even know where I am or when I would get to see you. It's just so good to talk to you, man. I can't believe…"

"I'm coming out for the weekend, you asshole, and don't tell me what I can and can't do. Just because you don't think you're worth driving that far for don't mean I don't know the friggin' score. I'd come and see you if you were in friggin' India, you dipstick. I'm worried about you. Steve said you almost took a bottle of pills this time. What happened, man? You and the little woman experiencing technical difficulties?"

I shook my head, though I knew he couldn't see the gesture. "She doesn't know I'm here and don't tell her. It isn't her, man. I mean it is and it isn't. She's probably back with that guy from Colorado again by now anyway. She told me she couldn't love someone who had nervous breakdowns and would cost her a ton of her money."

"Her daddy's money, Slim," Diresk corrected.

"Yeah, really. It's not her. It's just the same demons again, different volume. She just freaked me out when she disappeared last week when I needed her most. Man, I can't believe you found me. I was too embarrassed to call you. Here I am again in a friggin' nut ward. Screwed up again as usual, huh?"

"HEY!" Diresk yelled into the receiver. "Drop the ball, Topher! I understand, okay? I haven't hung out with you all this time without picking up on a few of your details. Yeah, I'm pissed at you and I hate it when you check into those places. Yeah, I want you to get your shit together so you can be happy. You've never been truly happy, Toph. Never, man!"

"You don't think so? Not ever?" I turned away from the nurse at the desk.

"I can't friggin' believe you, man. We've had some good times and shit, but you've always been dragging your feet. I just want to smoke dope and chase girls like before. I want you to live, man! Like you were born to. We got people to help and mouths to feed, Jerry. Bottom line is, I love you, man, but I'm scared for you. I don't give a damn what you do or where you end up as long as you stay alive, dig? Don't die, Topher. My feelings aren't ever going to change for you...no matter what shit you get yourself into. And I expect return coverage on that play, Bubba!"

"You got it," I whispered through rushing emotion. "Thanks."

"Just don't give up the faith, brother. All you've got to do is make it through another day, right? Don't do nothing stupid until I get down there and we'll do plenty of stupid shit together. Okay? Toph? Where you at, man?"

I was crying again. I couldn't help myself. He made me feel like I could do anything. He always did. Diresk was on the case. I knew I could hold on until he came to visit me.

"I better get off the phone so you don't have a huge phone bill. Diresk? Thanks for calling. You don't know how much it means, and the timing and everything is really amazing. I think I just...no, I know I just got this memo from the universe and you were the second one. I can't believe you are going to drive all the way out here, but I can't wait to see you! Hey, how'd you do on that Biology test you were freaking about?"

"Pretty damn fair since I got the answers from Tricia the night before. Believe I aced that one, Jerry. Want me to talk to your teachers for you? I bet some of them have noticed you haven't been to class for a while and you've got to do something, or they're going to flunk your schizo-ass."

"Yeah, I suppose that would be good. Just tell Dr. Durgin where I am and he can do whatever needs to be done until I get back and can figure out what I want to do. Just tell him I'm still sober, okay? Let him know I didn't screw that up."

"Sure. I'll see you Saturday morning, or maybe Friday night if I can cut classes. What the hell am I saying? I'll see you Friday night. Be cool and save me some happy pills, Junior. Hey. Seriously. You let me worry about how much it costs to talk to my best friend. You can't buy this shit with money, Topher. When are you going to get a clue about how important we humans are? Shit, I'd almost give away my last bag of dope for you, man. I've got to go. I love you, man. Keep the faith."

I closed my eyes and heard him cut the connection. The pain was still there, but I had a deeper feeling rumbling around inside of me. I had faith.

I thanked Marcia and handed her the receiver. I decided I would try to eat something. It really had been days since I had kept anything down. My eyes burned from crying so much and the cigarette fog in the unit. However, I noticed it was business as usual for the other patients.

I glanced toward "red eyes" and she was smiling at me. I quickly looked away but forced myself to search out her piercing eyes. I felt myself walking towards her and before I knew it, I was standing not more than two feet from the bench. She kept smiling at me as if she was right there with me, inside my thoughts.

She terrified me, yet I was drawn to her. She accepted a cigarette and tenderly placed it between her tattered shoes, hissing at me. My heart jumped against my ribs but I was unable to walk away or speak. Fear shot up from my stomach and the waves of a panic attack began their explosive assault throughout my body's nerves. My breath caught in my chest and I stepped back and scanned the room for help in the event I collapsed on the floor.

I felt the tender touch of a hand on my right shoulder and I found myself attempting to fight my way back to reach the safety of soft brown eyes. Marcia's eyes.

"Chris?" Marcia asked. "Can I help you with something? The blood is out of your face. You better sit down over here. How about some juice?"

I silently nodded and felt myself snapped back to the sounds and smells of the unit. I had to breathe and took in slow, deep breaths as Marcia led me to a chair. I could not help myself, and again turned to seek out Red Eyes, hunched over and quietly laughing at me. She leaned forward and I could read the words on her barely parted lips.

"Where's your God now?" she asked.

"What did you say? Excuse me?" I asked.

Marcia turned to look at Red Eyes and then back to me when no response was offered. Marcia gave me a concerned look that faded into compassion. She touched my hand and excused herself to get me some juice.

I sat with my back facing the toxic woman whose silent words had stung me like a hornet. She never spoke to me, or to my knowledge, to another staff or patient during my stay there. She would never again accept a cigarette from me and would avert her burning gaze whenever I approached her perch.

I did a great deal of thinking about what she said to me that night. Was it some kind of test? I knew I had not imagined it. It happened, and would be forever scorched in my memory.

Marcia and I had our discussion following our evening meal. She gave me a great deal of hope and shared her God with me. I do not remember what she looked like, except for her soft brown eyes. But I won't ever forget what she said.

"God is either everything or nothing at all, Christopher. There's no middle ground here. If God is everything we have nothing to worry about. If God is nothing, well, I guess we all just end up as worm food and none of this matters. I simply cannot believe that. Can you?"

Diresk showed up the following Friday and we spoke for a few hours, and then again on Saturday and Sunday. I told him what had happened with "Red Eyes" and after listening intently, he said, "Don't mess around with the dark side, man. It's no game. I don't know if there is or isn't a Satan, but I know there is a God and I'm going to give *Him* my attention. I recommend you do the same, partner."

I have spent a great deal of time in churches, Alcoholics Anonymous

Meetings, therapist's offices, and hiking around the beautiful Black Hills. I would never have expected to learn where God hangs out while locked up in a dingy state hospital with a bunch of psychotics.

God hangs out everywhere.

Three weeks into my hospital stay Paul would transfer my belongings into my van and move one of his friends into my apartment. My girlfriend would rekindle a previous relationship and I would learn of this the same day I became hip to the fact I was also homeless.

My psychiatrist would tell me the next morning it was time to get in touch with my anger as I homicidally related the disturbing details that recently surfaced.

I told him I had no fucking problem with that.

Chapter Twenty-Three

A few years after I got out for good, Diresk and I visited a mutual acquaintance who had been committed to the psychiatric unit in Rapid City. She had, the previous evening, piped exhaust fumes into her car via a garden hose and would have killed herself had she not lost consciousness and slumped against the car horn, alerting a neighbor to the suicide scene. It had been her seventh unsuccessful effort. She was twenty-five years old.

She had used the same hose Diresk had bought for her to fill up a water bed months before. My life was rather smooth by this time and I was in control of my emotions. The bats were still in the belfry but they were flying in formation.

Diresk, however, had been in the process of drinking and drugging himself into a stuperous indifference and intolerance of just about everything and everyone he came into contact with at the time. He was surprisingly affected by the hose incident and felt somehow culpable. He phoned and asked me to accompany him to the "Schizo Palace". I drove his truck as he was much too intoxicated and overcome by a molasses of melancholy to be trusted on the road.

We arrived at the hospital, parked in the visitor lot, and as I moved to open my door and exit, he grabbed my hand and held me in my seat. I turned to face him. His eyes wouldn't make contact with mine and he released his grip.

"What's up, D.?" I said, apprehensive in the face of a return to a building where I had excruciatingly pondered away the crippled hours that limped past me.

"If I ever lose it, I'm not going to go into one of these places, man. I mean it. Screw that! I'll blow my brains out before I waddle into a joint like this, Toph. I mean it, man! I'm not going down like that. I don't even know why I'm saying this shit to you, but you see me. You know where I'm at right now. It's really dark where I am these days, Toph. Feels like it's getting blacker every day and I can't find the light. I can't find the friggin' lights and I could always find the lights, man. Always before."

"Jesus, D. I didn't know you were hurting so bad. All you had…"

He glared at me. "It's not your problem!"

"Don't get mad at me! I can see your face getting red and everything. I know you haven't been feeling good for a long time now. Shit. I asked you if you wanted to talk about it a week ago and you blew me off. You know, sometimes I really do want to be there for you, but you won't let me. I'm not always so stuck on myself that I can't see when you're hurting, for God's sake."

"Just stop this shit, man. I hate talking about all this depressing bullshit. Let's just go in."

"No!" I insisted. "I want to tell you this and you are going to listen. You're my best friend, and I would do anything in my power to help you if you asked. I promise I would, D. I promise!"

"I know that, bird brain. *Jesus.* I didn't mean to open my friggin' mouth. It's just being here again and having to see Kate like I used to come see you."

I nodded and looked down at my knees, pulling at nonexistent threads.

"Why'd she have to use the hose, Toph? Jesus. I feel guilty about it for some reason, man. Like I bought her the hose and knew she was going to use it to kill herself with or something."

"You know that's bullshit, D. You bought her a hose to help her out once and…"

"Do you know that for sure? We don't know nothing about how this world works, man. Nothing at all. I can feel it, man. There's something weird about me getting her that hose."

"No way! No friggin' way, man." I shook my head and pushed myself back from the steering wheel, stretching the muscles in my arms and neck.

Diresk stared into his hands.

"She's in a lot of pain but it doesn't have anything to do with you. She's just fighting her demons and they are winning. Big time! She's tried to do this before, D. You didn't even know her then."

"I know how I feel, okay? Don't tell me how to feel about this, Topher! Something's going on inside me. It's big, okay? I can't explain it to you, but it's real, and it feels like it's going to take me down."

"I'm sorry, D. It just seems pretty far out that you would be connected to what is going on. I think maybe you are..."

I stopped myself before risking an explosion from him.

"What? You think maybe I'm *what*?"

"Nothing. You're right. I don't know how you are feeling and... Let's go inside."

"Say what you were going to say."

I felt myself shiver at the sound of his voice. He was on the edge and I would go over and down with him should he jump. I cautiously continued, feeling my way as my feet kicked rocks down the endless drop off in my mind. Finally I said my what was on my mind.

"I just think you're maybe tired and depressed and not thinking right."

I drew a breath and awaited the impending fist that would soon shatter my jaw on its way up and through my forehead.

Instead, his body deflated and sunk into itself. Maybe a minute hovered and passed between us.

"What's it feel like?" he asked. His eyes bulged forward full of fear.

"What does *what* feel like?"

"Going schizo? What's it feel like when you start to lose it, man?"

I squared my shoulders. I needed to be firm. "You aren't losing it, D. If you were, you are taking it a hell of a lot better than I ever did. You saw me, man. Remember how I looked and sounded all the time? You have never been like that no matter what you have been through. You must have a different foundation than I do. Built from better stock. Or at least sturdier, anyway."

"Yeah. I'm a friggin' mental health giant, man."

"I'm not saying you aren't messed up like the rest of us, but you have to admit, you've always had this inner strength I never used to have. I don't know where you got yours. Probably your old man." I hit him gently in the shoulder to soften my words. "Your old man's got concrete in his veins and your mom is solid rock, too."

"You really think I'm stronger than you are? What rock have you been hiding your head under? Jesus, Topher. I'm a drug addicted alcoholic! I know what I am. I can't put my medicine down for more than a couple hours, and you put yours away indefinitely. If my old man is so freaking strong, then why's he have to suck down a pint so he can sleep at night?"

"It's just his way," I said. "He's never checked into a mental hospital and I'll guarantee you he never will. You're the same way, man. You can somehow keep your shit together enough not to have it spill out all over you."

"It's not about strength, man. It's about doing what you got to do, and that's all there is to it. I got the same demons chasing around inside me that you got. I just keep knocking them down is all. But someday... maybe they're not going to stay down. If I go down crazy, then I go down crazy. I don't even know what we're talking about, Topher. What are we talking about?"

I grinned. "I'm not sure. Maybe we're just friends bouncing ideas off each other. Why do we have to understand any of..."

"Why don't you tell me the truth? Why won't you tell me what you think about how I live my life. What you *really* think? Huh? Why not?" Diresk punched me in the arm.

"What do you mean?" I asked. "What do you want me to say? That I wish you would get sober like I did? That I think you're wasting away with all those other people who gave up along the line? I wish we could go to meetings and talk about God and learn about all the magic that's around us everywhere, and be close again like we used to be, and all that shit! Yes. Yes, I do. I want you to be happy and healthy and I don't think we're close anymore because we have too much shit standing between us. It's not all you. I know that. But it doesn't help when you're messed up all the time every day. It isn't easy for me, either. I miss you, man."

Diresk eyed me with what I first interpreted to be disgusted frustration, and as I watched him soften and settle back into the cushioned seat, the lump caught in my throat was able to pass downward as we listened to each other's imagined thoughts.

"Let's go see Katie," Diresk finally said into the tight air in the car.

"You want to talk about this some more first? We got all afternoon to go in there."

"Nothing left to say, man. You're going down your road and I'm going down mine. Neither one's on a map."

I nodded, not agreeing with his words, but copping out due to my own personal agenda of finishing our visit and getting the hell away from the building. I again opened my door.

"I've got nobody in my life like you, Toph, and I don't even know if I got you anymore. I don't understand how this shit can get so messed up when you get older. What happened to them days on an inner tube and them days we used to play guns behind the rocks? I don't know anything anymore except I've got to keep on keeping on. It shouldn't be this hard. Oh, hell. Let's get this over with, man. I bet Katie could use a smile."

"She'll be glad to see you, man. I know that from experience. Maybe it will help to see me, too. She won't be the only schizo in the group."

Walking towards the building, Diresk stopped in his tracks. "That bother you? When I call you schizo?"

"Nope. Because I'm beginning to learn just how messed up you are, too. You've just kept it a secret all these years. You might be crazier than you think."

"Not possible, Jerry. You'd freak if you sat in on one of my little meetings in my brain. It's not pretty, and there isn't much air to breathe when it gets going. Got them smokes for Katie?"

I patted my breast pocket. "In my pocket. You're a good person, D. You treat people really good and you always think of others before yourself."

"It's all I got to keep the shivers down. That and my medicine. Even that isn't working like it used to. Everything's gotta change and get screwed up, doesn't it?"

"No," I shook my head. "Sometimes things change and we get to see where we should have been the whole time."

"Thank you, Socrates. How's my breath in case I kiss her?"

Ten years later...

I saw Kate recently in a small club in Rapid City. Still drinking like a fish. Still hoping some man will lead her to her pot of gold. She's on her second marriage and just enough antidepressants to keep the lava from scorching her patent leather shoes. She still laughs with the same Bette Davis growl. We danced and managed to jitterbug like college sweethearts.

God, Katie could dance.

Chapter Twenty-Four

ROSE

Rose was the only woman Diresk ever really fell for. I don't know why this was such a surprise to me. To all of us. We all fell hard for Rose. She would leave a string of open-mouthed men behind her as she would ooze through a room. Beautiful beyond script. Standing next to her was like taking the first drug of the day. Ethereal.

I remember the night he met Rose. We were drunk at Screamin' Elrod's in Spearfish, a favorite watering hole for the college crowd, to which we haphazardly belonged. Diresk cornered me in the men's room to brief me on a girl he had been introduced to by a couple of our friends. He was rather animated.

"Topher, you've got to help me," Diresk said, slapping my back and causing me to urinate all over my Chuck Taylors. He danced around like a boxer and attempted to coax even a hint of an obedient form of his tangled mane.

I cleaned off my shoes and watched in bemused horror as my best friend lost his mind.

"I think your favorite buddy is falling for a princess," he said. "Man, I can't get over the rush I got going inside right now."

"Was it necessary to make me piss all over myself though?"

"It's just beer, man. Check it out. I just met this goddess that knows Gary and Angie. She lives over in Harvard Estates where they do and I think she kind of likes me. Rose. I want to hose Rose. She's dialing my numbers, Toph. I'm not kidding here. I don't know what it is about her, man. I mean she's so friggin' beautiful, but when I try to talk to her I'm like a gorilla with a concussion or something."

"And this is somehow different in what manner from the seven hundred times I have seen you act like this?" I asked, grinning at him.

"I don't know." His reply stopped us both. "I don't know, Toph. She's like some movie star or something, man. She's got this power or energy or something. You have to see her! Tell me if I'm seeing what I think I'm seeing. But I know I am. Right when we first met there was something going on and it lit up the whole room. Listen to me, man."

He turned toward me. "See what I mean? Sounds like I been snorting stupid powder! Get out there and assume your position on the perimeter, Jack! We're sitting over by the dance floor. She's got long, black hair and she's wearing some kind of Japanese dress or something. Hurry up. I'll catch you later for the judge's scores. Hey, nice shirt, Fuzzy!" he tossed back at me before disappearing back into the loud music and bumping bodies.

"Thanks," I managed as I zipped up my fly and wandered to the mirror to see if he was kidding about the shirt, or if he really liked it. He had most likely been kidding. I looked at myself, wondering if I would ever find "my Rose". What kind of woman could conjure such an allergic reaction in the ultimate bachelor? I slipped into a stall to smoke some grass. I planned to be sharp for my appraisal.

Later, I tried to stay back in the crowd to look at her. I remember catching my breath when I saw them together, laughing, fingertips brushing casually as Diresk's eyes danced and drank from hers. Actually, it was more like a guzzle. It was as if she knew where to tickle his soul. I stepped further back into the gyrating bodies and began to memorize her every detail.

I had never seen him look so happy before. So content and tailored by effervescence. It was as if I could *taste* the two of them huddled together, if such a thing were possible. That two people could meet and the resulting polarity could season an entire room?

I was immediately jealous. I would wage with myself during their rapacious courtship the beginnings of a battle. I longed to be the one.

For him as well as for her.

I stood there and tried to take as much of her in as possible to prepare for the inevitable and brutal interrogation, but I could barely concentrate. All I could see was Diresk. He acted like he was in a movie. He looked like a man with everything going his way. His entire life spread before him like at some glamorous dinner party. I snuck away to an empty front row stool to resume the assault on my senses. Leroy, the owner and bartender, kept me flush with free beer and cigarettes for the next hour or so. My plan was to drink and smoke myself invisible, never to return to the throbbing complexities of real life.

Very intoxicated, I mumbled to myself. "What is she wearing a kimono for? Who does she think she is, man? Some foreign language freak? She probably thinks she's in some friggin' Bogart movie. What kind of name is Rose? It's a hooker's name is what it is. I'll go away and never come back before I watch him destroy his life over some she-demon like that! I'll go live on the beach under some blue tarp tethered to a bunch of rocks in a cove. I'll never come back to this place again! I'll grow my hair down to my ass and get the best tan on the beach and drink wine from a sack. I'm not selling out for some dame, man. No way!"

They would miss me. Oh, yes they would. I would silently haunt and hover over the two of them as they made love, listening and watching as Diresk would call out *my* name. I would smile and slowly caress my chin as he collapsed onto her sweat-beaded breasts, coughing his tearful lamentations into her lathered hair as he agonized the disappearance of his most trusted companion. She would attempt comfort, but his tears would not be assuaged. She would grasp the full measure of his impending sorrow and his inability to calm the pounding waves that tossed themselves against his inner soul like—

"TOPHER!" I spun around to face the sound of Diresk's voice, violently plucked from my self-pity swamp. The bar was closing down and I was finally able to locate his cloudy facial features amidst the layers of intoxicated collegiates filing towards the exit. Diresk waved at me with the free hand not holding hers as she leaned against his shoulder, smiling at me.

They swam through the river of bodies and soon stood before my stool. Leroy handed Diresk a cigarette and lit it, never taking his hungry eyes from the statuesque woman. I reached out to shake her hand and was quickly drawn to her tanned legs. She had flawless legs. Of course!

"This is the Toph Master. The one I told you all those lies about," Diresk giddily announced. "Topher, this is Rose, and she has my heart in her little black bag here."

"Nice to meet you, Toph Master. Angie showed me some of your poetry, and I really like it. She constantly raves about what a great writer you are. I live in her building. I would love to read anything you have written, if you wouldn't mind. I won't lie to you. I'm a tough critic, but I really enjoyed what I have read so far. You really should try to get published," she added.

"Naw," I replied. "That would be success and I can't have any of that. Right, D.?"

"On the money, Virgil," Diresk winked. "Topher has this problem with doing well with stuff. He calls it timing. I call it a human tragedy. We're going to an eatery to plug our arteries, and you have to come along to pay for all of this shit. Rose is driving because you and I are not fit for operation of a motorized anything. She's got a muscle car, man. Can you believe it?"

Wow, I thought, *she's the most amazing woman I have ever met! A muscle car? Why don't you go show her your muscles in the back seat and leave me the hell alone.*

"I'm going back to your place, man," I stammered, feeling panicked and not knowing why. "I'm really tired and messed up. You go ahead. I'll see you in the morning. I'm going to crash downstairs. Glen told me I could sleep in his bed this weekend."

Glen was Diresk's roommate and the only guy I knew who possibly knew more girls than Diresk. He also had a king-size water bed and an outrageously garish entertainment system in his bedroom which I borrowed whenever I could.

"Wrong again, Septic Tank Breath," Diresk insisted. "The night is young and there are still a few hundred people who haven't seen that shirt yet. I will not take "no" for an answer on this one. Finish that beer. We gotta git gone. You got the rest of your life to sleep, man. I'll even buy. Did I just say what I thought I said? Jesus, I must be happy tonight."

Rose laughed and touched me on the shoulder. Every negative feeling went immediately away. She squeezed my shoulder and my neck felt a shock.

"We would really like you to come along, Topher," she stated, drawing back her hand. "If I have to listen only to Diresk for the next few hours, I may have to do something drastic like cut his tongue out. We can come back for your car after you sober up and eat. Come on. I won't even ask you to recite your poetry."

I smiled at Diresk, who was obviously deep in the throes of Rose's spell. I liked her from that moment on. I had never seen anyone disarm my friend that way before. I swallowed what was left in my bottle and we made our way to Rose's car—a beautiful green Camaro. I remembered laughing to myself when I thought of her in a muscle car. She had already started to get inside of my brain and we had barely spoken.

She turned the ignition and the engine came alive. The soft whir of it made me feel safe, and I spread my arms to lean into the back seat. Power purred from beneath me and I closed my eyes to let the chemicals dance in my head.

"Buckle up, boys," Rose ordered. "You ride with me and you better get your affairs in order."

We both fumbled obediently for the straps and managed to secure ourselves in like a couple of children going to the zoo. I wanted to ride with her in that car for the rest of my life. Diresk couldn't take his eyes off of her and laughed at everything she said. But it was funny. She was dazzling, and we were powerless to deny her anything. We pulled out of the parking lot and the Camaro shoved off onto the highway.

I sensed something to be wrong in our direction of travel, opened my eyes and sat up to view the road as it dipped beneath the skyline. We had turned right and were heading up Spearfish Canyon. The restaurant was in the other direction, and I sat back smiling. I would not have cared had we driven to the ocean. Diresk decided to comment on the change in itinerary.

"Hey, screw breakfast. Let's go for a drive instead. Rose? Let's go up to the canyon instead, huh? Topher? Got any medicine on you?"

I arched my back and attempted to remove my pinch-hitter from my back pocket, succeeded, and handed it over the seat with my lighter.

"This is the kind of sugar that Poppa likes," Diresk said. "Wouldst thou be offended if I doest dope in you chariot, fair maiden?" He held the pot up and wiggled it for her like it was wet.

"IS THAT DRUGS?" Rose exclaimed, stomping on the brakes and throwing our internal organs towards the dashboard. "Get out! Now! Both of you!"

Diresk's eyes looked as if they would pop out of their sockets as he lamely turned to me for guidance and support. An extremely infrequent occurrence!

I was absolutely helpless, and deftly reached for the buckle to free myself in the event she was serious and we would soon find ourselves walking back to the bar with our illegal contraband.

"Hey, I'm sorry, babe," Diresk warbled. "We won't smoke it around you and you won't have to see it. We don't smoke it that much anyway."

In the unbearable silence that followed I could sense Diresk regaining some of his composed posturing. He gathered himself and began our defense.

"Look, we get high, okay? We are going to keep getting high until we are sixty years old. I am anyway, and Topher doesn't have any brains left anyway, so what does it matter? I like you and I want to hang around you, but I'm not going to pretend I'm somebody I'm not just so you won't wig out and spend time around me. Rose? Come on, Rose. Let's drive to the canyon and like each other again, okay?"

Rose bit her lip and withdrew into serious contemplation, leaving the both of us hanging in space, hands affixed to our seat belt buckles. Finally the prosecution continued.

"I am a liberal woman. I consider myself educated in the ways of this society and the world we live in. I am a lot of fun to be with and I know how to let my hair down. I will not, however, tolerate the use of illegal chemicals in my presence. I don't care how handsome or charming you both are. You have drugs on you, and I will have to ask you both to remove yourselves from my car and find your own way back to your cars. I mean it!"

The both of us sat there stunned. I can't speak for Diresk, but I felt like Scarlett must have felt when Rhett Butler told her to "screw off" in so many words. People just didn't say or do things like that to us. We were the coolest guys around! At least Diresk was, and I was his lieutenant. It had been new ground for both of us.

I followed Diresk's lead and drunkenly removed my carcass from the back seat of her Camaro. Diresk held the seat for me and as I exited the vehicle, I could see the utter astonishment in his eyes. He slammed the door for effect and mumbled something like it was a wonderful night to be walking home, drunk. I knew his feelings had been trodden upon, but he smiled without waiver to me. Then, he lit a cigarette like James Dean would have amidst a similar debasement.

Suddenly, the Camaro's tires clawed at the pavement and the car lurched forward and sideways, straightened, before she pulled over just ahead of us on the shoulder of the canyon highway. The lights and engine were cut. We stood smoking our cigarettes, watching the shadowed car. The metallic sound of her door opening was amplified throughout the base of the dark, canyon walls.

"She's going to apologize," Diresk whispered as if she was inches away. "What's she doing? She's messing with us, man, ain't she? She's going to ask us to come over and then peel out."

I was not so confident in his assessment. The whole thing had a strange feel to it, and I was ready for anything to happen at that point. Of course, I was unbelievably wasted and my judgment was highly impaired.

"BOYS? OH, BOYS?" Rose's scream echoed through the night.

We watched as she emerged from the Camaro and closed her door. She slowly approached us as the moon and stars dimly lit her image. We stood there and waited for her to arrive at the spot she had dropped us off. She took her time getting there and the three of us stood there silently posed on the graveled shoulder.

"Are you trying to risk your life being stranded out in the middle of nowhere with a couple of drug addicts?" Diresk asked. "My God, woman, you could be in danger beyond your wildest imagination. You come out here with us and you better get your affairs in order. Topher? You got the meat cleaver and the shovel? You cut her up this time because I'm not ruining another shirt, and I mean it! Speaking of shirts, I hope you didn't steal that one from some square dancer, because they're awful expensive!"

Diresk's humorous approach was offered as a diversion from the ambiguity we were both experiencing. We had our pride to protect, but neither of us wanted this new flower to turn and walk away from us. We awaited her next words, however I could not understand what was wrong with my shirt.

"I can be such a naughty girl sometimes," Rose said. "I can't help myself. My father says it's my mother's side. What's a girl to do with an affliction such as this? Do you think smoking pot would help? I really want to get better. I've tried therapy and not eating red meat. Do you think you can help me? I have money. I can pay. I have something here and maybe you can tell me what it is. I think it's supposed to be bad for you, but who can you believe these days?"

Rose reached into her back pocket and withdrew a folded piece of paper. The three of us smiled and began to laugh at the same time. Diresk plucked the folded package from her painted fingers and pretended to throw it into the trees as Rose gasped.

It was not the best cocaine I had ever sampled, but it was certainly the most interesting. I believe Diresk fell in love with Rose that night. I think Rose fell in love with him a few weeks later when he borrowed a horse from a guy we knew on the college rodeo team and galloped across the campus lawns dressed in full cavalry attire to pick her up after class. He got a standing ovation from hundreds of students and even a few faculty before being escorted off grounds by security. They would share the kind of love that sells romance novels in grocery stores.

As usual, I got to ride shotgun on the deal.

Chapter Twenty-Five

Rose, Diresk, and I were inseparable from that night on. 1984 was probably one of the most wonderful years of my life, but unfortunately I can't remember much of it. Due partially, I imagine, to the inordinate quantities of drugs and alcohol I ingested. I doubt I drew more than fifty sober breaths the entire year, though as before mentioned, it would be difficult to recall.

I dated a few girls on occasion, but it was usually the four of us, Grover holding court in the truck's box. We lashed out at normalcy with all the fervor of youthful splendor available to us. We absolutely insisted on having a grand time, every second of every day. There were to be no exceptions.

Man, I miss those times. It was as if the days would never end. They rushed by faster than I could have ever imagined possible. How do years slip by so effortlessly? I was twenty-three years old and the proud owner of not one concept of my life's direction or substance. I was a professional pot smoker who dabbled in tranquilizers and unmitigated sensual debauchery.

God only knows how I made it out of the bottom of that bag. I look at pictures of us during those times and I could almost swear I never met those people.

I remember going to a Bryan Adams concert at the Civic Center in Rapid City one summer day. We ate a bunch of mushrooms and drank tons of booze before embarking on the fifty mile drive from Spearfish.

It was Saturday. The three of us were enrolled at the university and were to attend the concert in order to earn extra credit for a Music Appreciation class we all took together. It was our kind of class. No tests, and the instructor got high with us.

Diresk used to say, regarding our educational experience at Black Hills State University, "Hey, it ain't law school…but at least it ain't law school."

Diresk and Rose were to graduate in the spring. It would take me another six years to finish a bachelor's in psychology after sobering up. All in all, it took me eleven years to complete a four year degree. Why rush into things?

Diresk's truck had the best stereo money did not have to buy. The two of us had meticulously stolen specific car stereo equipment over a three-year period and our patience had paid off. His automobile entertainment system was regionally famous in those days. Had we found it necessary, I believe we could have made extraterrestrial contact using an AC/DC tape.

Another crucial attribute of Diresk's truck was its ability to remain on the highway during feverish wrestling bouts between the three of us.

Tremendous alignment. Good tires. Possible spiritual intervention.

We had one hell of a match on the way to the Bryan Adams concert that day. We had spilled every beer and bottle, dumped an ounce of pot on the floorboards, and had ruined our favorite John Prine tape.

We had also managed to grab the attention of a state trooper who pulled us over and, in one of the truly great humanitarian efforts known to man and womankind, let us off with a warning without ever having searched our cab of iniquity. By the time he had turned around in the ditch and pulled in beside us, we had hid the bottles and cans, scooped up most of the grass, and painted upstanding Christian expressions on our faces. We could do nothing about our beating hearts about to escape our bodies.

We turned to watch him get out of his car and made a quick assessment of his character and our chances at redemption. Rose thought he looked like a grandfather and we all thought this was a good thing.

Thankfully, the mushrooms had failed to kick in, but we were by no means considered legally sane. The unfortunate interruption had served to sober us up some. Nothing like a highway patrolman pulling you over to compromise a really good high and initiate a bummer.

Diresk attempted a casual greeting as the patrolman arrived at his open window.

"Do me a favor and cease with the hanky panky while you are operating a vehicle, okay?" the patrolman said. "I know you are all just having fun, but I get tired of looking at dead bodies who weren't paying attention to their driving. I have this sneaking suspicion I could find a few things you would not want me to find in your truck here if I looked around a bit. Let me peek at your license and registration, sir."

"Got it right here, officer," Diresk politely announced as he handed over the documents. "I'm sorry about screwing around like that."

"How much alcohol have you consumed today, Mr. Webster?" the patrolman asked behind dark sunglasses.

"Well, more than you have…but less than I normally do," Diresk offered as my stomach seized and I exhaled much too loudly in front of the jury.

The patrolman sized us up, strolled back to his car and spoke into his radio, leaning against the door. Not more than a few minutes passed before he was at the window again, handing back Diresk's license and registration.

"Tell you what, Mr. Webster, I know you've been drinking today. For some reason I'm going to trust you to get where you're going and to stay the hell off the road until you get to thinking a bit clearer. Do I make myself understood?"

We all nodded in unison like three startled teenagers who realized they had been saved by God or the Devil. I do not believe I took a single breath until the man had finished speaking. Diresk even put on his blinker when we pulled back on to the interstate. He *never* used his blinker.

Five miles later we celebrated our good fortune with more mushrooms and wine. We were unstoppable. Untouchable. The universe was most certainly on our side and we would be young and strong until we were tired of being young and strong. Then, and only then, would we give permission to an aging process to enter our lives.

The mushrooms began to kick in for all of us, and a supernatural ecstasy was ours for the taking. It was beginning to look like a world record day when all at once Rose turned down the stereo and exclaimed,

"Shit, shit, shit! You are not going to believe this. I can't believe how stupid I am. I really can't believe how unbelievably stupid I can be!"

"What?" Diresk and I uttered in stereo.

"I forgot the tickets in my other pants. You know…the ones I absolutely had to change before we could leave. I took out my money and the mushrooms and I forgot the tickets in the pocket. Unbelievable! Shit! What do we do? We have to go back and get them, don't we? Shit!"

Diresk eased the truck to the shoulder and we sat in silence and waited for divine inspiration to take us back down the pleasure trail.

I always wish I could simply use a coupon for times such as that one. To erase that one pesky detail about to destroy an otherwise perfectly executed day. Just fix the one mistake and make everything wonderful again. In control. Where I always try to live, even now.

Turning around and driving an extra thirty miles or so is no big deal for the normal person. When you are hallucinating, stoned, and drunk beyond reason, thirty miles is an eternity. Who has that kind of time when you are immersed in absolute cerebral overload?

"Do we have enough money to buy new tickets?" I asked. "I have about eight bucks."

"I don't even know if we can get tickets because the radio said it's sold out," Rose answered as she attempted to fix the John Prine tape with the precision of a plastic surgeon using a pencil. I imagine her attempt at repairing the broken tape was a gesture to somehow cancel out forgetting the tickets.

"We can always get tickets, man," Diresk inserted. "People will be selling them before the show. I have five dollars but I forgot my credit cards. Either you got some green, Rosie, or we are on our way back to Spearfish."

"We're on our way back to Spearfish. I have fifteen bucks," Rose offered. "We still got plenty of time so we don't have to break any speed records getting there. All we need is to get nailed by that trooper again. I'm sorry about this, you guys. I'm going too fast. I'm speeding like crazy and I want to get there now! When we go back, I want to change into a skirt anyway."

This broke us up and we fell into a delicious fit of mushroom delirium. Tears flowed down our cheeks by the time Diresk managed to drive the truck through the ditch and jump on the interstate heading west towards Rose's other pants. I cannot begin to explain the effort that had been required to perform that simple act. When you are tripping like that, cars could be coming from any direction. Even from above.

We finally arrived at her apartment and got the tickets, stopped for more beer, grabbed Diresk's credit cards to ward off further tribulation, and jumped back on the interstate, laughing and chain smoking the entire time. We arrived at the Civic Center parking lot approximately an hour later, twenty minutes ahead of the dimming of the lights ritual. The lot was completely full and we were forced to park at a nearby high school.

There was just one tiny problem as we finished the tremendous hike from our parked truck to the facility.

"Son of a bitch!" Rose shouted. "I don't believe what I just did. Again! I forgot the tickets in the truck. What is wrong with me? I can't. Oh, Jesus. I've got to sit down."

"You forgot the tickets in my truck? Way over there in Montana?" Diresk responded amidst his own building laughter. "You mean to tell me you forgot the tickets you forgot in Spearfish...in my friggin' truck that is across the world over there? Over where eagles nest and cougars feast on speckled trout? Way over that mountain range? Honey, not the smartest thing you have ever done."

Diresk broke into his own hysterics at this point and could not continue comment. He fell into a pernicious pile with Rose as they both scraped skin onto the concrete walkway leading to the entrance doors. The two lit cigarettes as I donned a worried expression, fully aware it would be me hiking to once again procure the evasive tickets.

It could go no other way. I stood in helpless silence, waiting for the inevitable command.

"Topher? You have to wade over there and get those tickets. I'm sorry to do this to you but I can't...I can't make it, man. I'm going to puke." Diresk's face was a bright shade of red and Rose looked as if she would seizure any minute, hemorrhaging with laughter.

"Why do I have to go get the tickets?" I said. "I always get the dirty jobs, man! Why doesn't Rose get the friggin' tickets? I'm so messed up I don't know if I can make it, D. I'm serious, man! Twice, man. You forgot them twice in the same hour!"

It was a feeble gesture to avoid my inevitable quest. I was the only one not laughing. Penance for taking life so seriously.

I started to walk towards the truck and was called by Diresk who, observantly, threw me his keys which I did not even come close to catching. This provided a garnish for their uproar. I left them collapsed in each other's arms on the concrete path, surrounded by intrigued concert goers on their way to the show.

By the time I finally reached the truck and located the tickets where I had seen Rose place them so we would not forget them, my bladder screamed at me to release the gallon or so of alcohol I had poured into it. It had been a long trek. Must have been a couple hundred degrees out that day, too. There was no way I would make it back to a Civic Center restroom. I had the wherewithal to place the tickets in my pocket before I too forgot them again, and proudly locked the truck, keys in hand. I was winning, and if I could just relieve my bladder without being spotted, life would again be grand and there would be no stopping us this night!

It was not to be.

Why is it when you are stoned to the point of possible terminal paranoia and taking a piss in broad daylight that three girls you went to high school with casually stroll up to you to catch up on old times as they stare at your penis and fire questions like an Uzi?

I had not seen even one of these girls in five years. A rather odd way to bump into each other again. I broke into convivial greetings and converse until it occurred to me my genitalia was exposed to the elements as well as their judgmental appraisals.

Why is it that when you really must show someone your penis that it shrinks and shrivels like some embarrassed fungus? It is for this reason I will hate Jerry Serfoss for the rest of my breathing days. I shall never forget him strutting nonchalantly around our high school dressing room with a cobra hanging between his legs. Jerry Serfoss made most porno stars jealous.

By the time I was able to turn from them and place myself back in my jeans, I had deftly managed to soil my hands, jeans, boots, and Diresk's passenger door in an impressive display of incoherent incontinence. To add to this debacle, I had not yet finished peeing after garaging my shrunken member and sent a golden shower into my underwear and down my pant leg. It was a stellar performance. One of my best yet.

I do not remember a single word said by any of the girls on the walk back to the facility. I blacked out from the pure severity of the ordeal. I did, however, receive some support from one of my ex-classmates who had offered tissue from her purse.

Of course, I declined so as to not betray my utter powerlessness.

I found Diresk and Rose where I had left them, chatting with some people we vaguely knew from school. Diresk rose to hug our classmates and for a round of introductions. Then he noticed my boo-boo.

"What did you do to your pants, Jerry?" Diresk asked before he could take it back.

Under normal circumstances he would never have subjected me to such a crowded debasement in front of Rose.

"Well let's see," I began, demoralized. "I showed these girls my dick and then pissed all over myself. Here's the friggin' tickets and your keys!"

That quieted the crowd.

For only a few seconds I felt better, before the laughter exploded and shot at me like bullets. I rushed inside of the building, stopped, came back for my ticket as I had given them all to Diresk, and dashed back towards a restroom to possibly remedy my dilemma. I would have gladly traded all my "special circumstance" coupons for a quick rewind at this point.

An electric dryer proved most helpful. It took all of five minutes to dry my jeans, but I had destroyed the chemical wave I had been riding prior to my disaster.

I made my way toward the entrance areas and saw them waiting for me with serious faces and burning cigarettes. I approached them like a dog who knows it has done something very wrong.

"Oh, Topher," Rose said as she hugged me and kissed my nose. "Let's go have a wonderful concert and let's forget about all of the bad stuff that happened. It has still been a wonderful day. We just took some mushrooms and I have some for you when we get in there. You don't have your dope on you, right? They are checking pretty good. I got a couple joints hidden and they aren't going to check there, I'm sure." She winked at me and tugged a smile from my brooding face.

"Hey, don't sweat the small stuff, Tyrone. And it really is all small stuff," Diresk added. "Let's rock and roll, boys and girls."

The three of us filed into line with the throngs, and Diresk shoved me in front of him behind Rose. I will never forget what he said, although I can't remember much else of what happened that night.

He whispered, "Remember that night when I disappeared in Hill City and I told you I had to go make a call? That night we went to that party with those crazy bastards that worked at Mount Rushmore?"

"Yeah," I said.

"I didn't have to make a call. I left for another reason, man. I can't believe I'm going to tell you this shit. I drove up to a gas station to clean myself up because I had shit my pants. I shit my pants, man."

"You? Shit your pants? No way. No friggin' way."

I was stunned by the sudden mortality of my hero and quickly spun around to see if I had broken the ancient creed of confidentiality between best friends when one of them has just told the other something of such gravity.

"You shit your pants," I whispered cautiously.

Diresk pursed his lips and slowly nodded.

"You don't have to lie to make me feel better, D. It isn't such a big deal. I'm over it now. So I showed my little dick to some girls from school and then pissed all over myself like a circus freak. At least I didn't forget the tickets." I tried to force a smile.

"I don't lie to my best friend, Topher. If you ever tell anyone I did that, I will kill you, chop you into pieces, and feed them to Grover. They won't ever find your body. I mean it, man. This one's classified, Gerald! CIA shit."

"Tell anyone what?" Rose asked.

"Nothing," Diresk replied. "I was just trying to cheer up Urine Boy a bit and was telling him I'd kill him if he ever tells anyone about the time I shit my pants in Hill City and had to throw my undies away in a gas station. Got another cancer stick, Darling?" 1984—my best friends and I.

Chapter Twenty-Six

There was only one time Rose and I almost crossed the fine line we balanced on. I still feel a twinge of guilt and excitement for that moment.

I always wanted to kiss her. No! Wanted her to kiss me. Making love was entirely out of the question. I thought too much of her and Diresk to have pulled something like that off. Sex was always a precarious endeavor for me.

Hell, it still is.

I remember the night we danced together as our lips touched for one sweet second. Denver. To go back there and remember sends a jolt of high voltage through me still after so many years. I feel like I used to—before taking a big test or playing a big game. Like when I was in love with my best friend's girl. Searching for my Rose with her tanned legs and hushed voice grabbed my attention like an explosion.

And I'm still searching for my Rose.

"You are the prettiest girl here tonight, Rose," I humbly offered. "Sometimes I like to pretend you are with me when D. isn't around. That's silly, isn't it?"

"If I had never met Diresk, you would have been the first guy I would have kidnapped," Rose whispered in my ear as we swayed our bodies slowly to the music at an inner-city club.

We were both intoxicated as the three of us had spent the entire day assaulting the smog-soaked streets of Denver, smoking grass and drinking wine, pretending to be adults as the iron and concrete jaws of the city swallowed us whole, but we didn't care.

We were together and nothing was in our way.

Diresk bought me a beret and I wore it around the city all day and night. Rose painted Diresk's toes on a park bench and we thought we were the coolest people we had ever met. We gave a wino a five dollar bill and he drew us a picture of some building as his pencil shook between mangled fingers that fit perfectly and steadily around his bottle of gin. Rose kissed his cheek, and it took all the thinned blood he had left to raise a blush from the dead.

We later landed at a dance club to close down the night and Diresk passed out in a booth holding the picture and wearing my beret, leaving us to sway in the anonymity of the city's expanse. I danced with the most beautiful girl in the club that night, and for three songs she was all mine.

"I am very drunk, Mr. Topher. You?" Rose asked.

"I am semi-permeably incandescent, my dear," I proudly replied. Her clear chocolatey eyes made me want to lick them. Her aroma held me close to her shoulder.

"Wine makes me naughty. I'm having naughty thoughts right now. I wish we could go somewhere to another place in time and make love and come back and we would never remember it. Only deep inside our dreams. I could love you in my dreams, Topher. I could dance and make love to you and sleep beside the man I love. God, I am really messed up," she breathlessly sighed.

"Don't even say shit like that to me, because I have enough trouble with all of this as it is. If I thought you were attracted to me in any way, I wouldn't be able to…"

"Shhhh, I know," she whispered close to my ear. "I'm sorry. I just want one kiss. I have always just wanted to kiss you once to see how it would feel. I know how much you love him. It's only natural, Topher. All the time we spend together and all we have shared. There is nothing wrong with our feelings for each other. I am not ashamed that I love you. I mean, I love you like you love me. Is this making any sense?"

I found myself undeniably captured by her eyes, her skin, her smell. I did not even try to hide the fact I could not take my eyes off her legs—wearing a summer tan and her toes, a purple nail polish. She was barefoot. The way I will always remember her.

"I know what you mean," I said.

One more time I was the one who was forced to compose myself and watch the friends I loved more than anything in the world distance themselves from me in their own sacred bubble. A bubble I could see into, but never enter.

"Don't kiss me, Rose. I don't want to go through the rest of my life thinking about it. Okay? Not that you can't help yourself or anything, or were even going to—"

Then her lips brushed mine and lingered there, waiting for mine to join them. I closed my eyes and touched my forehead to hers, removing my lips from where I dreamed they could somehow rest forever. Her faced pulled away and startled me.

I opened my eyes and expected to see anger on her face. She was smiling. I will always treasure both the moment and that smile. It was the instant we crossed into most special friends. I wanted her ten times more than any drink or drug that night. I could feel her heart beat against my chest as if we had been separated only by cellophane. We danced to the music inside the music that only our souls could hear. I saw her soul's face for the very first time that night but I felt I had known her forever. Since the beginning of time.

We would never again cross that line or our understanding of the way things were certain to remain between the three of us. As I led her back to the table where Diresk slept, I could not hold down the feeling I would lose them both someday. It was a dismal feeling, hard to shake.

It took both of us to carry Diresk to the truck. I drove back to our motel with her head on my shoulder as we sang along with the radio and the crushing sadness beating within us.

Diresk slept the entire drive and would not remember either leaving the club or arriving at the motel. He sensed something between Rose and I the next morning at breakfast. He asked us why we were looking at each other the way we were and I could not help but feel I had betrayed his trust. Rose told him to mind his own business and kissed the syrup from his pouting lips.

We never brought it up again. I wonder if all close friends share such connections? Probably. But to us, we were picked especially to share in a magical friendship such as the world had never seen. We felt sorry for those unable to experience what we shared.

But maybe, we desperately sought to believe in the strength of three. Three against the world.

The world never had a chance.

Chapter Twenty-Seven

Rose took us shopping one day, and she wouldn't take no for an answer. She had threatened for months to "do something" about our blasé wardrobes. Diresk and I found combinations that worked for us and stuck with them until intervening factors prompted change. She, however, loved to wear purple. It made her skin look delicious, like a tasty caramel apple. She always reminded me of Arizona, and she changed clothes like most people change their minds.

On the other hand, I recall wearing the same pair of jeans for weeks at a time, and Diresk could usually be found in some neon bowling shirt with various advertisements. Shirts he usually picked up at a garage sale during our Saturday morning thrift period. His most treasured bowling shirt was a neon green and yellow number bearing the words The Pin Seeking Missiles.

I'll bet he wore that shirt five out of seven days. He was so happy when it was clean and he could initiate the cycle again. Rose attempted to destroy or lose that shirt on a number of occasions. Diresk protected that shirt with his life.

She led us through the mall one day like a couple of pouting ten-year-olds. Store to store, she yanked us along with her, barking orders at salespersons. It was her personal mission to clothe us like adults and she approached it with calculated focus. Diresk almost killed me after I had succumbed to hysterics when he had emerged from a dressing room sporting another of Rose's elaborate concoctions. He had silenced and disarmed me with a mere glance.

"You look wonderful, hon! You look like one of those rock stars. David Bowie," Rose said to Diresk as he shifted around in multiple mirrors, hoping against hope he would not be spotted by one of our acquaintances.

"Topher?" she said. "Tell him how good he looks. I dream of the day he loses that ridiculous bowling shirt and starts wearing clothes like this."

I knew I had to choose my words carefully at this point. I did not want to provoke Diresk, nor devalue Rose's efforts. To me, he looked like a disco freak. Something out of Saturday Night Fever. The clothes were cool and everything, but Diresk and I prided ourselves with our ability to skate around the borders of convention and hipness. We always believed we transcended such practices by never changing our styles. We would wait for the world to settle on our particular modus operandi. We did not have time to shift with the winds of change. Our plates were much too full as it was to dabble in such precarious nonsense.

"I like this style of clothes on some people," I cowardly offered. "Diresk would look good in anything, so I guess it just matters what he thinks."

"Thanks a lot, Senator!" Rose snapped back.

"I'll tell you what he thinks," Diresk sputtered. "He thinks I look like a friggin' cross between a professional golfer and a pimp! I'm not wearing this shit, Darling. You can wave those pretty lashes at me all you want, but I'm not walking around any place in this getup! If you laugh at me, Topher, I will beat you senseless."

"Don't get mad at me, man," I attempted. "This isn't my idea of a good time, either. Okay? If you hate the clothes, don't wear them. Rose has good taste and everything. I think you look good, and you could always teach disco lessons at a golf course. Maybe you could be the world's first used car salesman/bull fighter..."

I ran before I finished the sentence. As I emerged from the store, I realized he was not in hot pursuit.

That would prove to be worse. He would allow his wounds to fester and gather infectious momentum as he devised a diabolical scheme with which to traumatize me for, at the very minimum, my next two lifetimes. Not to mention the physical trauma. His strike would be timely and devoid of conscience.

Especially since Rose had been involved. I was a dead man. I would soon have a fist-shaped crater somewhere on my skull.

I considered trying to thumb a ride back to Spearfish in hopes he would never find me again. I knew he would not let it slide. Diresk could take a joke, as long as he was comfortable and in control of the situation. If anyone gave him shit when he was embarrassed about something? Well, suffice it to say this was something one just *did not* do.

And now, I had done the unthinkable! The unfathomable! The most serious infraction possible! I had insulted him in front of *her*.

There was nothing I could do but head for the food court and have my last Orange Julius before the slaughter. Hell, I even splurged and ordered the Raspberry Supreme. I was on red alert and constant surveillance, but there was no sign of him as I finished what was to be the last snack of my young adult life. I felt the impending doom approaching.

I was convinced Rose had run some type of interference for me which explained why I was still able to light and inhale a cigarette without a nurse's assistance. It would only be a matter of time until Diresk found a hole in Rose's web. My number was up!

I must have smoked five or six cigarettes as I contemplated my demise, but I could not stop laughing to myself as the smoke tickled my nose and face like a tiny fingered veil. I got him good. God knows he had it coming. He had humiliated me more times than I could count. Thousands of times. I always took what he dealt to me with a composed reverence. Finally, I had sprung from my self-imposed cell to fire back into the darkness of the waiting enemy.

It was truly a good day to die.

I sat there amidst fellow shoppers stopping for a snack before returning to the retail front, secretly afloat on my perilous conquest. It was one of those events I desperately wished to discuss with someone in order to process and explore all possible consequences and avenues of escape. Someone to share the broth with.

But I was alone, and the only friend I would dare invite into my coven of self-worship was somewhere with my foe. I felt like a spy waiting for a dissolving message as Nazi soldiers canvassed the area for my location. If successful in my mission, I would save the free world from Hitler's bloody reign. Failure could only end in tortuous testimony and assassination.

You must understand how very stoned I was and my prevalent leanings toward dramatic flair. After long moments went by, I waited with annoyance for the plot to unfold.

Minutes later, I spotted Rose hurriedly approaching the food court area, alone. I could not help but smile as I watched the male heads turn in unison as she sailed by in her short purple skirt, carrying her sandals as her bronzed bare feet padded along the polished tile. Her dark hair, teased and reckless, trailed behind her like a cape and framed her olive face with flowing chocolate.

She reminded me of a magnificent mare. Unbreakable.

I felt my body tense as my tainted senses simultaneously leaned forward to assess the data at hand. Was she a decoy? Sent to allow her villainous lover a blind-sided attack?

I quickly spun around in my chair to scan the perimeter for a lurking Diresk. My eyes searched through the crowd like a Secret Service agent struck suddenly alert by a gunshot, but he simply was not to be found. I returned my attentions to Rose who by this time had spotted me and was approaching with an indiscernible expression.

A grin inadvertently escaped from my clenched jaws and I felt myself calm as Rose responded in kind. I gestured her to a chair and she pulled up to face me, reaching for my cigarettes.

"Where is he?" I asked.

"He took off from the store and we got in kind of a fight," she quietly answered. "You didn't exactly help me any back there. He was starting to cave in about his clothes and now he'll never listen to me. He's really pissed, Topher. You embarrassed him pretty good."

"It isn't my fault or responsibility for any of this. He's going to wear whatever he decides to wear. You're the one making a big deal out of changing us, Rose. I've been dressing like this my whole life and I don't intend to change it because of anyone else's opinion. I like jeans and T-shirts. I don't feel right in anything else."

I paused before continuing. "How mad is he?"

"He's about a nine, I think," Rose offered. "I told him to cool his jets and that really pissed him off. I thought he was just kidding but he's really ticked off this time. He wouldn't even look at me when he came out of the dressing room. You better watch what you say to him. I plan to observe caution when he shows."

A strange smile and accompanying look overtook Rose's face and I realized I had let my guard down during our brief converse. I had failed to continue my perimeter check and was hit with a panic and feeling of disorientation. I caught a barely discernable shift in her eyes, and before I could form my next thought, found the top of my head covered in ice cream.

Chocolate Marble Fudge, to be precise.

Rose was immediately betrayed by her expression as an accomplice to my attacker's freezing assault. Through the chocolate haze impairing my blinking eyes I understood she had been dispersed to weaken my defenses by compromising my blind spot, thereby allowing Diresk a surprise attack with said frozen weaponry.

Oldest trick in the book. Send a dame to blink her lashes at the guard and then sneak into the enemy encampment to lower your boom.

Needless to say, his plan reached fruition and I was struck extremely uncomfortable. Physically as well as mentally. All I could do was sit there and bear the misery of the surrounding laughter and the sticky, cold bomb I had been hit with that afternoon. I never even broke stride with my next comment.

"So, do you think he will beat the shit out of me or just do something ridiculous like smear ice cream all over my head and face?"

Rose tried to extinguish the laughter brewing inside her, but was unable to maintain composure and fell in with the spectators at the surrounding tables. The moment was immediately sobered by the appearance of a disgruntled female custodial worker who stood no more than five feet tall, but had a voice that could crack drywall.

"I will have to ask you all to leave this facility, NOW! I will not tolerate a food fight and I will call security if you fail to vacate this area immediately!"

"That will not be necessary, ma'am," I angrily replied. "If you will just allow me to use your restroom facilities to tidy myself up a bit, we will be on our way."

I was not thrilled by her implication I was somehow remotely at fault for said event. She, in turn, was not thrilled by the sardonic tone I chose to address her with or perhaps the fact I was dripping a sticky dairy product all over her waxed floor.

"You will leave right this instant or deal with security! Do I make myself clear?" she punctuated.

I was promptly struck by a cornucopia of possible assaultive comments to toss like grenades at this minimum waged devotee, but was timely overcome in my malevolence by a sudden wave of rationality.

I was not going to worsen my dilemma and increase the potency of Diresk's strike. I swallowed what was left of my pride (and some chocolate fudge marble), un-tucked my shirt to wipe as much of my face and hair off as possible, grabbed my cigarettes from the table, and politely excused myself towards the exits. I briefly caught a glance at the curious look pervading Diresk's face as I departed from the battle scene.

I had nearly reached the exits when his booming voice rang out and halted me in my tracks.

"JUST BECAUSE I WANNA SEE SOME OTHER GUYS NOW AND THEN DON'T MEAN IT'S OVER BETWEEN US! I'M SORRY I THREW THAT ICE CREAM AT YOU, BUT THE THOUGHT OF LOSING YOU MAKES ME LOSE MY MIND, BABY! PLEASE, COME BACK TO ME AND WE CAN GO HOME AND TALK ABOUT THIS. Christopher! Please. Don't leave me like this! I'm begging you! Don't do this to us!"

A voice inside told me if I could simply leave the mall without having acknowledged his words I could possibly cut some of my quickly accumulating losses. But before I could stop myself, I spun around to view the wake of his attack.

Yep. Every person in the food court area was staring wide-eyed at me and my jilted lover. Rose was face down on the table covering her vibrating head, a victim of still yet another laughing seizure.

The custodial staff person stood dumbfounded with her hand on her radio, but her lips were pursed in silence as she waded through the details at hand. Diresk was on his knees, pleading, and had I found myself in possession of a firearm, would have fired with impunity into his carcass.

There are moments in one's life when clarity looms just beneath the surface of calamity, and if one is able to pause and allow the humiliation and momentum to wash through and pass, it can be readily accessed. I stood there like granite allowing the demons to surround and terrorize me. And then, as if my senses were drawn together and focused like a beam of light, I saw and sensed only Diresk. All other sights and sounds of the food court vanished. I steadied myself and opened fire. It was not necessary for my voice to reach the volume his had.

"Diresk, I shall always love you, but our time together has passed. I have been able to live with your temper, your emotional inconsistencies, and your unmitigated infidelity…but I can no longer tolerate your impotence. I need a man who can physically satisfy my passionate needs and desires. It saddens me that our relationship has reduced itself to such a public display of lunacy. You can send for your things, my sweet Diresk. I can only hope you are blessed with a medical remedy for your affliction. Good bye and God bless you!"

I actually heard a smattering of applause as I exited stage left, grinning from a place I had never accessed before. I lit a cigarette and strolled to Diresk's truck to await the arrival and next move of my competent foe and the lovely Rose. My wait was a short one. I was more than pleasantly surprised by the gesture of competitive respect offered to me by Diresk as he approached me.

"Man, I can't believe you just came up with that!" he said, laughing. "I am going to have to be careful in the future not to underestimate you when cornered, Cecil. Come here and give us a grab, you son of a bitch!"

I hugged him tight as my eyes found Rose and her obvious delight at the summation of our little event. Soon, the three of us were locked in each other's arms and laughter, with Diresk's eyes twinkling with mirth.

Even Grover amended her usual stance towards me and rode home comfortably perched upon my lap, licking the delicious dried syrup from my face and soiled T-shirt.

Chapter Twenty-Eight

Diresk used to say Rose could move in and furnish any brain she chose. I guess that would be true of mine. I still hear her in my dreams from time to time, this after a concerted effort to rid myself of her haunting fragrance I could smell in the days I hovered beside her.

My dreams always took place in or near water. Dreams that would take my breath away and leave me ignited. I dreamed of her often, but would never consider sharing this with either of them.

Rose also turned me on to the color purple because it made her skin such a beautiful luxury. I had simply failed to notice purple before Rose. Diresk detested the color, but would never mention it to her. I always wondered why he would leave this part of her alone. But then, he was always so careful around her. There rested below his usual brow-beating forays a most diligent restraint regarding his Rose.

I think he just wanted her to fall in love with him over and over.

He would sometimes touch her as if she was made from snowflakes, and he would kiss her as if drawing wine from her throat. God, how I envied his lips and their secret times together. The way in which he tried so very hard to keep his restraint in check. He was entirely reclusive in these matters, and would sidestep any and all conversation pointing towards his poorly-concealed vulnerability.

But me, I fell in love with purple, and the way in which it embellished her olive skin and seemed to backlight her eyes and teeth. Hell, I remember some of the outfits she used to wear. I will never forget her favorite swimsuit nor the effect it had on me. On everyone.

Rose had been ahead of her time and was the first, to my knowledge, to display the thong bikini in the Spearfish area. I actually witnessed the repercussions and reverberations during its unveiling in Spearfish's city park while sharing beers and Colombian marijuana with some pals as we tanned our skin and numbed our senses to loud music.

We usually hung out in our favorite spot in the park; a small plateau of plush, green grass nestled up against Spearfish Creek and directly opposite of the local fish hatchery. We would drown ourselves in tanning oils and arrange ourselves accordingly on lawn chairs in the middle of the cool creek. We developed an elaborate system consisting of coolers and a table we would carry out into the water with us to partake of our Earthly pleasures without having to ever move more than one muscle.

It was our place, and people grazed there by invitation only. Grover patrolled the area like some starving sentry, tethered to a twenty foot rope allowing her free reign of land and water. Every male who ventured into our private resort had to first obtain clearance from Grover in order to remain, usually preceded by Diresk's command, "COOL IT, GIRL DOG!"

Grover never restricted females from entering, though. In that sense, Grover was a very good dog.

On this particularly beautiful afternoon, I was entertaining guests in the absence of my two co-owners. A time-share agreement we adhered to cooperatively. I was surprised to see Diresk's truck pull into the parking area not twenty yards from our spot. I had incorrectly assumed my best friends would spend the afternoon chasing a tiny white ball around the Spearfish Canyon Country Club.

I abhorred the game of golf and still manage to avoid any and all invites to partake of this grim torture. Diresk hated it as well, but joined in because Rose loved it.

He would often say, "I hate the friggin' game, but I love the way her shorts sneak up her butt when she swings."

Rose would then counter with, "He just digs any sport where he can smoke, drink, and get a tan."

I must admit, I was inclined to concede to such manner of thought.

"Well, would you look at this," I mumbled to Tom Tolo, one of the greatest pot smokers of his generation. "Mr. And Mrs. Arnold Palmer must be taking time off from the links to join us for cocktails."

"I hope she doesn't wear that one suit again," Tom whispered. "I can't take that shit, man."

Curtis Pummel, basking beside us, concurred with a slight nod and tousle of his long blonde curls. Curtis was a great pot smoker as well.

He was also rather adept at helping himself to the hearts of fair maidens in our lovely little Camelot.

The particular suit Tom had mentioned was a rather slinky number sporting vertical black stripes upon a thin purple canvas. Tantalizing, yet pathetically pale, placed beside the incommunicable delight we were about to be exposed to, or should I say with?

I waved at Rose as she jumped out of the truck to liberate Grover from the box of the truck. She was clothed in Levi cutoffs and one of Diresk's bowling shirts. Diresk was moving around in the cab and accidentally honked the horn with his elbow, sending Grover on a barking spree and into the tan arms of our Rose. Diresk, having located whatever he had been searching diligently for, emerged from the truck wearing cut off football pants, cowboy boots, and his amorous smile nearly always present in Rose's company.

"Topher, your legs got skinnier overnight!" Diresk yelled as he fell into step and hand with Rose, still carrying Grover with her free arm.

"I love a man with thin legs, Topher," Rose countered. "You're a sexy man and don't listen to a word this barbarian feeds you. Hey, Tom. Hey, Curtis."

Tom and Curtis both nodded.

"It's hard not to listen when his mouth never stops puking words, man," I responded as they reached the edge of the creek.

Rose released Grover who finally ceased barking and began to vacuum the grass with her nose. Seconds later, our guard dog dove in, causing Tom, Curtis, and I to reflexively remove all appendages from the water.

Grover paddled towards us, growling deeply.

"Tell me you have beer in abundance, my lads," Diresk stated, ignoring my comment entirely. "GIRL DOG! Cool it now."

"We have beer in abundance, my liege," I answered. "And to make matters worse or better, depending upon the particular school of moral thought you attend, Thomas has blessed us this day with a golden spiked herb with which to deter our minds from the blatantly obvious detail of this lingering melanoma of reality."

"You have made me a very happy man, Jethro! What does a man have to do to get a drink and his pecker sucked around here?" Diresk inquired, bouncing his brows for emphasis.

"That sounds like a job for Tom," Curtis said with a smile that rendered many maidens helpless and without hope of recrimination when wronged by this virile knight.

"Right," Tom snapped back, splashing water in Curt's direction.

"What am I saying? All I have to do is lean down and I can do it myself!" Diresk exclaimed as he feigned the dirty deed.

"Why do boys constantly need to discuss penis size?" Rose said. "Don't you guys know that we don't care about the size of your organs?" Rose shook her head back and forth like a ping pong referee.

"I was wondering why you still hang around with Diresk," Curtis said. Curtis was not afraid to go head-to-head with Diresk and there was always a stretched tension between most remarks they made to each other.

"If you're looking to be seriously bloodied up today, I'm your man, Blondie!" Diresk answered, a slight smile betraying his comments which we all read to be a good sign that the two of them would not be at each other's throats all afternoon.

"If you can brave the dangerous rapids of Spearfish Creek and reach this spot, unscathed, you can help yourself to whatever medicine you desire," I offered to Diresk and Rose.

"I want your collective opinion on something and I want you to be honest with me," Rose suddenly said. "I bought something in Denver last weekend and I think it's really cool, but it may be a bit much for you right-wingers around here."

"Christ, Rose," Diresk announced. "It's only a swimsuit for God's sake. She's been yacking about this all morning and she wouldn't even show it to me. She makes it sound like she's going to get arrested or something."

"It's a European cut and it is rather risqué. I mean, for around here and everything. I absolutely love it but I don't know if I should wear it around here."

"Does it have a top and a bottom?" Curtis asked innocently as he took a long pull from the joint Tom had ignited and passed.

"OF COURSE!" Rose smiled.

"Bummer. Well, let us see it anyway," Curtis said as a fiendish grin began to overtake his smoking lips.

"Do I have to get up for this?" Tom asked.

"I don't think you are going to have a choice," Curtis whispered as he again pulled from the joint and passed it to me with a wide-eyed expression.

"Show us the friggin' suit so we can get on with our lives, for Christ's sake!" Diresk shouted.

Diresk was not happy about the unfolding of this event. It was in his tone and the cutting use of his words. He always pretended it never bothered him when other guys looked at Rose, but there were times, he was threatened by Rose's imposing presence. I think he must have sensed we were all in for something he believed he alone should have witnessed alone.

I passed the joint to Tom and opened another beer, throwing another to Diresk as a gesture of support. He caught it and waded out to Tom's chair and took his turn with the dope. I could sense his trepidation and could find no words of comfort to offer. Actually, validating his discomfort would have been a serious breach of diplomatic etiquette, and my silence more than likely saved us all from much turmoil.

"Okay, here goes," Rose nervously said.

She removed Diresk's bowling shirt and displayed a purple bikini top. Nothing out of the ordinary, but smashing just the same. Tom, Curtis, and I nervously glanced at each other and then towards Diresk, who pretended not to watch while cleaning a fingernail. Rose took a deep breath, flashed her eyes toward her brooding boyfriend, back to us, then gracefully shook her shorts to the grass and stepped out of them.

Had someone been watching the four of us young men, they would have thought we were watching a bomb squad defuse an exploding device. I know we had all been holding our breaths, though I can only vouch for myself. I'll bet we all looked like a bunch of idiots.

As I watched Rose remove her shorts, I was puzzled, as were my compadres, by the stunningly beautiful woman standing before us in what we all must have considered to be a sexy, yet fairly harmless bikini. She was gorgeous.

Curtis shattered our feverish silence.

"What the hell's the matter with that, Rose? I've seen you wear stuff like that before. It's no different than what a bunch of girls are wearing right over there," he said, pointing to a group playing beach volleyball on the sand court.

"You haven't seen the back yet," Rose added, dropping her head slightly.

"What about it?" Diresk shot back testily.

"There isn't one," Rose muttered under her breath.

Her comment was followed by a hushed silence, followed by

anticipatory jitters I could have cut with my tongue had I been able to remove it from the back of my mouth. We all looked to Diresk for guidance, who simply lit a cigarette and shook his head.

"It's called a thong, you guys" she said. "It has this string that goes up your butt and everything. Like that poster of those three girls in the back of that pickup out at Screamin' Elrod's, you know?"

We knew!

I couldn't take it any longer, and though aware I would distress our usually fearless leader, I spoke the words we all secretly longed to say.

"Turn around. Go ahead, Rose."

She took my cue and spun around on those purple painted toes of hers, announcing, "TA DA!"

"Oh, my friggin' God," said Diresk.

Tom, Curtis, and I spoke to each other only with our eyes, then immediately returned to the vision at hand. I could not bear to meet Diresk's eyes, and though I attempted to preserve his pride by not staring at his girlfriend's wonderfully sculpted behind, I failed miserably.

We all did.

The next words I recall hearing inadvertently escaped from the mustached mouth of Curtis. "Sweet Jesus and son of a bitch."

I admit I was inclined to concur once again, but I did so with a wordless nod of my pulsing head. Arterial explosion is what I now believe had struck me that afternoon. At the time, I had fully expected and braced for an aneurysm.

Rose could take no more of our scrutiny and again spun around to meet our helpless gazes. We were simply powerless to participate in the moment, other than to drink from our beers and light cigarettes with a perfunctory deliberation. Anything to focus on, aside from the raving beauty standing on the shore with a string running up her buttocks.

A purple string. Of marvelous design and strategic placement.

Yes, it was merely a thin piece of colored cotton that sunny summer afternoon. It is undeniably sad that a group of moderately intelligent young men could be moved and touched to such deep extent by something such as this, but we were utterly bombarded by beauty and sexually stung. An allergic reaction was had by all.

I remember Rose blushed as she was serenaded by several whistles coming from somewhere nearby. She self-consciously stooped to retrieve her shorts and was stunned by Diresk's surprisingly tender words. It is probably what I remember most about that day, and there was serious competition.

"Don't, Rose," he said. "You look beautiful in that suit. I'm acting like a shit-head over this. Don't put those shorts on, Honey. If people can't handle it, screw them."

Rose waded out to where Diresk was standing, and he jokingly covered her behind as they embraced in front of us.

Diresk shrugged his shoulders at me and I was again proud to be his friend.

Rose kissed him and removed his hand from its protective positioning as she leaned back as if in a dance dip to retrieve a newly lit joint from Tom's thumb and forefinger; crystal droplets of water leaked from the bare foot she pointed to the cotton ball cloud sky and I caught them in my mind's mouth.

"I love you, Diresk Nathan Webster," Rose whispered as her lips painted his with lipstick. "And I think you boys ought to buy yourselves some thongs so we can make a fashion impact on this dreadful place."

"If any of you ever see me walking around with nothing but a piece of dental floss up my ass I want you to shoot me in the head repeatedly," Diresk said. "Are we crystal clear on this, gentlemen?"

"If I ever see you walking around with a string up your ass I may have to shoot myself in the head," Curtis added, laughing and coughing pot smoke out of his nose.

That was our introduction to the thong bikini. Rose wore hers with pride for the rest of the summer, only receiving a few mild citations of reproach from concerned citizens of Spearfish. Personally, I loved the suit.

But I always loved her in purple.

Chapter Twenty-Nine

As the summer wore on, we all got closer, but Rose would never talk about her parents. I know they dropped her off with her grandparents when she was a child, but not much more. She carried a picture of her mother with her in her purse and whenever one of us would ask about her father she would say, "If he ever decides to come around, he can tell you what happened himself."

She told me something during one of our last visits before she moved to Arizona to be "closer to the sun and farther from the snow shovels" regarding her split with Diresk. She blamed it on her father. That is all she would say. No matter how much I questioned and baited her, she never bit. She made me promise never to tell Diresk what she had told me. And, I never told a soul…until now.

How could we have fallen apart? The three of us? If you could have but seen us then it would have appeared impossible to happen. But it did. It happened like clouds suddenly blowing in on the brightest summer day, carrying gigantic canisters of rain with which to ruin your one day off. How could that happen? Rain on my one day off.

I still feel guilty I was powerless to stop it. Guilty, because I have never attempted to track her down. Guilty for things that never even happened, but only flicker in my mind and are on the tip of my tongue. Guilty for the things I never said to them. For loving her so much in the shadow of their love. And, I still feel guilty for hoping she would come back for me.

I think they were together for almost more than two years. To this day, I have no clear sense of what drove them apart. I do not believe anything did. I think they just somehow flew away in different directions because staying together meant always having to be too close to someone. Maybe Rose got scared off by Diresk's drinking and self-destruction. Maybe Diresk got scared off by Rose's light. I wish I knew. Selfish for me to wonder, really. The answer never came to me.

Whenever Diresk would talk about Rose after she moved to Phoenix without him, he would get this look in his eye that reminded me of a James Taylor song the three of us used to sing. Every time I hear that song I shed a couple more tears from my heart.

The morning after Diresk died, I played that song over and over upstairs in my parent's house in Custer. Upstairs on the bed that Diresk and I shared during our early sleepovers, and where we practiced kissing pillows and hovered eagerly over hoarded pornographic magazines stolen from my step-father's den. The bed I sleep in when I return home to visit my family. It still makes the same noise when I get in and out. Like the screeching of hot air against the vocal chords of the demon who hid beneath my bed. The demon Diresk drove away because I asked him to.

I played the song but could not hear the words. All I could hear were the memories attached to the melody and movement of Taylor's often tortured past; I wondered if he had written the song in an institution. I cried so hard I feared my stomach would bleed. I wretched as bile stung my throat and gums as I curled up fetal-style against the cool plastered wall. There were not enough blankets in the house to warm me.

I could have begged some far away God to tell it to me straight, but why bother. Would God tell me? Really? Why couldn't he quit using drugs? Why everything has to end up hurting so bad and how the answers get buried so deeply in our tissues? Why Diresk could not sense what I had begun to find and not wish to at least request a sample? Why could Rose's love not save him? Save all three of us? How could I have missed so much? Why was I so blind and so selfish I couldn't see him drowning?

I remember praying for God to be real. Funny, looking back on the day I remember thinking please let there be a God so there can be a place to go when we die and I can see him again. Please. Would I ever see him again? Ever?

I miss you, Rosemarie. I miss you more, and less, with every passing of night and day. 'Just a matter of angles.' You told me that once.

I miss the way you always saw colors in everything, and the way you could make me laugh when it was so much easier to prune my anger and fears. I wish you would have told me of your father. What you knew of him. Do you have a child of your own? You would have a daughter, of that I am nearly certain. I'll bet she's as beautiful as the wild flowers you used to hang upside down in your tiny apartment. Was it their life's blood, rushing to their petaled faces that made them so?

Oh, Rose, if only you could have saved him too...

Chapter Thirty

One final ditty about Rose, though it is so difficult to relive these memories. How to edit any of this, so etched in the mineral matter of my mind? Fresh soil from this shovel I dig with these long nights, alone with the three of us. The hole is much deeper than I had intended.

If I could make a movie of our past together, I would certainly focus on the angels that must have followed and studied us with bemused glee. I would give Rose much more than her cameo. It feels like it would be black and white, but that would merely be a morose misdirection. Something about the absence of color always speaks to me.

I will remain forever in deepest debt to our Rose for the enormity and scope of her love, and for the alignment she provided for her boys. Rose taught me how to express love by throwing fuel upon embers and making it impossible for me to ignore my flame. Simple as that. She set me on fire with her own flame, and there was absolutely nothing I could do to extinguish it.

Maybe God sends people like her, bearing the ancient gifts, to remind us how alive we can be. Maybe we all are sent a Rose during our lives.

It was a Wednesday night custom for the three of us during our college days in Spearfish to attend the Hank and Christy shows at the B&B Saloon and Back Porch Bar. Hank on guitar and Christy on bass with the duo sharing vocals and humorous quips to smooth out the middle of the week for us overwhelmed collegians.

They are still playing together after all these years. More than likely playing the same songs upon the same stools.

Another Wednesday night custom we adhered to was to attempt to coax Rose on stage to belt out a tune with the band. We endured her private concerts every time we rode together in a vehicle, but we could never seem to convince her to share her vocal prowess with the hometown crowd. After weeks of cajoling, we wore her down and she finally relented.

No small thanks to the nearly lethal doses of hallucinogenics and wine consumed prior to her performance, provided by her talent agents. I was so delighted as she strolled confidently to the microphone that Wednesday eve to share her rendition of "Gold Dust Woman" by Fleetwood Mac. It was a song she could actually rise to on occasion, given her range limitations and abrasive vocal chords, sanded by years of a cigarette and coffee past. That night she fell short of our expectations.

Diresk and I writhed and grimaced into our seats during the performance as if we could somehow manipulate her voice into proper key. She was very close to nailing it, and had delivered both song and accompanying gestures with true compassion and heartfelt vigor, but to hyper-perfectionists such as myself, close only counts in horseshoes and breathalyzers.

If you have a good attorney.

The bar crowd was more that gratuitous in their response to her misguided, yet spirited crucifying of the Stevie Nicks tune and demanded an encore, which to my utter horror, she excitedly agreed to deliver.

One of my more lethal character defects has always been the inability to see the benefits of doing something just because it is fun, even though you may look less than perfect to prospective critics. Diresk was concerned with protecting Rose's feelings. Feelings insulated and befuddled by chemical assault, and in no danger of harm.

She absolutely had a ball!

Diresk and I quickly assembled for an emergency conference as Rose huddled with her accompanists in contemplation of her next selection.

"I've got to tell her to relax so she can show these assholes what she can really do," Diresk said. "She's not singing from her guts, man. She sounds like she's got a sore throat or something."

"Tell her she needs to sing from her diaphragm!" I shouted in his ear.

The natives were quickly approaching restless and began to demand action from the guest vocalist.

"What?" he yelled back.

"Tell her, she's singing from her throat and she has to use her diaphragm! Tell her she'll get much better range and be able to hold the key!"

"Jesus, you always have to complicate shit, don't you?" Diresk said.

"Just tell her!" I insisted.

Diresk nodded and approached the stage, pushing and shoving his way through the dancers gathered on the dusty barroom floor like a bear on his way to a buffet. Rose spotted him and assumed he was going to join her in song and announced his name in the microphone perched in front of her purple lips.

Lest I forget to mention a crucial detail of probable significance regarding the crowd's passionate embrace of our diva, Rose had been wearing a crotch-defying skirt topped by a skin-tight body suit. I believe she wore red pumps, and such dressings on women's feet seem to initiate a biological reaction in most males, often temporarily disengaging them from reality.

Diresk waved off his girlfriend's beckoning to join the show and gestured for her to present an ear for consultation, standing center stage beneath her. She eagerly complied and bent down to receive his message. She appeared to digest his comments, offered her own in his ear, and kissed him firmly on the lips before assuming her upright position at the microphone.

Diresk swung around to face me with a slightly opened mouth and a look of utter disorientation. Then, as if suddenly struck by a truck full of awareness, he exhaled, flashed me his grin, and began to slap his knee and laugh hysterically. He sat down on the edge of the stage, shaking with emotions, and began to vigorously clap his hands before leaning over to kiss Rose's right knee. It was my favorite knee, too.

He continued to sit there, shaking his head and smiling at me as I beckoned him over to share the latest, greatest, Rose. He soon ambled over and slid into his chair, eyes appearing to have glassed over with something I had not seen in him before. He spoke in near whisper and held my head in his hands. "I love that woman, Toph! God damn, I love her so much, man!"

"What did you tell her and what did she tell you?" I eagerly asked.

"I told her she sounded great but she needed to sing from her diaphragm, just like you said."

"Yeah," I said, "and what did she say?"

"She told me she wasn't wearing her diaphragm," Diresk replied and fell back into barely controlled hysterics.

In my current state of chemical imbalance it took me more time than

I would have liked to admit to catch on to the gist of the moment, but I got it. And more importantly, I laughed myself into total abandon of fear of judgment. I was able to witness the clarity and the magic of not taking one's life, or your best friend's for that matter, so damned seriously.

It is a night I often return to when faced with the proposition of performing some unfamiliar act I am not at all comfortable with, suddenly struck gullible by the mind-bred fear of not looking good. Thankfully, because of Rose and my noble Diresk, I am frequently apt to defuse such distortions by conjuring and coaching myself with their teachings.

"Sing from the diaphragm, Toph! Let her fly and don't worry about what the idiots in the cheap seats are thinking! It don't friggin' matter anyway, man. It only matters how much fun you have doing it!"

Diresk, where were you when you were handing out all of this free advice?

Chapter Thirty-One

FATHERS

I have never met my father. My biological father. All I really know about him is he left my mother two weeks before I was born and hightailed it to Florida to dive for treasure ships or something ludicrous.

He called me one day when I was sixteen and I haven't felt the need to speak to him since. He has also opted for passive avoidance. It's not that we actually reached any mutual agreement to not converse, but our one and only phone call sunk to a depth neither of us wished to return to, buried treasure or not.

"Christopher?" I could hear the panic in my mother's voice as she rapidly ascended the stairs leading to my room. "Open up, I need to speak to you right now!"

I obediently sprang from my bed and opened the dead bolt to my private fortress. I saw the panic in my mother's face when I opened the door.

"What's up, Mom?" I asked, stepping aside as she entered my room and sat down on my bed like a woman who had just spoken with the father of her child for the first time in sixteen years.

Her face was as ashen as the wedding dress she never got to wear in college. "Daddy" had been unable to cope with "the scene" and had split to become a pirate, promising to drop precious stones and bullion bars at her feet upon return. She held her breath for nearly seven years.

"I can't believe this!" she gasped. "It's Hank. I mean, it's your father...on the phone. He's down there on the phone and he wants to speak with you, Honey. I couldn't think of anything to say to him. He just asked me all these questions like he had left last week or something.

I froze up and couldn't answer any of them. I don't think I can talk to him again. Oh, my God, Christopher. It's your father. On the phone... calling from Florida because I guess he still lives there or something and..."

My mother continued with her digressions, deteriorating further with every spoken word, and I began to realize she was dangerously close to a nervous breakdown and could not be counted on for rational input or support. As the blank look in her eyes clouded and her wringing hands picked up speed in their attempt to smother some invisible flame, I began to question and fear for the sanity of my mother.

It terrified me to no end to see her in such straights, yet not nearly as much as the dangling downstairs phone with my estranged father attached to the other end.

My next thought had been to deal with the situation at hand. "I better hurry up. It's long distance."

The thought following that one was "Long distance? Screw him! I've been waiting for sixteen years for him to call me. He can wait sixteen minutes for me to talk to him!"

I believe my next conscious thought had been one of concern for my hysterical mother, still babbling supine atop my Dallas Cowboy comforter. I attempted to gain her attention. Instead, I was greeted by occasional glances and psychotically-induced smiles before she would return to her oral dissertations regarding the dangers of relationships, the absolute futility of trusting anyone, and an assortment of topics too numerous and perplexing to address.

The best I could manage at this point was to hold her hand as I deftly considered my next move.

Do I talk to my "deadbeat dad", even though there is a better than average chance my heart may soon be in my mouth and my breath cut off to a two-inch area just below my tongue? Or, do I stay with my mother who appears dangerously close to a psychotic break and thereby ignore my father who I have never seen or spoken to before. Who has suddenly reappeared on "the scene" and wants to chew the fat before boarding his next vessel to go tickle the high seas to see if it will laugh up some gold?

As luck would have it, I was struck hopeful by the voice of Diresk who had just waltzed in my home following a spirited debate with a local police officer, entitled what exactly constitutes coming to a full stop?

The officer, obviously assuming he had won said disagreement, promptly issued my client a traffic summons. Diresk had stopped over to air his concerns regarding the current system and to discuss and prepare our strategy for his impending court date and possible appeal.

He actually disputed the ticket in court and the judge was forced to throw the case out, as the officer in question failed to show up to testify on behalf of Custer County due to a rather nasty circumstance I am not at liberty to discuss.

"WHO'S ON THE HORN?" Diresk yelled up the stairs to my room.

"IT'S MY DAD IN FLORIDA!" I responded in kind.

"No shit?" he added, having reached my doorway in seconds. "Have you talked to him?"

I shook my head. "Mom did."

"He want to talk to you?"

"Yep."

"You going to talk to him?" Diresk asked, clearly curious.

"I don't know."

"What do you want to do?"

"Run away."

"We sound like we're on Dragnet, man," Diresk noted. "Mamma Topher don't look too hot, man. Should we get her a drink or something?"

"She's just in shock. So am I, man! I don't know what to do, D. He's waiting down there on the phone and I don't fucking know what to do. Sorry, Mom."

At this point, I knew my mother was in serious distress. Her not reacting to my saying the "F-word" was about as likely an occurrence as a Baptist minister with a mohawk.

"I don't know if I can face him," I said. "Feels like my heart is going to explode through my chest any minute now. I can't breathe very well, D. I always dreamed of this happening, but now I wish he would just go away and call back after I have a chance to think this all out."

"There's your answer, Slick. Tell him you can't talk to him now. That you need time to think this over and he can call back in a few days or something. You don't have to do anything, man. He'll hang up eventually anyway, but if you don't want to lose him again you best pop down there and at least say something. Want me to talk to him?"

"Yeah. No! Shit, I don't know! What would you do?" I asked, paralyzed by emotions as I continued to sink further into my mental quicksand.

"No way I can answer that one, Jerry," Diresk said. "I'd probably talk to the son of a bitch, but you know me, all guts and no brains. I know this has got to be Bummer City for you, and it may feel like it's going to bust your heart...but it won't. This is just another monster. Just like all the others, man. Feeding on your being afraid of it. Man, I can't friggin' believe he called!"

"Me neither, man. Where is this coming from? Out of the blue like this?" I wanted to sit on someone's lap and have them hold me like when I was a child, but I couldn't afford to freak Diresk out with a sudden barrage of intimacy, and my mother had regressed to the age of approximately five.

"Maybe you should go down there and see what he's got to say for himself, Toph. You don't have to be nice to him and you don't have to tell him anything you're not ready to say. Tell him the friggin' truth, man."

"That I'm about to shit my pants?"

"When the bowels got to move, the bowels got to move, Jerry. Naw," Diresk said, shaking his head. "Just tell him this is freaking your wig and you need some time to chew on it for a while. Tell him he can call back later. Or you can maybe get a number you can call him at when you're ready. Maybe you ought to just sit here and panic and make him feel worse than he already does. Tell him to screw off. Tell him to come visit you. Any of these options ring a bell?"

"I'm going to talk to him," I bravely reported, handing my mother's hand to Diresk, who slid into my vacated position on the comforter with the traffic citation now dangling from his mouth as he searched for something in his pocket with his free hand.

"Here. Take one of these," he whispered, blocking my mother's view and auditory acuity with his body. "If she gets any worse, maybe we ought to give her one, too."

I dutifully removed a single tablet of Valium from Diresk's palm and began my arduous trek downstairs to speak with my father for the first time in my young adult life. I swallowed the tab on my way down the stairs as a precautionary measure. Someone had to keep this family afloat for crying out loud.

Just before finishing my descent, Diresk's voice issued a final instruction. "Hey, Toph? It's your game on your turf, man. You tell him what you want, and then tell him that's the play. Relax and let him do the heavy thinking!"

I reached the bottom floor kitchen and was seized by an overwhelming fear at the sight of the phone receiver, dangling ominously like a tree serpent. I must have reached for it four of five times, my hand recoiling each aborted time as if from a flame. Finally, I succumbed to my conscience and palmed the receiver as I instinctively drew a deep breath and closed my eyes.

"Hello?" I hoarsely inquired to the obnoxious droning of a dial tone.

I quickly hung up the receiver to prevent an inadvertent re-connection, feeling not just a tad relieved and remiss, simultaneously. I stood there tasting the bitter tablet, my hand still affixed to the phone on the wall as if I could somehow feel what my father's voice would have sounded like. I began to sketch a mental picture of his features and was overcome by an enormous sadness that flooded my stomach and chest.

I nearly fainted when my artwork was violently interrupted and erased by the metallic ring of the phone still resting within my tense fingers. It would beckon twice again before I would swallow hard and rip it from its catch.

"Hello?" I answered in a near whisper.

"Christopher? Is that you, boy?" a deep voice yelled into my right ear.

"Yeah…it's me. Hank?" I asked, speaking over my pounding heart.

"What took you so long to come to the phone, boy?" the voice barked at me. "I ain't got a million dollars in quarters, here!"

My chest felt as if a razor had sliced down my sternum. Soon to follow was a rage that welled and crested liked a hurricane. An electric explosion of white heat started in my head and deluged my senses like flood waters. For the first time in my life, I spoke the words of a man.

"What took *you* so long to call me?" I shot back. "If you are so worried about the money, why didn't you call collect?"

"Okay…listen to me, Chris," my father quickly said. "I don't want our first discussion to turn into a bummer. Okay? Look, I know I should have tried to get in touch with you sooner, but I was worried how you would react. I didn't want to screw up your life any more than I already had, you know? Chris? Come on, man. Let's start again."

"My name is Christopher and I don't know how to react to this. Haven't you ever wondered about Mom and me? You don't know what this is like! Mom is upstairs freaking out like she just saw a friggin' ghost and I feel like a car is parked on my chest. Why now? Why today?"

"It was just time, man. Like I woke up the other day and I was thirty-six years old and I looked around and I ain't got no family, no home, and I want to get... I need to get some of that in my life. I want to... hang on a minute, man. Jesus Christ. Two and a half bucks?"

I listened to the clicks on the line as he inserted coins and was brushed by a gentle breeze of contentment and clarity. I smiled to myself and waited for my father to continue. I no longer felt cornered. I suddenly felt an elated pulse throughout my entire being.

"Hey, man," my father continued, "why don't you call me back at this number because it's going to bleed my ass dry if I have to keep feeding this hungry animal quarters. What do you say, kid? Everything copacetic?"

"No," I said with a new-found peace and direction. "Everything is not copacetic. Why don't you give me a number I can reach you at some time? I need to think about this some more. I'll call you when and if I feel ready. That's the play, here, Hank. Take it or leave it."

I took a deep breath and waited for a bomb to explode in my ear.

"There is no number I can give you, Christopher. I'm always moving around and out on the water all the time, man. Speaking of, you've got to come out to Florida so I can show you around the sights. It's a God damn paradise down here and you can't believe the babes. I'm looking at two of them right now that would melt your retinas, man. Can you call me back now? Don't leave me hanging out here, man. I'm about tapped on the coinage until I can get another diving gig. You got a pen? I'm in Lauderdale. It's going to cut me off and I have to keep what I have so I can party hearty, dig?"

The metallic voice had again barged in to trade coins for time.

"Come on, man. It's going to cut me off pronto?" my father begged as the second round recording issued a more assertive plea.

"I told you what I was going to do," I firmly managed. "If you want to talk to me, you can somehow get a number or address to me and I can..."

"Forget it, man!" my father erupted. "I don't know why you have to bust my balls, kid! All I wanted to do was see how you were doing and see if you needed anything. Jesus! If you can't forgive me for..."

The line went dead.

I stood there holding the phone, oblivious to the bothersome noise in my right ear. My silent reflection was invaded by Diresk's voice directly behind me. I felt his hand on my shoulder and I slowly turned to face him.

"What'd he say, Toph?" he softly inquired.

"He wanted me to call him back. I told him I wasn't going to and we got cut off. Said he didn't have enough money to keep the call going," I said. "Did I blow it, D.?"

"Hell, no!" he answered as he removed the humming phone from my hand and replaced it on the wall.

He patted my shoulder and wandered to the refrigerator to remove two of my step-father's Coors beers, bouncing his brows in invite as he opened and handed one to me before delving into his own frosted can.

"Where's Mom?" I asked with mild paranoia.

I looked up the stairwell for signs of possible maternal intrusion. I was not allowed to drink alcohol during family holiday meals, let alone in my own house for the hell of it.

"She's crashed like a wino on your bed, Junior. Don't sweat the small stuff but please do tell your best buddy D. the skinny on Pops."

Hesitantly, I drank from my beer as he flashed his patented grin at me. I had, however, remained in good standing with my encompassing calm, and could not wait to share my good fortune of inordinate demeanor with Diresk, who had already drained his first beer and was en route to his second.

"I can't believe it, man," I began. "When I first started talking to him, I thought I was going to get cut in half because I was so pissed at him. I hadn't felt anger like ever. Anyway, we started to kind of argue and I was starting to get that panicky feeling. I was expecting some panic freak out to overtake me so I would pass out or just go blank and have a stroke."

"Get to the meat, Jerry . Before I turn fifty!" Diresk said.

"Sorry, but this was kind of heavy for me. I'm just trying to tell you I think I'm getting better with managing my feelings. You are always talking about how I can't keep a handle on my feelings, and when I go to tell you about how I'm beginning to do just that, you jump all over me and don't let me tell you about it! Maybe I'm getting stronger is all I'm trying to say here, if you'll just cut me some slack."

"Yeah, maybe," Diresk nodded. "Or maybe you got a little boost from the medicine I gave you. What do you think that was, man, a friggin' breath mint?"

I suddenly felt vexed and rather foolish. The Valium had entirely slipped my mind. Or had my mind slipped on the Valium? Blinded by my arrogant assumption I had somehow temporarily vanquished my pesky nemesis, I had conveniently overlooked my ingesting of a potent tranquilizer prior to conversing with dear old Dad. Dang!

I immediately launched into a sedated self-pity and was soon ready for my second mood altering beverage.

I replayed my conversation with my father as best as I could as Diresk listened intently, inserting timely perceptions and insight with dramatic waves of his burning cigarette. We checked on my mother, and after pooling our collective wisdom regarding medicine, psychiatry, sociology, and religion, we were able to determine an immediate transport to a health care facility was not warranted, and merely covered her in a blanket and escaped to the quiet confidentiality and comfort of Diresk's truck.

Grover tried to bite me and I spit in his hairy face. I was in no mood to take canine shit, and though Diresk was not pleased, he let it slide.

As we drove away, I could not help but wonder why I was not in tears. It seemed the appropriate reaction to such a situation, but I could barely get a feeling to rise toward the bait.

"Look," Diresk said after crossing the city limits. "You can't sweat this because you're the kid and it's not your responsibility to figure this shit out anyway. He's the parent. He and your mom are supposed to be adults and deal with all the necessary details. Problem is, most adults don't know what the hell to do when they get themselves in these situations. Shit, my mom and dad act like twelve year-olds whenever something goes wrong at my pad. Your dad probably isn't that bad of a guy, but let's face it, man, he's a burned out hippie who thinks he's going to get rich finding some buried treasure for Christ's sakes. That should tell you one thing and one thing only, Larry.

"It's high time for Topher to let the grown-ups fend for themselves and find a father figure he can depend on."

He let that comment just hang in the smoky cab as we both watched the Custer State Park Highway roll under the truck as if the Earth was spun by its tires.

"How in hell am I supposed to find someone like that?" I asked, turning down the stereo to maximize philosophical absorption.

"You don't have to find him, man," Diresk replied, turning to burn his next words into me with his cutting eyes. "He's not the one who's lost, pal."

That said, he turned up the stereo signaling, at least for the time being, the discussion was to move into a quiet reflection on my part. He drove his truck like some redneck shaman, rocking to the beat of the music and nibbling the skin off of his chapped lips.

It would be several years before I would catch the gist of his comments spoken on that day; just in time to save my life and be able to stick around to witness the end of his.

Somehow, I have to learn to accept the injustice of it all. I'm just grateful I finally found a father figure who calls me all the time. If I will just listen.

Chapter Thirty-Two

"Do you remember the first time you ever saw a picture of a naked woman and what you were doing?" I asked Diresk, eyeing him peripherally one day.

"I think I was wondering who shot Kennedy. *Shit.* I must have been about four or five, something like that. My old man's Playboy was under the sink in the bathroom and I brought it out to show him. My mom freaked out and they got in a big fight, man."

"How can you remember that far back?" I asked. "I can't remember anything that far back, man. I can't believe how people can…OUCH! Shit!"

"What happened?" he said.

"I sat down on my balls wrong. God, I hate doing that. Son of a bitch! Does that happen to you when they catch the inside of your leg once in a while and it feels like you're going to puke or something?"

"Oh, yeah," Diresk laughed. "Sometimes I stand up from my desk at school and catch a ball like that. That friggin' hurts, man. Girls don't know what that pain is like, man. Kick us in the balls and think it's cute when we're about to friggin' die."

"Yeah. Though I'll bet having a baby doesn't feel too good," I said, carefully rearranging my scrotal belongings and wincing with every touch.

"Not as bad as getting kicked in the balls, man. I don't care what any woman says. That's the worst pain in the world. Worse than getting kicked in the shin or anything! I got kicked in the balls by Greg McDonald once. Before you moved here. I saw red for a friggin' hour and my dick even started to bleed."

"He did it on purpose?" I asked, curious.

"He said it was an accident, but I know he meant to do it. We were playing football and creaming his team. He hid from me for about a month that summer, man. But I caught him behind the pool one day and made him eat a piece of dog shit I found. I told him I was going to kick his balls if he didn't swallow all of it, and he did it."

"Dog shit? Oh, God. That's evil, man."

"No, evil was kicking him in the balls even after he ate the shit," Diresk replied, winking at me and grinning.

We laughed together in our flannel pajamas and wrestled on his bed. We were in the eighth grade at the time and I had been granted temporary leave from my home for a sleepover at Diresk's house. I would never have dared have him over for the night at my house. I was too embarrassed by the tight reign of my step-father. Chains tied to my very soul. But that night we had fun.

Chapter Thirty-Three

"Didn't your old man prefer blondes, man?" Diresk quizzed me. "What?" I lazily replied as my fingers attacked my step-father's pornographic magazines I had brought with me. My step-father had hundreds of such magazines in the bedroom he no longer shared with my mother. Under the mattress, tucked away in the closet, in boxes under the bed and hidden in a crawl space in the walls. I knew all the hiding places.

"Blondes, you dimwit! Your mom told you your old man likes blondes, and every time you see one in a magazine, your friggin' eyes fall out of your skull."

"Do they really?" I answered with minute interest.

"I've been doing a little research with you, and you don't hardly ever look too long at redheads or brunettes. Always blondes. Your whole body gets all lit up, and shit, when you see one. Bet it's because your old man likes them so much, huh?"

"You are out of your mind," I shot back defensively, marking my page and closing the magazine. "I like brunettes and redheads just as much as blondes, man! You're the one who is always talking about how girls with brown hair and brown eyes drive you crazy. I think you may be…"

"I'm not blind and I'm not dumb, Gomer," Diresk said. "You got the blonde fever and you got it bad!"

"So what if I do?" I shrugged. "What's your point, Dr. Freud?"

"All's I'm saying is what I been noticing. Don't get all spasmodic and shit. I'm making a simple point and you can listen or throw it out. It makes no difference to me."

"I've never even met my father," I said. "You know that. How could

I be just like him if I've never met the man? Just because I like blonde hair doesn't necessarily mean anything other than…"

"Whatever you say, Jerry. You believe whatever you believe, but I know I'm right, so it don't matter what you say. Just trying to point out something that may help you down the road. I think you better think about it and see if I'm not right."

"Whatever!" I shot back and rolled over and away from him.

"Know something?" Diresk softly asked.

"I know lots of things!"

"Every time we talk about your old man, this happens. You always get pissed and I always want to get you more pissed. Sometimes, I think you should go find him and have it out with him once for all the good it would do. It's not good carrying this shit around like you do."

"Why can't you just leave me alone? I don't want to talk about it and I don't agree with what you are saying, so just knock it off!"

"Ice cream."

"What?" I answered, turning again to face my interrogator.

"Ice cream. We need some ice cream to cool off, man."

"What kind you got?" I asked, quickly losing ground on my brave stance.

"Butterbrickle, Slim. Fudge sauce ready to pour."

"Cool," I said, licking my lips in anticipation.

"Topher?" Diresk asked as he swung his legs over the bed and stood up.

"What?"

"Do you think blondes taste different than redheads?"

"Go straight to hell and don't collect two hundred dollars."

What angered me most about what he had said to me was I had to admit he was right. I had the blonde fever. A chronic case that was traceable back to my first grade school crush over Sue Tennyson, a platinum blonde. I've been blonde-crazy ever since.

Just like my father.

My blonde fever was cyclical as I glance back over the love trysts of my life. Every two years, a peroxide-tipped sheet seeking missile would blow through my life like a hurricane with a hangover and toss my delicately balanced sanity around like a sandwich bag full of nitroglycerine. I would hear the storm coming, the warning siren and the ominous shift in surroundings, but would invariably exit my protective walls to naïvely strut directly into her jaws in a state of mystical absorption, only to be filleted like some moronic trout that keeps striking at the same rusted lure.

I knew better. Deep down inside. There's always time to abort the mission before going down with the boat, but I was powerless to resist the addictive, melancholy melodies slowly escaping from these women's pores. Always blonde. Always anorexic or bulimic.

Always a disaster.

We continued the discussion, well into our twenties, and it would always follow the same invisible trails leading into the same old canyon.

"All blondes can't be bad, D. Just because a girl has a specific hair color does not necessarily denote disaster. Some people like to drive red cars. Some people only wear blue jeans. What's the harm in a color?"

"It's not the color of these girls' hair that's got you up a tree, Slim. You keep picking the same kind of girl under the hair."

"There you go again," I said. "Lumping all my relationships under one handy, little…"

"Like I was trying to say. You keep picking princess types who are supposed to be perfect and you can't live up to it. I don't have all the details worked out here, but we been talking about this for years now and you keep getting bent out of shape every friggin' time. Christ, Toph, it's just a detail of your life. It doesn't mean you're hopeless or bad. Hell, you don't need to…"

"Don't need to what?" I combed my fingers through my hair in agitation. "Jesus, D. It's real easy for you to sit back and pick apart my life. You don't exactly have the girl thing worked out yourself, do you? You don't have a perfect picker either."

"Never said I did, Slick. All I'm saying is you have to admit you get screwed up over chicks like nobody I've ever seen. You almost get killed every time you break up with one, man. Throwing up and in bed for weeks and shit. Ending up in nuthuts for weeks until you can get your brain working again."

"It always has to come back to the hospitals, doesn't it?" I glared at him. "You just can't live with the fact that I've had emotional problems, can you? Why not, Diresk? Why is that so hard for you to swallow? Why?"

"I don't give a shit if you have to check into a million of them. I'm just a friend who is trying to show you shit that keeps knocking you down, man. If you don't want to listen, it doesn't mean I'm not going to keep putting it in front of your face. It's not about no hospitals or any of that shit, man. It's about you, and me having to watch you go down in flames every time you fall for some chick who pulls your trigger!"

"I still don't see the connection with my father who I have never met and know virtually nothing about and the girls I have relationships with. You seem to think I'm stuck in some paternal mud or something, but I just don't get it."

"Haven't you ever listened to what your mom says about…"

I shook my head. "All my mother ever said about him was he chased women and cheated on her all the time."

"With blondes, man."

"Yes, blondes. My mom is a blonde, Asswipe. So he likes blondes. So do I. Most men do, for crying out loud. It's a known fact. Look at all the advertising and movies and shit."

"Big titties and…"

"You're a sick person, D. And you're giving me advice about women? You think most of the men in America have the same hang up my old man has? Just because most of them like blondes? Do *you?* Do you think everyone but you had this Freudian paternal noose around their neck and are hanging themselves by falling in love with blonde women?"

"You're losing your marbles, Chuckie, and one of these days you're not going to be able to get them back in the bag. I'm tired of this shit, anyway."

"Then let's drop it!" But I wanted to keep going.

"Fine by me, man. Fine by me. Didn't mean to step on your toes again, Toph. Consider it dead and gone."

"Good. I'm tired of talking about it. We never get anywhere with it anyway."

"No use beating a dead blonde to death. Let's talk about something we both agree on. Smoking dope!"

"I don't want to get stoned now," I said.

"Roll me a fat one and I'll grab us a couple beers from the cooler."

I smiled as Diresk went to retrieve some beers and began my appointed task. I had rolled a cigar-sized joint by the time he had returned to the canvas tent.

"Toph?" he said.

"Yes?"

"Do you think because your dad left you like he did that you keep trying to grab some piece of him by…"

My ears were plugged, and I was loudly singing nonsense.

Chapter Thirty-Four

He was known around Custer as a man not to be messed with in town. Decades spent hefting chainsaws and large brush through the pine forests surrounding our majestic community had chiseled and sculpted the upper muscles of his long torso. It was said he could cut more trees in a day than any two area loggers. Diresk had once seen his father carve his own name in a large pine using a thirty-six inch chainsaw blade and only one arm.

Jake "Thunder Fist" Webster was a powerful and domineering man, prone to violent tantrums, frequent alcoholic binges, militant leftist reform, and impromptu displays of gregariousness and fetching theological philosophies.

Although the man often terrified me, I was drawn by his meticulous pursuit of and adherence to the convictions and principles by which he lived his life. His periodic expressions of tenderness and love served to distract from his often brutal behavior towards his family or anyone who crossed him the wrong way. Diresk loved his father desperately and was burdened by such mixed emotions.

On one hand, Jake Webster was the father all boys could look up to. His scarred and callused hands could demonstrate amazing feats of strength, yet appeared to constantly shake with a confused sense of tenderness and compassion.

I had seen these hands hold Diresk's frightened face like some fractured eggshell, caressing his son's crimson skin as if to transfer all his love through the tips of his fingers. I had also seen these hands lift Diresk off his feet and toss him into a wall with such force as to shatter glass from picture frames ten feet away.

Diresk carried with him many scars from such events. It was almost as if he wore them as badges. Medals of a secret honor society he shared with his father. I more or less envied him for these scars. My step-father and I never battled physically, and my scars were hidden deep beneath the surface of my skin like the pornographic magazines beneath the mattress I had stolen from him.

Jake Webster was a golden gloves boxing champion in his twenties and passed on much of his pugilistic tendencies to his only son. Diresk began to swing boxing gloves at various targets as soon as he was able to lift them. Throughout the years, father and son would spar countless hours away in the basement den and weight room. Celia Webster had hoped her only son would pursue her musical interests, but that was not to be. Jake Webster simply would not hear of it.

"The last thing the kid needs to learn is the piano, Cele!" Jake would lecture his portly redheaded wife. "He'll end up trying to become some rock star and throw away any chance he'd have at a future. He ain't gonna end up like me and spend the rest of his life ruining his body! He ain't gonna! He's gonna use his brains at some college and get a good job! If he wants to play the damn piano after he gets settled into some career…fine by me. Until then, he ain't gonna waste his time or yours sitting on some damn bench trying to teach his fingers to sing. Period!"

"Honey," Celia Webster would plead with her sad smile. "I just want Diresk to have a hobby he can enjoy for the rest of his life. He has a wonderful ear for music. Have you heard him sing? Have you?"

"Just because I don't go to them choir shows don't mean I don't love or support my boy, dammit Celia! I always see his football and basketball games, don't I? I always…"

"You always support him when you think it's a good idea. Honey. Diresk is a gifted and intelligent boy. He is so creative. It won't hurt him to take music lessons."

"NOT IF HE'S IN MY GOD DAMN HOUSE! Why don't you listen to me? I said, he ain't gonna do it and he ain't gonna do it! I know how smart my boy is. I know how everyone thinks he's the funniest damn kid in school. That ain't gonna get him down the road to where he needs to be. What about all this trouble from the school this year? Clowning around and playing jokes and shit. That's where creative will get you."

"Oh, Honey, he's just having a good time. He's got a wonderful sense of humor. He's still just a boy. He'll grow out of this phase."

My step-father disagreed. "It's just an excuse to get out of hard work is what it is. World doesn't need more comedians and jesters and guitar pickers, Cele. World needs great minds and men with courage and smarts to get us out of these dark times. World's losing touch real fast. It needs heroes, not love songs. Got enough friggin' love songs to blast on the radio to last us for eternity and where's it getting us?"

The room fell silent. I heard something crash against the wall.

"I ain't having my son throw away his life chasing no music dream and growing his hair down to his ass and taking drugs! Now if you think I'm wrong about it, I'm sorry, but it's the way I see it and it ain't gonna change. All God's got is us humans to get His work done and He ain't got time for us to be fiddle-fucking around! We gotta get this world turned around in a hurry, Cele, or it's gonna throw us all off its back."

We were both thirteen at the time.

I listened to the heated conversation in Diresk's bedroom. Diresk and his parents were discussing this situation in the family room. I remember having all of these rebuttals come to mind and wishing I could telepathically transfer them to my best friend's brain and rescue. Diresk wanted to learn to play the piano, his mother's instrument. He came home from school requesting parental permission to sign up for band.

But as I listened as Diresk made his brave attempt to sway his determined father, I doubted he'd get his way.

"Dad, I just want to play like Mom. It's not like I'm going to ruin my life because I want to play music. Besides, can you imagine how much the girls will like me after they know the coolest and toughest kid in school can play Mozart? I'll have to hire a bodyguard. I'll have to beat them off with…"

"You got my final word on this, Diresk," his father hissed in a lowered voice. "You ain't playing in no band and you won't say another damn word about it again. You understand me? Answer me, son."

"Yeah, I heard you," Diresk meekly answered.

I heard something crash to the floor, followed by an immediate scuffle.

"YOU WON'T ACT LIKE SOME SPOILED BRAT IN THIS HOUSE, GOD DAMMIT! PICK IT UP! PICK IT UP NOW!"

"JAKE, DON'T BREAK HIS ARM, HONEY!" his mother yelled above the sounds of bodies struggling and Diresk's cries of pain.

"I'll pick it up, Jesus!" Diresk cried. "Let go and I'll pick it up! It was an accident anyway. You don't have to twist my arm off. I know you can beat the hell out of me, okay? I know how tough you are, okay? You're the big man! Throw your son around the room some more, why don't you?"

Silence invaded my heightened nerves as if the family room had suddenly fallen into a chasm. I had no idea what to expect next. The sound of my name made me jump off of Diresk's bed and scan the room for an available exit or concealment possibilities.

"Is Christopher here?" his father asked in a deliberate and measured tone.

"He's in Diresk's room, Honey." Mrs. Webster chimed as if hoping to tame the monster precariously perched for attack in her husband's being.

"CHRISTOPHER?" Jake Webster's booming voice announced.

"IN HERE," the words escaped through my lips on instinct.

I would have hidden in that room for the rest of my life had I the choice. As I heard his heavy steps approach Diresk's bedroom door, I backed into the farthest wall away to shake and quiver like a scared puppy.

The door opened slowly to the blood-reddened face and intimidating chassis of Jake "Thunder Fists" Webster. He was wearing a stern brow and clasping meaty hands together near his groin as if to prevent them from injurious measures.

"Christopher…we're having a little family talk here and I think it's best you go on home now. If you need a ride, I can give you one now, son."

"That's okay, Mr. Webster," I choked out of my dry, burning throat. "It only takes me fifteen minutes to walk home and it's real nice out and everything. I'll just get my things from the kitchen and go on home."

It took all the courage I had to address him again.

"Um, Mr. Webster? Would you ask Diresk to call me later tonight if he can. I mean, I don't want to get in your business or nothing, but he sounds kind of upset."

"I'll tell him to call you after supper, son," he firmly stated. "Thanks for giving us some privacy for this. I hope we didn't scare you, son. I just lost my temper a bit and we need to talk this thing out some."

I nodded my head and snuck past him, closing my eyes as my body brushed his. I quickly made my way through the family room, catching a glimpse of Diresk's sunken and defeated form on the couch, and sped into the kitchen to retrieve my jacket and backpack. I was aware of a presence behind me as I hurried to zip my coat and start my walk home.

Mrs. Webster's soft voice startled me, but I was physically relieved to hear her. "I'm sorry if we seem like a strange family, Christopher," she nearly whispered, tugging back at emotions that were fighting for escape. "You are welcome here any time. Diresk will call you later tonight. Are you sure you don't want a ride? Jake can run you home."

"No, thanks," I replied, offering my back to her, pretending to struggle with the zipper.

Finally, I turned to face her, though I fought to meet her eyes. They were Diresk's eyes.

"It's okay, Mrs. Webster," I began with a forced smile. "Every family has fights now and then. I think my family fights more than we do anything, actually. Thanks for the cookies and juice and tell Diresk he can call me any time tonight before nine. Bye now."

I tugged open the oak door and walked out into the bright, snow-covered front yard, illuminated by a tired sun on its way down for the night. Mrs. Webster closed the door behind me. I remember feeling angered and sorrow-laden as I crossed Montgomery Street and a field where I would eventually play countless games of football and baseball in the following years.

Life just wasn't like television. Well, not like the television I was allowed to watch.

Diresk called me later that night. I was reading in bed and was called to the phone by my own unpredictable step-father who lectured me on having friends call late at night and informed me he would be timing my discourse. I dejectedly swallowed my medicine and picked up the kitchen phone with my constant companion—anxiety—churning in my stomach.

Why could I not be like Diresk? Why could I not stand up to my step-father's insolence and fight my own battles? Mother always fought them for me. I was the tenuous child who could not be bothered by such stressful notions. It would be many, many years before I would begin to learn to set the boundaries that would safeguard my emotional stability.

"Hey, man!" I announced to my waiting friend. "I can't talk too long because my Dad's on the prowl tonight. Said he's timing this call."

"I don't feel much like talking anyway," Diresk muttered. His voice sounded sad. "Sorry about today, Larry. The husband and missus were in fine form, huh? Doesn't look like I'm going to be the next Elton

John. Something really freaked the old man out. I don't even think it's about band or anything like that. Something deeper. Really deep! Just a minute."

There was a pause and I heard Mrs. Webster's faint voice say something to Diresk and then he continued.

"Mom came downstairs for a sec," he reported. "Anyway, I should go, but something strange happened today. To Dad. He took off and went somewhere a couple hours ago. He was drinking pretty heavy after you left. All he told me was he loved me and he was sorry for grabbing me like that, and shit. Then he bit his lip real hard and kissed me man. Kissed me for like fifteen seconds."

"On the lips?" I asked, horrified.

"Naw, man. On the forehead. He's not a friggin' pervert so stop your detective brain in its tracks. It's just weird is all. Like he was never going to see me again or something. I'm kind of worried about him, Toph. I also wish I was big enough to knock his friggin' head down inside his neck! My neck still feels like I got grabbed by King Kong. But you know something? I love that son of a bitch more every time this shit happens. One minute I want to blow his brains out with a shotgun and the next I want to sit in his lap and be five years old again. He's not that bad of a guy, man. He just can't let go of nothing. Wish I knew more about head shrinking so I could figure this shit out. I think something bad happened to him when he was a kid. I ever tell you about Grandpa Webster?"

I shook my head, realizing he couldn't see my gesture. So I added, "I don't think so."

"If you had met him, you would understand why Dad took up fighting. Gramps hated everybody. Equally. Blacks, Jews, Mexicans, Indians, mice, dogs, cats. Insurance companies. Shit, he used to bitch about insurance companies for hours, man. I was four years old and he would tell me to never pay for insurance. Hell, I probably won't," he said, laughing then coughing.

I imagined he was probably smoking. Talk about fearless!

"Why don't we just run away and get the hell out of our father's lives?" I jokingly inquired.

"Can't run from nothing, Zeke," my best friend said. "Anyways, I love my old man, man. Man, man. Man, what do you think of my old man? Does your old man grab you like a vise? Shit."

I joined in his laughter regarding his careless nomenclature. I loved the way Diresk talked. *Man.*

"Know what my dad said to me when I got in my first fight at school?" Diresk asked, coughing away his laughter. "He said, 'If you are gonna fight for something, fight for something you believe in. Don't fight someone just to beat him up because you want to or can. I taught you how to use your fists so you could defend yourself and the ones you love from filth! I don't want you to ever use your ability to fight to hurt someone that's afraid. If they're scared, they don't believe what they're doing is right. They're just fighting because of what people might think about them. That boy you whipped today might've had it coming, but was he afraid?"

He sounded far away, like he always did when he talked about memories of his father.

"You know Danny Wiles?" Diresk asked. "He was the one he was talking about. Anyways, he called me a name and I kicked the shit out of him. I told my dad that Danny was crying before I even fought him and he said, 'You wanna fight someone to prove you're some big man, you can fight me! I want you to stick up for others who can't do it for themselves. I seen you looking at my boxing trophies and maybe you think I want you to be some great fighter so I'll be proud of you. You'll make me the proudest if you just use what God gave you to make the world a better place. I love you because you're my son and that ain't ever gonna change. Don't fight with your fists, son. Gotta fight with your mind. Get an education and you can be lots better than me. Be a lawyer or a doctor or someone like that. That's where the real power comes from. Not from fighting your whole life and cutting down trees like I've done. Use your brain, son. I hate myself for not doing all the things I could've done. I ain't nothing but a broken down logger who ran out of time to change. You're gonna go places and it's my job to make sure you do.'"

As I listened, the parallels of my own life came into view. I didn't understand it then, but we were faced with the same dilemma coming from opposite approaches. Diresk was the imposing oak that pounded and drove his roots through his doubts and fears. Hard, durable wood used for shipbuilding and furniture. I was the brittle aspen sapling, whose leaves quivered in the slightest breeze, shedding my leaves in the cold wind.

Neither one of us had a clue as to how to wrestle or finesse true contentment from the intrepid tentacles of the monster our fathers had conversely painted for us. Of life. Of the pursuit of happiness. I would finally develop an inkling of how to grow into the fruition of a rather handsome tree as decades passed. Happiness is not, in fact, to be attained through pursuit; it is a necessary and inevitable response to the act of slowing down enough to allow appraisal and for us to cherish our innate treasure maps leading to bliss. In short, each of us finds the place where our energy fits.

"I've got to go, Toph," my best friend added as if to cross the T he had just dropped in my lap to ponder.

"Wait!" I blurted. "What in the hell are you trying to tell me? I'm not following your point. What does this have to do with what your dad did today? I mean, the story about fighting and becoming a doctor or scientist or whatever?"

"I got so much work ahead of me with you," Diresk sarcastically sneered into the ear attached near my befuddled expression. "Don't ask me to explain it to you, Jerry. It just makes sense to me, and that's what's important to this cowboy right now. I'm too tired to dig into this anymore. Hey, don't wear your purple shirt to school tomorrow because I'm going to wear mine."

The phone died in my hand, mere inches from the smile that had begun to crack my lips. He had done it to me again. Delivered some crucial message in code when, if deciphered, could have saved me from thankless hours of emotional carpentry.

Stricken by insomnolence, I measure, sawed, and pounded throughout the night, working on my newest existential structure.

Chapter Thirty-Five

The first time my lips tasted alcohol as the fiery brew poured down into my skittish belly, I felt as if God had reached down to touch my nose.

The first time I smoked marijuana, I felt as if I could reach up to touch God.

Booze prevailed over many of my assorted tools of indifference and distraction from reality, and though it proved to be a most pleasant ally, I was often able to gaze upon and engage it with a rather disciplined nonchalance.

Pot was an entirely different ally, and I fully intended for it to finally fill the pesky hole in my being. For a time, I believe it may have, at the very least, provided a makeshift dressing.

Smoking pot was like putting a pair of sunglasses on my brain. A delightful rush of numbness followed by a soothing mitigation. Absolute wonder and a sense of propriety with my world.

It was as if I had inhaled tiny tendrils of tranquility that coiled and climbed throughout my body. It was always my first thought upon awakening. To kiss my lover's lips and inhale her sweet breath. Then, to sink back into my pillow and allow her to fill me with love. I would do nothing, could do nothing, without first getting high.

I stayed high for nearly ten years. A decade's dance with a demon. She left me at the altar and I would have stayed married to her forever had she not turned and bit me with such vengeance and bitterness. My world shattered when dope quit working. It was like waking up in a coffin, buried alive with bare inches to move and no one to hear my screams. My solution to everything deserted me.

My step-father was a beer drinker. Not a connoisseur, mind you, he drank only Coors in a can. He would nightly sip himself into oblivion in front of the television, submerged in a recliner in our family room. He was not a hard man to locate.

He has since sobered, and we now enjoy an understanding that is rapidly approaching a friendship. He has replaced beer with Pepsi, and now flips through the Internet as opposed to cable channels. He walks five miles a day and has lost nearly thirty pounds. He no longer takes blood pressure medicine, nor finds it necessary to coat food with a thick layer of salt.

I love him. He's my dad.

Growing up, I cannot recall having spoken more than twenty times with the man—Richard Hammerquist, my step-dad. Our repertoire of conversation consisted mainly of him screaming at me which nearly always led my mother, Sandra, to my cowering and rescue. This, of course, predicated the countless parental battles that echoed off the walls of our small, stucco home. My step-dad would invariably retreat to his chilled Coors. My mother, tearful and victimized, would again vow to leave her alcoholic husband, then disappear on another of her marathon walks. Such was their marriage. Separate lives lived under the same dark roof.

Our house seemed so much smaller then. Today, I find it rather spacious, and it feels like a place I could once again call home.

And mean it.

In the old days, I'd simply retreat to my room and private kingdom to disassociate from the family woes. But on October 31, 1974—Halloween night—I'd stroll through a corridor and enter new and improved chambers.

"GET IN!" Diresk ordered as he pulled into my driveway and spotted me, in costume, impatiently waiting for him beside our towering wood pile. He picked me up in his truck for an evening of debauchery, and dressed as drag queens we spun out of our driveway and into the ripe night.

"I can't walk in these heels, man!" I giddily informed the well-muscled blonde sitting next to me. Diresk wore a black leather miniskirt, a curly blonde wig, a flowered blouse, full makeup, and his basketball shoes.

He had insisted I wear the pumps we had borrowed from some friends of ours and had pledged to do so in kind. Last minute, he'd grabbed his high-tops. We were five blocks away from my house before I discovered his violation of the discretion.

"You promised me you would wear the high heels," I pouted. "If you aren't going to wear yours, then take me home so I can change. I am not going to sprain my ankle in these friggin' things if you get to wear tennis shoes!"

"What time do you have to be home?" he asked, ignoring my protestations.

"Diresk! Take me home! I mean it! I am not going to the school dance with these on and that is final! You lied to me, man. What am I saying? Like that should surprise me. If you would just…"

"What time do you have to be home, Henry? I'm cut loose till two bells. Ma got me an extra hour," he proudly announced and held up two fingers, which dropped the burning cigarette that had been perched between them onto the vinyl seat cover. It rolled under the edge of my mother's dress and I nearly knocked myself unconscious in my feverish attempt to avoid scorching the borrowed garment.

Thank God for thick wigs. I managed to save my bodice and skirt.

"Jesus, D.!" I scolded.

"Didn't get you, did I?" he shot back.

"Here…and watch the friggin' road," I stated as I handed his cigarette back to him and witnessed a near miss with the curb of the Piggly Wiggly store parking lot.

"What time do you have to be home, Little Topher?" Diresk asked me again, this time in sing-song fashion.

"Midnight."

"MIDNIGHT? That's when shit starts to hit the fan, Leroy! I'm not taking you home one minute before one."

"He'll kill me if I'm late tonight," I said. "Mom had to pull off some wicked bank shots just to get my ass out of there tonight. He's still pissed about what you said to him."

"Screw him! Let him be pissed. He's not going to treat my best friend like some kindergartner," Diresk barked and returned a stern glance my way. "I mean it, man. You can't keep taking that shit from him like you do. It's going to mess up your wiring inside and you're going to go schizo on me some day."

Neither of us had any concept of the accuracy and clairvoyance of his statement. Well, I didn't anyway.

"I'm not like you, man!" I cried. "I can't help it. He scares the shit out of me. He could break me into tiny pieces if he wanted to. I would give anything to be able to tell him off like you did the other day."

Diresk smiled and handed me a cigarette, which I in turn lit with his. He shook his head, blowing smoke from his nostrils and pounded on the steering wheel with both of his painted hands.

"I don't want to talk about this shit no more tonight, Topher. Let's just have us the best time we can and get home when we get home. Okay?"

I gave him the best nod I could, but I'm sure my eyes looked as if they would leak at any moment.

"Besides," he inserted. "I got us a special treat for tonight's festivities."

I could take no more of his knee driving and took the helm as he rummaged beneath his seat for his surprise. He glanced at me and shook his wigged head as if to say, "Have I ever wrecked before?"

He winked as his hand found its mark and produced a black film canister from beneath his legs. My heart sped up and it suddenly became hot in the cab.

"What is it?" I asked with hesitant mirth.

"Marijuana, Jethro. Cambodian gold or some shit like that. I got it from Slack who says it's the real deal. I know we were going to wait till after basketball was done, but this was too good to pass on."

Slack was the apropos nickname of a casual acquaintance of ours who was known regionally to have smoked so much pot that his first born would be stoned for a year. He was Custer's number one drug dealer and he always passed out candy bars like business cards at our school.

I never trusted him. He was a drug dealer, for Christ's sake. For all I knew, he had given us heroin or an even more dangerous narcotic. I was not ready to lie in alleys with hypodermic syringes protruding from my shriveled veins, jaundiced by the fever and disease carried in my blood, passed out in vomit-soaked Salvation Army rags. I was not prepared to spend the rest of my life in a prison going steady with some rabid sodomite who would force me at knife point to fellate with him in front of his buddies. I was going to law school. I was going to win the Pulitzer Prize and lecture intellectuals well into my nineties, for Christ's sake.

And my step-dad was going to kill me!

"I'm not sure I want to do this, D.," I countered. "Let's just get some beer or wine tonight and think on this some more."

"'Think on this some more,'" he mimicked. "If I had to wait for you to think on shit before I would do anything, I would kill myself from boredom and embarrassment. The game is going now, Toph! We're not just warming up for it. You've got to grab life while time still lets you see the handle! It's only reefer, man. It's not even addictive. We'll just smoke a tiny bit and see what it does to our brain waves. By the way, you look hot in them shoes!"

"Yeah, right. What if it's laced with PCP or something? Remember that girl from Spearfish who smoked PCP and locked herself in the closet? By the time they got her out she had chewed off and swallowed three of her fingers. She thought she was smoking 'just pot,' man. She nearly ate her friggin' hand!"

"Without mustard?" he said in a serious tone.

I held off as long as I could, but soon joined him in laughter and my first marijuana joint. Diresk rolled it and really messed it up, but I knew I couldn't have done any better. We pulled into our favorite spot behind the football field on our way to become drug addicts. I remember we played a Doobie Brother's tape in his eight track stereo which was strapped to the bottom of his dashboard with baling wire. We had to usually stick a matchbook cover beneath the tape or it would refuse to play. We borrowed it from the local Gambles Store.

For about five years.

I must have swallowed fifty times as I watched him labor with the rolling papers, panicking at the sight of every set of headlights that approached on the dirt road below us. All I needed was for the FBI to nail us with dope and haul us off to Alcatraz.

"Just take it in like a cigarette, but don't take too much. You've got to hold it in your lungs as long as you can," Diresk instructed and then took a very long drag from our haggard looking joint.

Within seconds, he launched into a convulsive coughing spell. By the time he had regained control of his lungs, his eyes were blood-soaked and my nostrils were treated to their first whiff of the sweet and pungent breath of Cannabis sativa.

"That looks like a real blast," I quipped. "Cough your feet up through your mouth and then throw up all over yourself. I like it. Let me at it!"

The look I received from Diresk was one of mild amusement, but I also understood I was not going to escape my turn at the hemp helm. I removed the burning member from his pinched fingers and maneuvered it to my pursed lips. I was careful not to repeat the fiasco endured by my partner and took in short, deliberate puffs. My lungs were soon filled to capacity. I hurriedly handed the drug back to Diresk, who was making faces at me in an attempt to sever my emotional control. He failed, and I held my breath as long as I was able to.

I released the smoke from my itching lungs and waited for the first signs and symptoms of insanity to overtake me.

Diresk took a conservative pull, grinned, and passed the torch back to me. I was not at all convinced a second round, before careful documentation and discussion of the first, was such a great idea, but I found my lips inhaling again before the rational intervention could be proposed and implemented.

To make a long joint finally end, we finished it, lit some cigarettes, and sat back to see what happened next.

What happened next could be construed as my very first spiritual awakening.

Actually, it had been more like a spiritual falling out of bed.

Although Diresk's report had been favorable, I do not recall him reacting in a like manner as I had. I do not remember him having anything but smoking pot on his mind for the next eight years.

And I was absolutely transformed! I had finally arrived, or had been found. Marijuana gave me a feeling I can only describe as one of omniscience and ascendancy. Indisputable mastery of the human condition. Of fear. Of everything in this beautiful word, and so much more. In smoking pot, I was finally given equitable opportunity to not only join the human race, but I would finally be able to show everyone how special I was. That night, I had been able to kick off my pumps and feel the freedom of spirit I always assumed burned inside of Diresk. Pot was to become my new religion. I stepped forward to accept my discipleship with an uncanny stroke of certainty.

Diresk and I smoked another joint and never made it to the school dance. We were so high, we somehow must have understood that mingling with other humans would have been a grave error in judgment. We did manage to flag down some friends who provided us with alcoholic beverage to take some of the edge off of our new and exciting discovery.

By the time I finally snuck bare-stockinged into my house at 2:20

am, my central nervous system had been in such disarray that when my step-father found me making faces in the bathroom mirror, I screamed at the top of my soot-stained lungs and fell laughing to the floor. I was in direct violation of curfew, drunk, and stoned out of my mind, and my father figure did not appear in the mood for a pardon.

"I've been waiting up for you for two hours, son! You think you can slide away from this, don't you? You think your mommy is going to save you and jump on my ass for grounding you for the next month?

"Your ass is grounded and belongs to me for the next thirty days! I should wake your mother and let her see her little angel like this. 'I don't drink or get in trouble, so why's he so hard on me?'" he sneered. "I smelled the booze from my room, young man. What else have you done tonight? ANSWER ME!"

His last statement had been accented with a kick of the bathroom door and it got my attention. He never struck me. His assaults were predominantly verbal. Still, I was terrified he might really flip out and kill me!

"I'm sorry, Dad." I somehow found my voice and begged for my safety. "I wanted to get home earlier, but Diresk was driving and he wouldn't take me home. We did drink some beer and stuff at the dance."

He entered the bathroom, closing the door behind him, and whispered to me with a voice brimming with rage and vengeance.

"I know what dope smells like, young man. You're as high as a kite. Aren't you? Answer me Christopher or so help me, I'll beat you!"

"Some of the kids I was with were smoking it, but I didn't!" I attempted. "I drank some beer and that's it. I don't care if you don't believe me. You never believe me anyway, so why would you now? I don't know why you hate me so much. What did I ever do to you that was so bad? You treat me like I'm the worst kid on the planet! I'm not that bad of a kid, Dad. If you knew what some of my friends did…"

My words were extinguished as his large hands encircled my face and pressed my skin taunt. I met his eyes for the first time and they had tears in them. I tried to look away, but could not. He held me there by the grip of his hands and the pain in his eyes. All the pot I have ever smoked could not have insulated me from his next words.

"I love you more than anything I have ever loved in my life. I wanted to be your father more than anything I have ever wanted before. Your grandfather would never let me be your father. Your mother would never let me be your father."

His tears had begun to overtake his speech and I helplessly watched as he sunk to the floor and rested his back against the porcelain tub. He hid his face and tears behind his trembling hands. I slid against the opposite wall and watched him cry. I had never seen this man cry before. I had only seen his rage. My mind was so cloudy that night I had difficulty just trying to take in everything that was going on before my bloodshot eyes.

He crumbled. All he carried inside of him every day was leaking out of the pasted cracks of his being. Cracks he had tried to mend. Cracks like mine.

"I'm sorry, Dad," I whispered, not sure if he'd hear me or if I wished him to. "Dad?" I asked, louder.

He looked through his fingers and shook his head at me. I wanted to bolt from the room, but was held to the floor by the adhesive voltage of my step-father's suffering. I believe it may have been the first time I had allowed myself to participate in my feelings of love for him. I wiped my face with my forearm and noticed the smear of makeup and lipstick, tattooed just above my wrist. I looked down at my mother's dress and torn stockings.

We sat there like that, in silence, backed up against the wall and the tub. Words were not necessary. Only breathing. It was the first time I had ever ached for him.

Chapter Thirty-Six

"**B**OYS! Come over here and give me a hand," the booming voice of Jake Webster reached us in the scattered pines behind their home.

"Shit!" Diresk mumbled under his cigarette-stained breath. "He wants us to help him lift that new gas tank he bought. He's not even going to give me a key to it. Can you believe it? Says I'm irresponsible and would use it all up too fast. Where's he getting this stuff from?" Diresk asked as he fired a grin at me, putting his cigarette into the rock outcrop near our fort/hideout.

"A purely uninformed and hateful admonishment. Oh, responsible One," I cracked out of the side of my mouth. "How heavy is this thing and who will pay for my hernia surgery upon completion of this task?"

"It's really friggin' heavy, man, I can tell you that," Diresk said. "If Dad needs help lifting, you've got no business helping us. Hey! If you do get a hernia you can have that nurse shave your crotch. Remember that babe who took care of Knutson? What the hell was her name? Judith? No. June or something like that. When I saw her, I was ready to knock Knutson out of bed and jump in there myself."

We reached the back of the house and were on our way to the shed when Celia Webster's musical voice escaped through her bedroom window, instructing us. "Be careful, you guys, and make him do most of the work! When you guys get tired and can't manage, just call me and I'll put that darn thing up for you."

Diresk received his sense of humor from his mother. She was amazing and I loved the times the three of us were in the house alone together. Diresk and Celia Webster were like a comedy team from Hollywood.

"That's okay, Mom. Just see if you can't slide that retaining wall over a couple inches to the right," Diresk countered, straight-faced. "You slid it too far the last time and about cracked the foundation. Hey, the Broncos call back yet?"

"They said I want too much money to play nose guard," she whined. "I told them they could keep their money and I was going to sign with the Cowboys. Right, Christopher?"

"Best team in football, Mrs. Webster!" I proudly chimed in Diresk's face, who hated the Dallas Cowboys almost as much as wearing a tie and going to chemistry class.

"Bunch of whining pussies is what they…" Diresk started.

"If you don't get your lazy asses over here to help me, I'm going to show you what it feels like to get hit by a real nose guard!"

The sight of Jake Webster always struck me. No matter how many times I saw him, his entrance into any situation was always somewhat unsettling to me. This particular day, his head appeared around the corner of the house wearing a huge, tobacco-stained smile.

"How about a little tackling practice when you get done moving that tank?" Mrs. Webster hollered to her husband.

"My seventeen-year-old ears have been tainted for life," Diresk said. "Do you two mind not talking dirty in front of my best friend?"

Mr. Webster's head disappeared from the end of the house, signaling the end of the game with the effective efficiency of a loud whistle. It was time to go to work.

Diresk and I wandered around the house to the old shed where I received my initial appraisal of the gigantic object we were to lift and transport to the foundation Mr. Webster had prepared for it. It was a very large tank. I have no idea how many gallons. It was conceivably four feet tall and about eight feet long. I threw a helpless glance towards the abandoned spot I had last seen Diresk, then spied him fiercely circling and stalking the behemoth with his father. Hard work fit well and looked good on these two.

Me? I always felt kind of like Liberace at a construction site when invited to shoulder up with those two for a project.

"I can get this end, if you munchkins can get the other," Jake Webster firmly stated.

"No problem, Pop!" Diresk said. "Topher's been doing pushups for the past four days and he's turned into an animal."

"Let's cut the comedy routine so we don't get nobody killed, okay?" his father said with a barely discernible grin. "We gotta lift it high enough to get on that ledge. We can roll it from there. Let's roll it over as close as we can right now. Topher? Diresk's kind of a sissy, so you're gonna have to pick up his slack."

I was relieved by his good-natured teasing, after which I was even able to speak to him occasionally. If I wasn't too stoned and paranoid.

We rolled the tank over to the awaiting foundation. It felt impossible to lift. I kept looking at Diresk for support of my fatalistic notions, but absolutely lived for moments like that with him.

"Okay, I'm gonna count to three and we'll lift it together," Jake Webster announced as he maneuvered his powerful torso and arms around the tank. "Make sure you gotta good hold underneath before we start. Bend your knees and lift with your legs. Keep your backs straight. READY? One...two...THREE!"

My arms immediately sent a signal to my brain, yelling, "Just what in God's name do you think you are doing?" Just the same, I grunted with the two of them and gave it my best. Slowly, our end began to raise to meet the other end that had already risen off the ground and was awaiting our arrival. The veins in Diresk's neck and arms bulged like earthworms. It felt good to stand beside him, puny as I was.

"Son of a bitch...son of a bitch," Diresk grunted as we both fought for position and leverage under the tank. "I don't know if we can get it! I can't....let me just get a better...son of a bitch this weighs a friggin' ton."

"HOLD HER STEADY!" Jake Webster calmly stated. "I'm gonna set my end up and I'll come around to help you. There. Now don't let it move, and I'm coming around!"

I felt the other end land on the ledge and was ecstatic to see Jake Webster's imposing bulk closing in to assist us with what felt like a baby elephant we were carrying. Suddenly, the tank was lifted out of my straining arms as if it had never been there at all, and our end was safely transferred to the ledge.

"We got her now...easy now...just another few...inches and... THERE! Good job, men. Diresk, watch your language around me, Son."

From there it had been a simple matter of rolling the tank, spinning it to fit the iron arms, and easing it into place. Piece of cake.

Diresk was struck silent following the lift. I could sense something was bothering him, but would not have dared ask him in the company of his father.

Jake Webster stood back to admire his new gasoline tank and inserted some chewing tobacco into his lower lip. He'd scream at Diresk for smoking. So, I puzzled over such hypocrisy, but would postpone any surfacing comments for time alone with my friend.

I sat down in the shade of a tree to rest my aching back and to admire the culmination of our concerted efforts. It was late August and an uncommonly hot day for Custer. Diresk turned and started for the house without uttering a word to either of us. After he disappeared into the front of the house and my anticipatory jitters had turned into near convulsions at the prospect of facing converse with Jake Webster alone, I decided to join Diresk and his mother in the coolness of the house.

I had barely taken a step when the sound of his deep baritone halted and spun me around.

"He's mad 'cause I had to help him," Jake Webster quietly reported. "He's got so much pride. Can't imagine where he got it at all. You?"

"I was wondering what was bothering him," I slowly answered, failing to acknowledge his humorous invite.

"You got a minute?" he asked.

"Yeah. I guess."

"Ride with me. I gotta check on something downtown. They'll be okay without you for a few minutes," he added, following my longing gaze toward the house.

I initially felt honored by his request to accompany him, but was soon congested with befuddled trepidation regarding his possible motives.

What in God's sweet name did Jake Webster want to talk to me about? Ask me about? Confront me about? All at once, it struck me like an embolism! And I was scared.

Would he ask me about the drugs we were taking? No. The girls Diresk was having sex with. Oh my God! He knew I was stealing from my gas station job and was going to drive me to the police station! I instinctively reached for a cigarette, but I rarely carried them on me and my hand groped my left breast through my empty shirt pocket. I was cornered with no chemically induced abandon in sight.

As I got into Mr. Webster's Scout, it was all I could do to suppress my pleas for him to not turn me in to the police for whatever I had done. I managed to keep my cool intact and closed the door to the staggering silence of the cab, my heart aflutter.

It makes me swallow hard just to think of it still, and I already know how it turned out. You see, this was the paranoia I lived with on a daily basis during my drug-induced days. I always assumed and portrayed myself as being on top of my game, but the truth always lingered close behind. You can't outrun the damn truth and even I know most of the back trails and shortcuts. It's like my student loan officer who could find me in places even my mother's maternal extrasensory perception could not penetrate. He would've made an excellent FBI field operative.

"Thanks for riding with me," Jake Webster said as the engine fired.

I stared ahead at the image of Christ on the glove compartment, maintaining my strategic silence.

"I don't know how to say this," he began as the battered vehicle moved beneath my quivering legs. "I know you're his best friend and he tells you all the stuff he must think about and everything."

A calm began to fan out and infiltrate my being, as did the awareness that I was not to be incarcerated nor chastised for questionable behavior. I nodded and awaited further data.

Jake Webster steered the Scout out of the driveway and towards Main Street. I could almost feel his struggle for words. I continued to wait in silence as the big man gathered his thoughts. Suddenly, he began to empty himself as if his words were burning the flesh in his mouth.

"I don't know how to reach him," he said. "We used to be so close and everything, but now we hardly talk about anything important. His mother says I'm too hard on him, but you gotta be firm. Maybe this ain't right bringing you into this, but...he's my son and you know him better than anybody."

He glanced sideways towards me, an interjection of sorts, as well as an invitation to comment. I had absolutely no clue what to say.

I took a breath before speaking to delay the inevitable. "Um, I don't know exactly what you are looking for me to do here, Mr. Webster," I replied as my skittish glances danced around and landed on his pulsating temple. "Is there something wrong with Diresk?"

I felt the car begin to slow and we pulled over and parked next to the Custer Community Church, the site of my first French kiss with a girl named Latonya. I watched as he primed his lower lip with more Skoal and then took hold of the steering wheel with both hands as if to gain leverage for what he had to say next. His forearms bulged and trembled as if they would suddenly rip the mechanism from the dashboard as the engine purred in front of us.

"Why won't my son talk to me anymore, Christopher?" Jake Webster cried. "He acts like I'm a monster. I know I can be rough on him and

Cele. I don't mean to get that way, but I'm just trying to keep us all above water! We used to spend days together and we were best friends. I was his hero. I used to be the one he looked up to."

There was nothing left for me to do at this point but to try and comfort the giant of a man who was trembling beside me. I had a difficult time focusing on his words as my mind continued to drift to my own step-father and our precarious relationship.

I braced myself and began, "You're still his hero, Mr. Webster. He talks about you all the time. I think all parents and kids go through what you are going through to some extent. My dad and I hardly even look at each other. You guys have a much better relationship than we do. I don't want you to take this wrong…but you can be pretty scary sometimes. Diresk just wants you to be proud of him. I know he loves you both very much."

Jake Webster turned his head away from me, and though I never saw them, I could sense his tears as they slipped down his tanned cheeks. His right hand released its grip on the wheel to brush them away, and I was struck with a whim to touch him in comfort, but tucked my hands between my knees instead. We sat in silence, listening to the rising tension of the moment.

"It ain't easy for me to talk about my feelings," he finally said in a soft, vanquished manner. He rolled down his window, continuing to avert his eyes from mine.

A slight breeze entered the cab and I could smell the freshly cut grass on the church grounds. I waited for him to continue. Eventually, he turned to face me with reddened eyes and a grin laced with such sadness I would not have been surprised if he had leaned in to request my embrace.

"I know I'm a hard man, Christopher. I've worked with my hands my whole life and I ain't the best at using words to get things done. I love my son more than anything I have ever loved in my life. I would die for him. All I ever wanted was for him to have a better life than I did. I know I gotta tell him this myself. Guess I wanted you to do it for me, but I know now that ain't right. I don't know if I can change. Don't know if I want to. I just don't want him to leave and not wanna come back like I've seen some kids do. Like I did. My dad died before I ever got a chance to make up with him."

I felt the need to touch his arm, but stayed put. "Diresk doesn't want to get away from you and Mrs. Webster, I can tell you that for certain,"

I said, looking into his eyes. "Maybe if you tried to tell this stuff to him, you two could work something out that would make you both feel better about everything. If my dad and I could talk like you and I are right now. Man. I have learned more stuff about life from Diresk than I have ever learned from anyone. And he always tells me he learned most of it from you."

Jake Webster's piercing eyes burned into my own before returning to the church building, sprawled out in front of us through the windshield. He nodded slightly and reached over to softly squeeze my shoulder before I felt the Scout move again.

"You wanna go back to the house or go home?" he asked me as we rode together towards nowhere in particular.

"You can stop wherever you need to and then run me back to your place."

"I don't have anywhere to go. I lied to you," the big man chuckled. "I'll run you back to the house. Then, I think I'm gonna weld that tank in place."

We again rode in silence and I assume, due to the nature and intimacy of our discourse, I pulled off my next uncharacteristic gesture. I was honest with him.

"Mr. Webster?" I asked and was met with his full attention. "Diresk is going to want to know what this was all about. I don't know if you want me to keep this between the two of us, but I rather doubt I could. I'm not going to promise you something I can't deliver. I can't keep anything from Diresk. We're best friends and we share everything."

"I appreciate you telling me that, Christopher. I guess I'm gonna have to talk to him about this sooner or later…and this'll just make me do it sooner. You just do whatever's right for you, son."

We soon pulled into the Websters' driveway to the background music of Grover's barking. Just when I thought I was in the clear and had survived my time alone with Mr. Webster, he floored me with his next comments.

"Christopher? I think you may be a good kid. I know all about you and Diresk's shenanigans. I know about the dope and the booze you two been taking. I hear things. I was a young gangster once. I want to thank you for talking with me today. You and my boy got good hearts. I feel good about that and I hope I had something to do with Diresk's."

He was silent a moment as he put the Scout in the front of the driveway, and opened his door to spit out his tobacco wad. My restlessness began to crest as I braced for the impending lecture I believed I was to receive.

"I did some things when I was your age I ain't proud of," he said. "Things have changed since I was young. I know that. It ain't easy living in a world that tells you kids you don't have to wait to feel better. All you gotta do is take a pill and not worry no more. I'm willing to let my kid be a kid and learn from his mistakes like I did, but if you two get too far away playing with them drugs and such I'm gonna bring my kid back. I will do this…believe me, son. Yes, sir."

"I understand, sir," I replied.

"You're too young to see it, but this world ain't going in the right direction. Everyone thinks they're smaller than they really are and that's why everyone acts so greedy and foolish."

I nodded, not sure what he was after.

"Son… Every human being on this planet is a chrysalis just waitin' to spring wings. If you do anything with your life…help folks to see that. But first, you gotta know it for yourself. Ain't nothin' more important in this life than helping people know how important they are. That's all God wants for us to do. People run around like idiots trying to find God's will. Hell, all HE wants us to do is water each other so we can grow."

His eyes never left the driveway as he finished his statement and parked the Scout next to the old shed. I felt compelled to respond to him but was unable to do so. I was barely able to remove myself from his vehicle. Our private encounter had been tainted by my sudden awareness that Diresk and I were not the cunning "gangsters" we assumed ourselves to be. Our chemical jig was up!

Diresk and I would need to rethink any future outings.

Though Mr. Webster and I visited a special place that afternoon, I was never able to return there with him again. Diresk was more than mildly stunned after learning of his father's cognizance, and had bypassed his father's expressions of love and well-being for him.

"SHIT!" Diresk exploded during the telling of my tale. "Does Mom know?"

"He didn't say," I replied.

"Think he's bluffing?"

"I do not believe so. I think he knows a lot more than we think. I just can't figure out how he would have found out. He said he'd heard rumors around town. How much does he know?"

"SHIT!" Diresk again emoted, lighting a cigarette as we sped away from his house in the pickup. "This is beautiful! My dad thinks I'm a drug addict and he gets closer to my best friend in fifteen friggin' minutes than he has gotten to me in seventeen years! Well, if he kills me he kills me. I'm going down medicated, Virgil."

That said, my best friend rolled a joint the size of a magic marker, and we proceeded to launch a carefully crafted assault of our senses. It took us nearly twenty miles to finish smoking that monster. And by the time we arrived in Newcastle, Wyoming, neither of us could locate our faculties.

"Slick?" my heroic leader said. "If I am not mistaken, I believe I have exposed my noggin' to a bit too much wacky weed. I've got to pull over before I lose motor skills completely."

"I can't feel my friggin' feet," I added.

"If you can say that fast five times, I'll French kiss Grover," Diresk stated as he gestured back towards his hound.

"I can't feel my frigging feet. I can't freel my figgin' feet. I can't speak," I attempted.

We both laughed and lit cigarettes as he pulled the truck into a service station parking lot. Diresk shut off the engine and we smoked and watched a very obese man emerge from a small sedan to fill it with gasoline. He must have weighed close to four hundred pounds and he waddled like a duck. Needless to say, the sight struck another humorous chord in us.

"How'd you like to go to a buffet with that cat?" Diresk laughed.

"As long as I was first in line," I chimed in with my guffaw.

Our laughter subsided and we watched the man waddle to the office to pay for his gas. Quiet minutes passed as we lit another round of cigarettes and inhaled.

"I love him, Toph!" Diresk finally shouted.

"The fat dude?" I asked, baffled by the seriousness of his tone.

"No, idiot," Diresk glared at me. "My dad, man. He gave you the chrysalis speech. Huh. He must like you, man. He's crazier than I thought."

Within seconds, a fit of laughter seized the both of us and would not let go for a duration lasting through several illegally purchased cigarettes and beverages.

Chapter Thirty-Seven

I was attending college in Vermillion and Diresk was in Spearfish. Diresk and I had both returned to Custer for the summer, and I was employed by the U.S. Forest Service to work on a survey crew. There was an incident that occurred between my step-father and Diresk. He had opted against gainful employment. For his twentieth summer running. Mr. Webster could always be counted on to put his son to work in the woods beside him, and basically allowed Diresk to drift his summers away due to the fact he was so enthralled by Diresk's collegiate attendance. Mr. Webster was also quick to respond to any compulsory financial needs his higher learning son might accrue. Mrs. Webster was also known to supplement her son's coffers on occasion. She was always the first to respond to Diresk's fiscal supplications.

The incident of which I speak was an altercation between my step-dad and best buddy in our family's kitchen. Diresk and I had just returned from playing an afternoon basketball game at the school gymnasium. We had stopped off for a few cocktails at a local watering hole on our way home and my step-dad had not been impressed by either our unconventional parking job or our rather booming entrance.

"I would like to speak with you in my room immediately!" my step-father stated as he descended upon us seconds after we had staggered into my home.

"If you're looking for advice on what to wear to church Sunday, Richard, don't come to me," Diresk said with a straight face. An obvious shot to my step-father who, to my knowledge, had set foot in a house of God only twice in his adult life.

"I don't need your comedy routine today, Diresk!" my step-dad barked with beer in hand. "Get in here now, young man! This is still my house and you will play by my rules if you are going to live here."

I took a step towards his room in the back of the house when my momentum was halted by Diresk's hand on my leaning shoulder. I quickly flashed him my concerned expression and was met by his piercing eyes, blazing with confident luster. I was surrounded by a sense of impending doom and torture, but was forced to remain in my current position to await my step-father's wrath.

"You stay the hell out of this, Diresk!" he said. "This is none of your business and you are a guest in this house! MY HOUSE!"

"Why don't you just plug yourself back into your television and have a few brews, Rich. Toph and I will get out of your hair and you can sit in your throne and bitch at the screen."

"You get out of my house right now!" my step-dad hissed and grabbed my upper arm. "Get in my room now, Christopher! You have no place in this house anymore, Diresk. You are not welcome here ever again. Do you understand me, Mr. Funny Man?"

"Fine by me, Rich," Diresk drawled and pulled my body from my step-father's painful grasp. I was spun around like a tiny doll and placed behind my best friend's protective stance. Diresk's eyes blazed and the veins in his arms and neck were at attention and pulsing in preparation for combat.

They stood there, frozen, assessing each other like large jungle cats. Although my step-father was a robust man, he was not prepared to face Diresk in a fist fight. I believe Diresk had sensed this all along and this knowledge had greatly enhanced his gallant stance.

I, on the other fist, was terrified beyond comment or gesture as I stood helplessly awaiting a fight between my best friend and father.

"We're going to get out of here now," Diresk announced. "You're not going to touch him, man. Not while I'm standing here. You don't even know your own son, man. You don't even see all the kick-ass things about him! All you see is that screen and your beer cans. Just because you're so friggin' miserable doesn't mean you get to make everyone around you feel the same way, man. Yeah, we had a few drinks and we're having a blast being alive. Life's supposed to be a good place to be, Mr. Hammerquist."

My friend's words hung in the air like frozen smoke. I watched as my father's shoulders sank into a humiliated arch as the sound of Diresk's heavy breaths provided the room's only sound. To my utter astonishment, my inner-allegiance swung to my fragile father, and I shoved my way past Diresk to solely confront, and if necessary support, the man who had raised me.

"Let's get out of here, man," Diresk insisted as I stepped in front of him.

"I need to talk to my father alone for a second," I replied, requesting entrance into my father's eyes. He was shaking now, and I wanted to help him somehow save face. He looked like I usually felt in that home.

"For Christ's sakes, Topher," my friend said. "What are we doing here? Playing some friggin' junior high game? You don't have to bow down to no…"

"I need to speak with my father. Alone." I tensed as my words snuck out between my lips, but as I turned to face Diresk, I thought I caught a respectful glint in his stern expression. He again glanced at my father, nodded his head slightly, and backed out of our front door.

As the screen door slammed in my face, I sensed my father's presence shift and leave the room.

"I want to talk about this," I offered to the back of my father's moving form. "I don't even know what to say, but I think we have to at least try to discuss this, Dad."

My father stopped in his tracks, gestured me away with backward, cutting slices of his hand, and continued into the solace of his bedroom. I stood and watched him disappear with the slamming of his door.

A rage rose from inside me.

"Open up, Dad! You started this and we need to finish it now!" I yelled at his locked door with pounding fists.

The sound of the television was audible through the door and I found my ear pressed to the wood, straining for evidence of any response. I again called his name.

"I'm not going to stand here much longer, Dad! If you won't talk to me I'm going to go with Diresk and I don't know when I'll return. I want you to know I don't agree with everything Diresk said out there. I don't like our relationship, but it's not entirely your fault that it doesn't work and I am well aware of this. Dad?"

The door swung open and I found my face no more than six inches from the anger etched on my father's. My pulse began to race, and at first, I thought he may strike me. When he didn't, I stood my ground and waited for his words.

"This is still my house," he hissed, "and if you don't want to listen to me, then you can find another place to live. I'm tired of you and your mother hating me."

"We don't hate you," I said in my defense.

"BULLSHIT! That's bullshit and you know it, Chris. You two are always behind my back. How are we supposed to be a family when I'm always on the outside?"

"You put yourself on the outside. We never just decided it was going to be us against you. You did. You're the one who hides in your room all the time. You're the one who always seems unhappy. I never see you happy, Dad. Never! Maybe you and Mom don't get along, but even that could get better if you two would stop screaming at each other long enough to just communicate. We walk on egg shells all the time, wondering what will set you off next and what you might do."

"Oh, Jesus Christ, Christopher." He started to close the door.

"No. Hear me out," I said, holding the door open. "Hell, the minute I hear you pull into the driveway, I always get this queasy feeling in my gut. So does Mom. Ask Her? That's no way to live, Dad. We aren't meant to feel like that in our own house. I'm not that bad of a kid. I'm not. I get good grades. I don't hurt people. What is so bad about me? What, Dad? Why do you have to treat me like some prisoner all the time? Don't you want to be happy? Do you want to end up like Grandpa and hate everything and everyone the rest of your life?"

I knew I had tapped into only a miniscule portion of the words welling up inside to be finally released. I do not recall ever having spoken in such a manner with him before. I just remember feeling good that day. That instant. I felt like a man. I felt like I belonged somewhere, I just was not sure where.

My step-father sank down on his bed and shook his head at me, gathering his response which arrived in a whisper.

"You can't see yourself, Chris. You never could. You think this is all me and you are this perfect child. Same as your mother."

I shook my head. "I just told you it wasn't all your fault."

"Easy words to say. You're a good talker. You probably even believe most of what comes out of your mouth, but *I* don't. I've watched you play your mom and your grandfather. I know how you can con and manipulate everyone to get what you want and to hell with the rest of us! Maybe I'm not the great father you wanted, but I'm not a phony. I'm me. I don't run around acting like God's gift to everybody. You think you're going to be twenty years old forever? You're sorely mistaken. You don't know what the real world is like. You live in this fogged up fantasy world and probably think someone is going to take care of you for the rest of your life. You're going to have one hell of a rude awakening one day, Son! You are the most selfish, self-centered and narcissistic person I have ever met. And you don't even see it."

"Nope," I said. "I guess I don't. You don't see yourself either. How many people have told you what I'm telling you today and how many have you listened to? None. You can never hear anything if it's about you and you don't agree with it. Why can't we both be wrong and both be right? Why do we have to have this epic struggle all the time? Don't you ever get tired of living like this? Don't you ever tire of being pissed off all the time? Is it because you don't want to feel something else?" I had pushed his buttons but didn't care.

"Get out!" he yelled. "Go play with your best buddy. Don't worry that your mother worries herself sick over what you may be up to next with that hoodlum. Don't worry about being on time for meals or ever helping around the house."

"Like you really go out of your way to help Mom around the house!"

"Just run around and act like the world owes you, Chris. The rest of us will stay out of your way and let you use up your family and friends till you're all alone."

"All alone?" I asked. "You're a great one for talking about being alone, Dad. When do you ever go out with Mom? When do you ever spend time with friends? Do you have any friends? I don't see them. I don't hear them on the phone. They don't come over to see you. You just watch television or sit in your room drinking like some leper. Don't tell me about *alone*, man. You got the market cornered on that!"

I knew at this point the best outcome I could hope for was below dismal and I opted to jump ship while I still could float. My step-father dismissed my last comments with a wave of his hand and a touch of his finger to the television volume on his remote control he brandished like a pistol.

Without further ado, I closed his door behind me, scribbled a note for my mother who had been, as usual, walking away her woes, and ran out to Diresk's truck.

I found him in the back with Grover, licking each other's tongues in one of their obnoxious kisses. His eyes met mine in question, but I shook my head. I wasn't ready to talk about my father.

"Hey," I said as I startled them both. "Let's get out of here before he finds where I hid his bullets, man."

"You're not exactly on my favorite human list, Freddy," Diresk groaned as he removed Grover from his chest and sat up against the back of the cab.

"Because I asked you to leave so I could talk to my father? Well, you shall most certainly pardon my remiss, Oh Great One."

"I'll take your remiss and shove it up your ass and see how you like that," Diresk barked.

I was not able to determine the gravity of his comeback and merely hushed myself and entered his cab. The best defense with Diresk was always to feign flattering submission, so I prepared for his arrival by lighting him a cigarette and inserting his favorite Jerry Jeff Walker cassette into the stereo we had been in illegal possession of at the time. This type of behavior would often render Diresk reasonable, assuming his disposition was less than ballistic. This particular instance, it had done nothing to defray his consternation as he assumed his position behind the wheel.

"I can't believe you bowed down to him again like that, man!" Diresk started as he snatched the smoking cigarette from my fingers and inserted it between his front teeth. "He's the friggin' reason you're scared of your own shadow and act like some damned neurotic all the time! He's not such a big man, now is he? What the hell did you talk to him about? Topher, if you apologized to that asshole, I'll friggin' tear your tongue out!"

"He's not that bad and..." I said, putting my hand through my hair.

"Am I hearing this? Who do you think you are talking to, man, some friggin' social worker? Every friggin' day you're telling me about the shit he's doing to your mom and the shit he's doing to you. I get so tired of hearing it. *Shit,* Topher. He's not right in the head, man. He's got some type of miserable disease and he's trying to give it to you and your mamma."

"Yeah, I know," I conceded. "But you don't see it all. You only see and hear my side, D. I don't like what he is and what he does either, but you have to be able to look at the entire picture here. It's never black and white, man. There's got to be some middle ground in there somewhere."

"I don't believe this! You're defending him. This is just beautiful, man. What has he ever done for you or your mom but screw up your heads? Huh? What great purpose has he served? Come on, Topher. Inspire me, man."

I knew I was standing on shaky ground and believe me, my heart was not entirely invested in the prospect of defending the man I had feared and resented for nearly twelve years. The man I had always blamed my defects of character and emotions on. Yet here I was in my best friend's truck—my best friend who had just stood up for me and threatened to fight my step-dad to protect me—and I was about to bolster an argument that would certainly be considered a breach of our friendship. Diresk did not take saving others from themselves lightly. He thrived on it, so I gingerly proceeded.

"Look," I said. "You don't know how much I appreciate you being here for me. I get so much strength by just knowing you are there for me as my best friend."

"Save the shit for some other asshole, man. I don't need to hear this now, okay? I think you're swell, too, okay? Don't got nothing to do with what that prick is doing to you."

"Can you please just hear me out and then you can talk? Please?"

Diresk glared at me, then nodded. Barely.

"I can't fight battles like you can. I can't stand up to my step-dad like you can stand up to your dad. But do you want to know the truth? My real dad left me as a child and could care less about me. Richard has been the one who has helped give me food and clothes. He's the one who went to all my games and tried to support me and tell me he was proud of me in his own way. He's the one who showed up to see me get awards from basketball and praised me for my scholarship offers. He gave me comic books every day when I was in grade school. Maybe he's not the best at being happy and expressing his love but he's been there, man. That has got to count for something." I took a breath before I went on. "I can't blame him for everything. He's responsible for a hell of a lot that isn't right in my home and in my head...but I'm in there, too. So is my mom. He's not the only gear that isn't grabbing in our family, D."

Diresk started the truck and backed out of our long driveway. We headed down Pine Street and out towards Custer State Park. I was shocked by my own words. I had never given any consideration to what I had just told him, let alone voiced it. We drove along and listened to Jerry Jeff slam the government and talk about whiskey. I was not at all certain how my words sat with Diresk, as he had not offered any feedback or response to my statement back in the driveway. He smoked and drove.

I waited and wondered.

"I don't agree with some of what you said," Diresk finally noted. "I don't like him and I don't like what he's done. You've got a way of putting things, Toph. I guess me and my old man are kind of the same in that way. You see all the shitty stuff he does and I know about how great a man he can be. All the cool shit he's done for me. I was ready to kick his ass, Toph. I was, man. My old man would tie you up in bloody knots if you had pulled that shit on him!"

He turned and smiled at me and the cab felt like home again. I lit a cigarette and Diresk swatted my shoulder with his free hand.

We both learned something that afternoon that would come back to me years later, and allow me to tell my step-father how much I loved him during family week of his alcohol treatment. Sitting there, holding hands with him and encircled by other families and patients, I was able to return to that day and my conversation with my best friend and the insightful discussion and drive that followed.

I think it had been the reason I was able to cry with my step-father that evening. Gangsters, you see, are not supposed to cry.

Even broken ones.

Chapter Thirty-Eight

Bob had murky bottomless eyes, and when you tried to look into them when he did not want you to they sent shivers down to your toes. Quick with a gripping tale or joke, he was like the wise old man often written about who lives in a cave and hands out spiritual road maps to all who dare seek his advice. His empathic self-disclosures of the footprints left behind his often perilous path were legendary in my school.

His breath always reminded me of the old western paperbacks my grandfather kept on a dusty shelf above his bed. Almost as if his bodily organs were smoldering. Diresk and I spent every lunch break at his arcade from junior high on. I can't place his last name. We all called him Uncle Bob, or just Bob. Proprietor of Bob's Arcade located less than one block from our school building. It was the place to be if you were a teen in Custer in the 70s.

Bob must have been in his fifties when we knew him best. Diresk and I loved to pass away the hours on Saturday, uninterrupted by school or other such nonsense; eager sound boards for the owner of the town's only arcade. He stood not much over five feet tall. A graveled voice spun tales like a web through a tight-lipped grimace encircled by gray-whiskered spikes. My mouth would itch just looking at him. He had lost most of his black hair somewhere behind him, and he constantly rubbed his shiny head as if he would somehow recall just where. Bob always wore the same tattered jean jacket and urine-colored cowboy boots. And I can't recall a time when a Lucky Strike was not dangling from his lips. He never lit them.

"I ain't lit one of these devils since 1971, lads," Bob once informed us. "I got so close to emphysema one time I could feel it sucking the breath right out of me. You boys best quit while you're ahead on that one. They'll kill you faster than you think. Last thing you need is to go around pulling some oxygen tank behind you like a little red wagon when you're my age. If we were meant to smoke cigarettes God would've given us a hell of a better filtering system than the one we got."

Bob was considered eccentric by most of the people who lived in Custer. He saved up to buy a ranch on the west side of town and had, to the consternation of nearly everyone, torn down all of the fence lines immediately upon gaining residence.

"Most folks spend their lives putting up fences but I'm gonna spend mine taking them down. I like it that way. If my neighbors don't like it, they can move!" Bob said with a burned out twinkle in his empty eyes. "You oughta see all the deer and animals I get hanging around my place since I took them down. Hell, I feel like Noah sometimes, lads. Makes me feel good that they take the time to drop in on me."

Rumor had it that Bob had left a wife and kids in North Dakota, but he never really did say either way. Whenever we would ask him, he would tell us to mind our own business and to "let a man worry about his own life because you kids got too much to think on as it is". I tend to believe he did have a family. Somewhere. Probably back where he had lost most of his hair.

The only adult friend, to my knowledge, that Bob gave any attention to was Hank Webster. Hank thought Bob was an honorary member of a dying breed of "free thinkers." Bob thought Hank was "one tough son of a bitch!"

Diresk and I used to watch the two of them shoot pool at Bob's place. Those afternoons were like taking a class in manhood, and the closest I ever got to experiencing any rite of passage. Those two talked about and pretended to know everything you could imagine. God only knows how much of that I digested and implemented into my own being.

One afternoon Diresk and I stopped at Bob's to hang out and see what the man had on his mind that particular day. I believe we were juniors in high school and the discussion swung to our basketball season. Bob was a voracious sports fan and could be seen at all Custer boy's sporting events, home or away. In the midst of a heated debate over zone defenses and my lack of confidence, Bob's door was filled by the looming presence of Jake "Thunder Fists" Webster.

Jake was usually a welcome addition to our afternoon sessions, but this also signaled compulsory amends of our usual verbiage. Diresk, Bob, and I were avid admirers of the slang and profane. But Jake did not approve of such immature derisions of the language. At least not in front of his son.

"Well, if it ain't the big man!" Bob eagerly greeted his valued customer and confidant. "I believe I owe you a whipping from the other day, my friend. Why don't you rack them up and I'll see if I can scare us up some snacks."

"If you want to get destroyed again, who am I to stand in the way of a man getting his much needed lesson," Jake Webster said, then looked at us. "Thought I might find the two of you wasting away down here."

"Someone's got to monitor the exploits of this vagabond," I offered, hoping I would be rewarded with at the very least a tiny hint of a grin from the unpredictable man.

"Hey, Pop," Diresk said. "We'd rather be out making something of ourselves, but a guy's gotta do what a guy's gotta do. Someone's has to help this handicapped urchin out. Who am I to turn my back on the handicapped. Even Bob."

"I'll handicap you in a minute, Mr. Smart Alec," Bob delivered over his shoulder as he disappeared into the back of his store to retrieve some special snacking material.

"Have you talked to your mother today?" Jake asked his son. His lip resembled a front loader, filled to the rim with tobacco.

"Nope," Diresk said. "I haven't been home since this morning. Why?"

"She needs some help shoveling snow and I've got to get back out to finish up on them brush piles. I want you to get them walks done today, young man. You can have your fun when the work gets done."

"Did you just rhyme that on purpose?" Diresk smiled with open-mouthed astonishment. "I can't believe you just did that, if you meant to do that."

"I'm not exactly without talent, boy," Jake Webster replied with a smile. He then gestured to the pool table and Diresk reluctantly abandoned his stool and began to gather the billiard balls to rack them for his father's next competitive encounter.

"How's it going, Christopher?" Jake said. "You played a fine game the other night, son. If you'd had some help on defense we would've whipped them."

"I'm good, Mr. Webster," I said. "Kind of sick of this cold and snow though, I guess it could be worse. Yeah, we should have destroyed those guys. I thought we had them down until Rick fouled out and we quit pressing. I should have never missed that shot on the baseline, either. Man, I wish I could have it over again."

"How many points you get? I didn't see the paper," Jake continued.

"Eighteen. Diresk had twelve rebounds."

"Yeah, but he didn't play defense worth a hoot," his father noted, pointing a thick finger at Diresk's chest. Diresk stuck his tongue out at his father.

"Yeah, all I did was hold a guy who was five inches taller than me off the boards all night," Diresk shouted. "He only got about twelve points on me, Pop."

"I'll tell you what lost the damn game," Bob's voice rang throughout the arcade as he appeared, arms filled with sandwiches and sodas. "You can't let them push you around underneath that…and why in the hell didn't you guys full court press in the first half? That point guard couldn't have dribbled down his chin if you would've scared him some. When you finally did jump on him, he threw the ball away two or three times in that last quarter."

"Thank you very much, Bobby Knight," Diresk teased. "Would you mind sitting on the bench with us next time so you can tell us all how to play?"

"I know a thing or two about basketball, junior," Bob shot back. "The only way you ladies are going to get to the big tournament is by cramming the ball down people's throats and using your quickness to cover the court on defense; not to mention, force turnovers and slow down their game. Like you did against Spearfish. Now that's how to win basketball games!

Chris has to have room to move the ball around, and you've got to work harder to get open underneath. You guys play like you did against Spearfish and Sturgis then nobody can beat you for the rest of the season and that's a God damned fact! Who wants mustard?"

The three of us voiced our affirmatives and I found myself attempting to breach the silence.

Finally, I began with, "Diresk's getting open is not the problem, Bob. The problem is we can't seem to work like a team. We spend more time arguing with each other than playing basketball. Don't we?" I nodded at Diresk, who responded with his own as he put his finishing touches on the racked balls.

"Too many chiefs and not enough Indians," Bob mumbled through a mouth full of ham, cheese, onion, and lettuce. "That's the coach's job to take care of that stuff. If a kid doesn't want to be part of the team, he ought to get his ass put on the pine for a few games and see how he feels then. You've got to nip that attitude crap in the butt right away."

"In the bud," Diresk stated firmly.

"What?" Bob rebounded.

"Nip it in the bud," he repeated.

"Whatever. What the hell's that supposed to mean anyway?" he asked.

Diresk's grin switched course, flipped upside down, and he swung to me for support.

"I believe," I said, "it means to take care of a problem while it is still in its early stage of development. A bud is an undeveloped plant shoot or a flower that has yet to open. That would be my guess, anyway."

"My boy is not stupid," Diresk proudly announced. "Now if I can just get him to shovel that snow for me."

"If we can work out proper compensation for this task, I can possibly assist you."

"How come I don't get money for shoveling, Pop?" Diresk directed his question to Jake. "A guy's got to have coin in his pockets, man."

"You get a roof over your head and you keep me broke buying food for you," Jake Webster replied. "The fact I don't break your jaw so you can't keep smart mouthing ought to be worth a hell of a lot, too."

The discussion continued and eventually changed course several times while the men shot pool and Diresk and I basked in the comfortable rivalry and good-natured bantering before us, inserting what we believed to be timely and amusing anecdotes between bites of chocolate and soda swigs.

In time, Bob managed to commandeer the billiard lead and strutted around his pool table and establishment like Napoleon spewing personal accolades and speculations. One could not help but perceive Jake Webster's growing frustrations which led to an eventual self-sequester in Bob's back room. I imagine to gather his thoughts as well as his shooting eye.

"I think your poppa is a might upset over his pool playing, Diresk," Bob chuckled. "He usually doesn't get this bent out of shape over our little games. Everything okay on the home front?"

"How the hell should I know?" Diresk shot back, causing both Bob and I to take note of the facial expression accompanying his outburst.

"I think the Webster boys need some sun, Chris," Bob commented as he left to join his disgruntled nemesis in the kitchen.

"What's up, man?" I asked Diresk who had begun to pace the carpeted floor.

"I just hate how nosy he gets! It's not his business what goes on with my family. If Dad wants to tell him about him and Mom, then he should be the one Bob should ask, not me. Just because Dad lost a few pool games don't mean he's getting a friggin' divorce!"

I sat there and watched him pace the arcade like a dog in a tiny pen. It was during times like this one I often struggled.

I knew Diresk was upset. The emotional culprit festered under the surface of what had been happening at Bob's that afternoon. I knew it was my job to diplomatically incite his response and that would lead to an eventual disclosure. The key was to present it in such a way as to allow it to be Diresk's idea. Usually, I was able to accomplish this with an attitude of strategic aloofness, but not today.

"You want to take off?" I began.

"I want to talk to Dad before we split. I know Bob's a cool guy and everything. I'm just so pissed off, I don't even know for sure why."

"I can tell you're upset. Maybe your nicotine level has plunged and your brain is organizing a revolt. Maybe we should drive out to Stockade and see if the ice will hold us. It's thick enough, don't you think?" I said, trying to distract him.

"That's what I need, man. I need a cancer stick. Hang on a second and I'm going to tell Pop something. Here, start my rig and warm it up, Cecil." He tossed me his keys and disappeared into the kitchen, pocketing a couple candy bars on his way, grinning and shaking his brows up and down.

I grabbed my coat and gloves and went out to start the pickup, gathering my thoughts and insights for the discussion that would accompany whatever tape we would choose to play. I started the engine and pumped it until a steady idle was achieved. I considered lighting a cigarette, but decided against it to avoid possible confrontation by Jake Webster and his sinus detectives. I tensed against the biting cold and sprinted back into the heated store.

The pool game had resumed. So had Bob's mining of Jake Webster's precious metal.

"All I'm saying is if you can't talk to your best friend, then who can you talk to?" Bob said. "You're not as self-sufficient as you think you are, Jake. I know something is really gagging your ghost and you better spill it before it joins up with the rest of your secrets and eats a hole in your belly!"

There had been a split second when Jake Webster's rage had come dangerously close to spilling out of his grinding jaw. We had all sensed and braced for it. It was as if the room had suddenly become thick with an electric and ominous fog. All breathing in the room had been cut to thin wisps of the heavy air, and my eyes captured the deft shift of Diresk's body a mere instant before his voice attacked like a striking serpent; gathering force and volume with every biting word.

"Why don't you MIND YOUR OWN BUSINESS! JESUS CHRIST! You don't have to know everything about everything, Bob! If you are so God damned curious about what happens in our home, then why don't you come over and see for yourself?"

"You will not speak with that tone or tongue, Son," Jake Webster annunciated through his tobacco-stained, clenched teeth. "I mean it, young man! I don't want to hear that come out of your mouth ever again. Do you understand me? Diresk? Look at me, boy!"

"What?" Diresk said. "Can't I stand up for my own family for God's sake?"

"For God's sake? Language like that has got no place with God's sake, Son! You get on home and we'll talk about this later on tonight. Give Chris a ride home and you get some of that snow moved before I get there. You got something to say to Bob before you go, Diresk?"

"I don't have to apologize for saying what I believe. Bob and I've had a million arguments before and we'll be okay. You think I'm wrong?" Diresk asked as he turned his attention and blazing eyes to me.

I shrugged. "I don't think I better say anything about this, because it's not really my…"

"I'm not asking about that, Topher! I want you to tell me if you think I'm out of line here, man. That shouldn't be too hard for a smart guy like you!"

It wasn't until much later that I understood he'd been taking his aggressions out on the only perceived safe person in the room. His best friend. At the time, I was very disturbed he would place me in such a delicate position. What was I supposed to say? Diresk's friendship was my most treasured possession, and he knew how terrified I was of his father. What amazed me more than anything was the quiet of the room as Jake Webster and Bob awaited my reply.

I cautiously dipped my first toe into the stream rushing before me.

"Well...as far as the cussing goes, I think words are just words and one doesn't really have more power than another. I don't think it's always appropriate to cuss, but sometimes it just seems to fit the situation the best. Words are just words and they only have what we give them.

"I mean, you shouldn't try to hurt people with words or insult them with words, but that's probably a lot better than hurting them with fists. Words are just tools; sometimes one tool is just as good as another. But sometimes you can only use the right tool for the job."

I paused before inserting my entire foot, hoping I had not confused my words or contradicted myself. It was not every day I was allowed to address such an esteemed crowd, and I got lost somewhere between the moment and my pulsing ego.

"As far as the stuff with your family goes, I don't think Bob was trying to harm Mr. Webster. I think he was trying to be a friend. This really isn't my business here. I do agree that Diresk has a right to speak up regarding his family, and he just wants to defend Mr. Webster, and that's a good thing. Now I don't remember what else I was going to say."

I did not draw breath for considerable duration following my impromptu, oral interpretive treatise. To be entirely honest and true to my wares, I fully expected to be pummeled by Diresk upon our exit from Bob's meager establishment. Thank the Lord, I am often plagued by misguided inclinations.

"Now don't get mad at me if I said something you didn't agree with here. You were the one who put me on the spot and I didn't know what the hell to..."

"Damn, I like to hear you gab, Toph!" Bob humbly stated, turning to face Diresk for the first time since my best friend's explosion. "Look, Diresk, I didn't mean to upset you. I can see I did maybe I owe you the apology. Your daddy has been a good friend of mine. Hell, my only friend. Guess that makes him my best one. Like you and Chris. I may not be a genius but I can tell when a man's burden is starting to bend his shoulders to the ground. Any fool can keep his own counsel, but that's just what he's going to stay being. Life isn't always pretty. Sometimes you've got to kick a man when he's down because that's the only way to get him to stand up again. Sometimes you lay down there with him. Depends on the man and the situation. The point is, you can't step over him and pretend he's not there."

"I'm sorry too, Bob," Diresk offered. "I shouldn't have cussed you out like that. I like hanging around here. You're always good to the Topher and me. I guess I must be upset about something else and I don't even know what it is. Dad? I'm sorry that my cussing bothers you so much, but I talk this way when I'm not around you."

Jake Webster's reaction hung above us all like a water balloon, struggling and stretching as its boundaries fought to contain an impossible flow. Bob, sensing his friend's overwhelmingness, inadvertently shut off Jake Webster's pressurized valve by blanketing him with a hesitant embrace.

It hung on the powerful man like a poorly tailored suit, but managed to calm him and even conjure somewhat of a grin. Jake Webster, proud and strong beyond measure, softly escaped from HIS best friend's arms and sent him a "thank you" with his eyes. He turned to face his son with aching amusement.

"Get over here!" Jake Webster ordered his son.

Diresk, his arms held impotently to his side, stepped with a perplexed ambiguity toward his father as emotions battled for control of his face. I managed to catch Bob's wink out of the corner of my eye as I followed my friend's penchant stride.

Diresk stood toe-to-toe, face-to-lower chin, with his imposing father. There were no words for the moment, and neither Bob nor I would have dared an attempt as we stood and watched father and son communicate with matching eyes. It had been an honor to be in that arcade in that day, but not because of the culmination of events or even the fragrant repose that followed.

It was a gathering of men!

Together.

Generations of bloodline and intimate association danced blithely among us that afternoon like ancient spirits in a fire-lit cavern. The sharing of ideas and all that is man, and the disposition of all that is not. Exploration of passageways leading to true essence of spiritual and psychosocial development. To a young man, these are moments of delight and wonderment. To many, the only representations of discarded myths and the mirth of donning paternal garments, sadly infrequent incidents for boys hot in their pursuit of manhood.

Hell, at first I thought we were having a disagreement and billiards game.

Diresk and his father stood like granite statues, inches from each other's measured breathing. I will remember their embrace for as long as I am able to close my eyes and open them again.

It had been, I now am inclined to accept, a hug meant for us all.

Chapter Thirty-Nine

"You are a troglodyte!" I yelled at Diresk from the kitchen of my house in Custer. Diresk and my mother had been sitting at a card table in the family room, awaiting my return to resume our heated game of Scrabble.

"How do you spell *that*?" Diresk shouted back at me as I removed three sodas from the refrigerator, tucked them under my arms, and palmed three glasses of ice and a bag of chips. Intermission snack and a chance for me to regroup for a change. Mom was killing us.

"Like it sounds, Dipnode," I tossed at him as I set the drinks and chips in the center of the table near the game board.

"Christopher, don't talk like that to Diresk," my mother said with a slight smile.

"T-R-O-G-L-A-D-I-T-E?" Diresk attempted with an unlit cigarette in the corner of his mouth. He looked like a gambler in an old west movie. We were both early twenty-somethings at the time.

"No cigar, Wet Brain. T-R-O-G-L-O-D-Y-T-E," I proudly stated.

"Takes one to spell one, Luther."

"You don't even know what a troglodyte is," I said.

"Some kind of prehistoric being who lived in a cave or something."

I was stunned. I nodded and opened my Pepsi, short on a comeback.

"Like your father," Mom lithely inserted.

I turned to face her unexpected quip with a dropped jaw reverence. Diresk offered her a "high five" and chuckled noisily as my mother slapped his palm like one of the guys and sat back in her chair to celebrate. The three of us shared laughter that felt like a beer and a cigarette.

Every now and then she would let her keen sense of style and humor peek out from behind its curtain and blow me away. As I grow to love and know her more deeply, I am thoroughly amazed at how little of my mother I was aware of growing up in Custer. She just never had anyone to believe in her. She was so secretly proud of her card playing prowess and was anyone's first bridge partner pick. Too bad there is not an Olympic event testing walking and card playing proficiency.

"We've got to get Mrs. Topher, man. She's wiping us off the map again."

No matter how hard I tried, my mother would always defeat me at Scrabble or Gin Rummy, and it pissed me off to no end. Diresk would have to be drug kicking and screaming into any card or board game. Every once in a while, my mother could coax him in.

"I'm only fifty points ahead, you guys," Mom noted in her usual well-hidden beleaguering tone.

"Fifty ahead of Toph. Hundred ahead of me," Diresk whined.

"Maybe if you knew how to spell it would enhance your score," I tossed at my partner.

"Christopher, he's never going to play with us again. Be nice."

"Never fear, Mrs. T. I'm used to his abuse. It bounces off me like a tiny little bug. He's just trying to make up for his low self-esteem is all. He doesn't mean to be so rude."

He paused as I smiled and awaited his next stab.

"I think he's getting kind of tired of you beating up on him so much. He ever beat you?"

"Oh, every once in a while he beats me. I think he beat me at Gin about six or seven years ago," Mom delivered with a poker face I would not have believed possible for her usually rather staunch demeanor.

By God, she was better than I thought.

Diresk shot Pepsi through his nostrils and covered his face as if to somehow shut off the pressurized spurting. Somehow, he managed to keep the cigarette on a dry lip.

Soon, the three of us were locked in mutual chortle at my mother's rarely displayed humor. We continued to laugh and rub our eyes as my step-father suddenly appeared in the room's arched doorway wearing an angry mask on top of a just awakened face. My stomach immediately seized and I could feel my mother's own reaction like an electric shock as the two of us wound down from our laughter like a light touch placed upon the spinning tire of an upturned bicycle.

"Do you think you can keep it down a little in here?" he said. "I'm watching a movie and I'd like to be able to hear the dialogue if it isn't too much to ask."

Kind of hard to watch a movie through closed eyes…isn't it, Father?

If Diresk had thought it, he would have asked it. I held my silence like a breath, peeking from the side of my eyes towards a possible Diresk rebuttal.

"Oh, Richard," Mom began with a suddenly serious tone, "we're just having some fun here. Go back in your room and forget about us for crying out loud!"

"Dammit, woman, you have to use your smart mouth, don't you? All I ask is for some peace and quiet around here. I don't need to get my head snapped off every time I want something to go my way for once! If you can't…"

"For once?" she asked him. "My God, Richard. You get your way every time around this house. No one else gets a say about what goes on in this home. Chris can't even open the refrigerator without you…"

"There it is again! Defend him. Defend your little angel who can't do anything wrong for his mommy! What's he going to do when he doesn't have you to take care of him? What's he going to do?"

"Richard, that's enough! Go back to your room and leave us alone."

"Are you going to have him live with you forever so you can wipe his butt whenever he makes a mess? Are you ever going to let him do anything for himself?"

"Diresk, I'm sorry you have to hear this," Mother stated, her eyes burning through my step-father like laser beams. "Richard, we can continue this upstairs…but I will not do this in front of Christopher's friend."

"Shit. We wouldn't want anyone to think we aren't the perfect family now, would we? Jesus Christ, what would the Websters think of us?"

"Careful, man," Diresk whispered, sliding his chair back on the worn rug.

I shot a glance towards Diresk to attempt to halt any advance. It would not be necessary. My best friend and I had discussed such situations. He graciously agreed to stand aside so I would learn either to spit the tainted medicine back at my step-father, or continue to taste the consequences of consumption.

Diresk leaned back sipping from his glass as his eyes prompted me from above its rim.

The four of us, silent in the tense fog of the room, measured each other like two street gangs in an alley. My mother rose slowly in her chair and approached my step-father, who stood panting in the doorway.

She offered her hand. I tried to blink away the sight of her yield, pregnant with another likely miscarriage of cornered courage. I tasted my self-loathing as it rose like bile in my throat and screamed for release or redemption. I swallowed hard and ground my jaw, drawing the breath I would need to launch the words, foaming throughout my entire being.

"NO! Mom!" My words seemed to stop every molecule in the room and were out of my mouth before I was aware I had spoken them. I had not yet met my step-father's eyes, and was startled by the explosion of wooden letters and ice cubes and Pepsi as my fists struck the table surface.

"Clean it up!" my step-father hissed, ignoring my mother's outstretched hand. "I want you to leave now, Diresk."

"You're the king, Richard," Diresk replied and abandoned his attempt to divert the stream of Pepsi from cascading onto the floor with a dismissive shrug of his dripping hands.

His eyes drew mine like magnets and poured into me. I was helpless. Held up next to the moment, I felt like a twig beside the trunk of a large Pine. I watched as my best friend slowly rose from his chair. I winced as I saw the wet stain in his jeans, giving him the appearance of a table wetter. Diresk took deliberate steps past my mother and stopped only inches from my step-father's rage.

"Excuse me, Richard," he said, his tone casual. "Got to get my coat."

"Get it and get out!" my step-father ordered, moving cautiously aside and into the family room.

I began to gather the soaked game pieces, then angrily shoved them off the table riding a Pepsi wave. I was sick of myself. Sick of the fear holding my hand like a child molester. I nearly upended the table, dropped my head into my cupped hands and pushed myself up and off my chair.

"Thanks for the game, Mrs. Topher," Diresk's voice again appeared in the doorway. "I guess you win by default, huh, Mrs. Topher? You got lucky, Jerry. I was fixing to drop a doosey on you."

"My wife's name is Mrs. Hammerquist and I would appreciate it if you would address her as such," my step-father growled.

I turned to face them and watched as Diresk started for the front door. I watched him pause and consider addressing my step-father, shake his head, then flash me a peace sign before disappearing behind a slight slam of the screen door. My mother pushed the oak door shut. Her eyes were so far away and the room got darker and heavier as if a gigantic tarp had been tossed over the house. All I could think about was striking him with every ounce of rage and strength I could gather.

I played it out in my head. Every punch and kick to his body was like a drug rush inside my brain as I brutalized my step-father in my private theatre. I could taste the blood spraying on my face as my fist sunk deeper and deeper into his flesh until all I could see and feel was the life pumping out of him and into my veins. I sucked him dry and with one final blow I tore through his ribs and crushed his heart like a sponge. The blood was black and hot like a summer highway tar and I let it ooze through my clenched fingers, humming to myself a song I had never before heard.

Finished, I tucked his bloodied body away in my thoughts and returned to the room and the sound of my mother's crying. My step-father was gone. I heard the slam of the bathroom door as my mother turned to face me. Her tortured face pushed everything else out of the room. I so wanted to cry with her, but all I could do was wear the lie of our family like the smile of a demonic clown.

All at once the room began to spin in foreign angles and my heart blasted inside my head like a tremendous tin drum, pounding faster and faster until I thought I would collapse.

My mother spoke to me as if she was ten-years-old.

"I'm so sorry I did this to us, Honey," she said. "To you. I just always wanted you to be so happy. I'm so tired of it all. So tired."

Cloudy. She looked out of focus or like she was standing behind some thin veil. We embraced and I smelled the strawberry of her favorite shampoo. I wanted more for my mother at that moment than I have ever wanted for another human being. It was as if I could sense every line and crack on her skin, every ache of every nerve in her body. The woman who had fought wind gusts with every step her tiny feet had ever taken, only to have worn a circled path. I begged God to give her peace and love and joy.

I knew I could not.

It broke my heart.

It still does. Why could we not be close? Why did we keep our distance? I hugged my mother, but neither of us took a breath. It was almost as if we were auditioning for parts in a play. My mother. The life blood of my body and the ship that again sailed over my soul. I could not feel her and I could not hear her. I was simply too far away to ever come home.

The flush of the toilet caused us to break free from each other, and our eyes caught for a split second. They darted away and I reached for her without any intention of touching her.

The bathroom door opened and my step-father's steps disappeared behind his ever locked bedroom door. Not a slam, but loud enough to warn us not to follow or knock. My mother's eyes danced around my face as if trying to locate a way inside. It was the only time I ever remember holding her face in my hands.

It was the first time I ever remember missing her like that.

To this day, whenever I see her, I kiss her and miss her desperately.

Chapter Forty

I only recall a few instances when the four of us spent any real time together. Diresk and I had once joined our fathers for an afternoon fishing trip at Pactola Lake. We borrowed a neighbor's boat and trolled for trout to the hypnotic whine of the tiny motor. My father and Jake Webster could not have been considered friends. More like compelled acquaintances, bound by sense of duty to connect.

For my father, who preferred the solitude of alcohol and daydreams, it had proved to be quite a stretch to attempt kinship with Jake Webster. Jake was a man's man, and I believe my step-father viewed himself as neither manly nor fit for such duty. His father had managed to quarantine his sons from much of the informative data available to all.

He had also beaten my step-father and his two brothers with a mop handle on a regular basis.

My earliest memories of Grandpa Hammerquist are of a ten-foot tall giant of a man whose tantrums whirled and crashed like tornadoes through the tiny family home, destroying the spirits of those unfortunate enough to be found in his path. I swear to God I remember him growling like a caged animal. I remember the dull gray of his skin, as if his malice and venom held fresh air at bay.

I watched him die like a twisted branch in a room that smelled like anger and fungus as cancer's straw sucked his lifeblood away. I held his chilled fingers in the warmth of my own, bent to hear the final whispered words escape from his lips.

"I'm sorry. So sorry. I wasted your time. Any time. Please forgive me, Lord. I'm so sorry."

We caught a ton of fish that day and shared much laughter. I believe my father had a great time. He held back on his drinking throttle and we sat next to each other in the back of the boat as Diresk and Jake Webster faced us from the front in a good-natured competitive stance as they caught nearly all the trout that day. But not the biggest. Richard caught that one, and I was so happy for him. Diresk netted and landed it for him and even slapped him on the back after it was safely in the bottom of the boat. It was the best piece of ground they had ever shared. I loved it!

I wanted the day to continue forever.

I carry a faded memory of receiving a "pep talk" by these two men prior to a basketball game in the state tournament. Our fathers had inadvertently arrived together at the motel where our team was staying in Sioux Falls near the Arena, and stopped in to prime us for victory. I remember my own delicious bliss as Diresk and I were consecutively serenaded by them, barely able to contain their beaming pride.

We won that night.

Funny, I can barely recall the game we had worked all season to play, but I remember what my father was wearing that afternoon as he stood proudly in our motel room. I can still recall much of what was said, too.

The instant in time I shall treasure the most happened with the four of us together on a cloudy morning in a candled room adorned by red roses and a sorrow that clung to my skin. When I close my eyes I can still feel the intensity of that room.

My step-father and I had found Jake Webster collapsed on his knees, his callused hands dangling from the velvet edge of his son's coffin. The crucified Christ hung above his head, peering down with a knowing silence.

240

I had been previously unable to find my tears since learning of my best friend's suicide. I received the news of his death and discarded it like some tainted beverage on the walls of my room. Walls that closed in on me and forced me to breathe deeply into Mrs. Webster's ear who had called me with the news of his death as I was cutting a pair of jeans off above the knees. Patrick Simmons from the Doobie Brothers sang "Black Water" somewhere in the spinning room.

I refused to hang up the phone after she had.

I found my tears in that heavy room that morning. The day the sun had shattered my oblivion, and my dreams of frozen trout and crimson soaked snow.

My step-father drove me to visit Diresk after I had initially refused. As we turned the corner off of Main Street and approached the funeral home, I was stung by the sight of Jake Webster's Scout parked near the alley. Beside it, water-beaded with waxen sheen, a gray hearse stood ready for the following day's appointment.

Diresk and I had once considered stealing that same vehicle and parking it on the Hot Springs football field the night before we were to play them in their homecoming game. We were foiled by our inability to "hot wire" the station wagon. We had even dressed in black camouflage, wielding assorted screw drivers and rubber gloves. True gangsters.

The very next day, April 22, 1989, it would start with a key and deliver my Diresk's physical shell to be covered with dirt and a marble crown. He was twenty-eight years old when a a .38 caliber pistol shut up the voices in his head—voices I had little knowledge of due to my own design. All I can think about right now is wondering whatever was done with the gun.

My step-father and I saw Jake there, pressed against the son he would never again watch through a lifted curtain to stagger from his pickup and into their darkened home. The son he would never again scream at or shake a fist. Whose face he would never again cup in his hands. Who would never again stroll beside him through the trees and meadows of Custer's majestic surrounding forests. Their special places on God's Earth.

He would never again sneak from his room to watch his son sleep.

Jake Webster had taught his son how to clean, load, and fire handguns and rifles at the age of twelve. He had given a silver plated .38 caliber pistol to Diresk as a Christmas present.

To celebrate the birth of Christ.

"Jake? Sorry to bother you. We just wanted to pay our respects, and then we can get out of your way," my step-father tensely whispered.

"Hi guys," Jake Webster managed through his muffled tears, turning to greet us with an extended hand. "Thanks for coming. Christopher, I meant to stop over last night but I was too tired. I had to stay with Mother. He wanted me to give you something. I got it at home. It's a package. Come over and get it when you want to. Cele wants to see you, I know."

The quiet in the room began to crush us all and I stepped forward as if to view his body, but stopped myself short and searched for Diresk instead in his father's eyes. Before I could speak, my tears began to flow and soon my body was convulsing as I stepped back from the coffin. I struck the wall behind me, sliding down into an upright fetal position. My eyes remained open as I watched my tears paint the denim covering my thighs. All I could do was to release the waves that rushed from deep within my secret walls.

I do not know how much time elapsed before I looked up and wiped the fog from my eyes. I recall how the candles caused the shadows to dance around the room and how unbelievably large Jesus appeared above the generic altar. At first, he had appeared to me as an angry titan, but as I pushed and pulled myself to standing, his eyes seemed to follow my movements. I felt something shift inside me that I can only pretend to believe was the tossing and turning of my sleeping faith. It would take years for it to open its eyes, but that morning, I knew Diresk was no longer in that body, I was not alone, and somehow, I was going to be okay.

For that split second, it was as if he had reached down to whisper something in my ear that I would not fully comprehend, but was a planted seed I so desperately needed to continue to travel where he could not.

My next conscious moment was that my step-father and Jake Webster had left the room and were quietly talking in the foyer. I turned and could see their shadows on the wall directly opposite the doorway. I watched as my father reached out to comfort Jake Webster, draw his hand back, and then again replace it on the huge man's shoulder. I could not decipher their words, but by my father's movements and gestures, Jake Webster's posture and the way in which he cradled his own face in his lost hands sparked a new flow of my tears. But tears from a different place and a different time.

So many memories brushed past me in that instant. I was treated to countless harmonies of Diresk and I as they drifted across the front of my mind like a highlight film. I could not keep my eyes open as my head rocked and swayed to the soundless music of our lives together.

I loved him like a storm. My earliest recollections will always contain him, regardless if he was present in them. He was my hero, my protector.

I love you, Diresk! my mind screamed. *I will love you until I see you again and then, we shall see what we shall see.*

"Chris? You okay in there, Son?"

My attention was forced to shift towards my step-father's voice, whose face had appeared in the doorway.

"Yeah, I'm okay, Dad. I didn't know you guys had left. How long have I been here like this?"

"About an hour. Jake wants to tell you goodbye. He's heading home for a while and he's going to come back with Celia. Why don't you run out and catch him real quick? I'm going to say my goodbyes here. I'm so sorry about this, Son. I wish there was something I could say or do to make it all go away." He made to reach out towards me, but his hand fell short. "Thank you for letting me come with you. I had a nice talk with Jake. I don't know what I would do if something—"

"I'll be right back, Dad," I quickly said and rushed out to speak with Jake Webster. I hurried away from my step-father's emotional release, and felt so confused as I paused and attempted to gather myself behind the front door. Soon, I realized this to be a ridiculous proposition, shared a faint smile with myself, and pushed out through the heavy oak doors, past the parked hearse, and into the alley where Jake Webster waited in his idling Scout.

"Dad said you wanted to talk to me, Mr. Webster."

"Yeah. Thanks, Chris. Maybe I've got nothing to say. I don't know what the hell I want right now. I keep trying to figure a way I could get him back and I can't stop trying to remember all the mistakes I made when he was still here. Look, I gotta get home to Cele. I got the package for you at the house and I want you to have it. You don't have to tell me what's in it because my son wanted it to be just for you. He told us so in the note he left for his mother. You can get it whenever you feel ready, okay?"

"I'll come and get it maybe later tonight. Waiting won't make it any easier, I guess. I'm sorry, Mr. Webster. I can't believe he's gone, and I can't believe I couldn't do anything to stop him from doing what he did. God, I never knew he was that upset. He always just seemed to get through stuff like I never could. I figured if I could keep going through what I've been going through, he could, too. When I talked to him the other day, I just didn't see it coming at all. I didn't have the faintest clue he wanted to...die like that."

"You know something?" he said. "I always thought you should call me Jake, but I never said so. Would you do that for me? Call me Jake and drop the Mr. Webster malarkey?"

"Yeah. I would like that. I like that better. I always wanted to call you Jake but I didn't know how you would take it."

"Settled! You still off the booze?"

"Yes, sir. Jake."

"I'm not done yet, but it's coming soon, let me tell you. I'll know. It's never never done me much good, but I need it now more than I ever needed it! I'm proud you gave it up, son. I kept hoping Diresk would take after you, but who was I to tell him to dry up? He told me he was proud of you. I'll bet a hundred times or so." He shook his head. "How you got through them hospitals and just kept on going. I asked him one time what was wrong with you and why you kept ending up in them funny farms. I don't mean nothing by that, it's just what we always called them."

"I understand, believe me." I tried to smile.

"Anyway, I don't mean nothing by it. I probably should've been in one myself, but they never caught me. I asked him what had you so bothered all the time. Know what he told me?"

I shook my head, bracing myself for something I knew would shake my very essence.

"He told me you were the only person who didn't know how special you are. Said you were going be a big star someday if you didn't keep getting in your own way all the time. If you didn't...oh, I don't know if I can take this, Chris."

Jake Webster inhaled and braced himself against the storm swelling in his soul.

"He said you were going to find out someday about all the best parts of you and he was going to stand back and watch you take it to the sky. You were going to become some famous writer, if your brain didn't talk you into killing yourself." He stared at me as if I wasn't standing in front of him, then said, "Anyway, I best get on home."

His tears fought their way through his immense pride, finally falling like waterfalls down his sunken cheeks.

"I've got to go. Come on over tonight and we can talk some more if you like. Thanks for…um…being his friend. I'll see you later."

I was forced to step back from the Scout as he pulled away to continue what had started again. I turned and faced the hearse, and for a moment considered kicking it as hard as I could. I ran my finger down its polished steel curves, still drying from its recent wash.

"You've got to look fancy when you bury someone, don't you, you son of a bitch?" I asked the car as my finger dropped from the grill and I went back in to find my step-dad.

Chapter Forty-One

I wish I had never erased the last message he left me on my answering machine. Who can know when someone offers their last words to you? One press of a button and it's gone. One slight movement of a finger and a tiny hammer pounds a bullet through a polished steel tube. Life goes on and on like a brain. Like gravel. Like the sound of the ocean.

Five messages. His was the third. My mother had called to complain about my step-father's delay on completing their taxes and to remind me about removing a roast from the oven. My friend, Steve confirmed a card game for the weekend and gave me grief over not returning some books I had borrowed. I quickly climbed the stairs to my room as the machine continued.

It took about ten seconds for Diresk's voice to appear on the tape. I stopped halfway in my bedroom doorway to catch the delayed message, removing tennis shoes and socks as my ears perked for words. He sounded breathless and somewhat irritated. I walked barefoot down the stairs as I listened to him slur his way through his labored delivery.

"Slick! In case the parents are listening, I'll make this suitable for all ears. Sorry about my attitude today. Thanks for bringing back my poems. I know you didn't read them, but that's okay. I kind of like them and I don't give a shit what anybody else thinks anyway…ha! Anyways, I'm feeling better and I'm going to sleep now. I'm going to sleep now, Toph, so don't go calling me tonight and ruining my dreams. I wanted to tell you that…you're my best pal, Toph! No one would've hung around me as long as you have, man. I'm drunk…again. Imagine that, will you. Anyway, keep your powder dry, Jethro. World needs cats like you to keep the fever down. I just might be crazy about you, man.

You're the best thing I ever had in my life and I want you to know I'm not afraid of going crazy no more. Okay? Remember? I'm not scared of it no more. I'm drunker than ten skunks, man. Topher? I got something to show you, man, and I really want you to think hard on it when you see it. You're not going to believe it but it's true, man. It's really true and I'm crying if I'm lying. Well, I guess I may be lying then, huh? Later days, my brother."

I must have stood there for a couple minutes, digesting his words and the punishment and pain they seemed to carry with them. I thought he might be getting close. I thought he had had enough. Maybe this time he would quit. God, he must have been blasted. I knew he had been crying. I almost called him, but it was getting too late.

So I didn't. Now, I wish I would have.

He left a note for me along with a package filled with pieces of what we shared together. When I first opened it, my heart was pierced by a thousand tiny needles and I cried so hard I thought I would faint. The world felt so big again, and too small. Like the morning we first moved to Custer.

His note was written only to me and I will not share it now. It belongs only to me and that is that. Sacred words written as death patiently waited at the doorway, holding Diresk's jacket and hat. I shall take them with me into the dirt as my floating ashes blow and drift through the next door. They will burn with me in whatever oven they shall choose to use to take my bones.

Will he be there waiting for me with his wrinkled grin and ugly bowling shirt? Will I be bent from seven decade's weight, grayed hair and skin melting down my body like wax? Or will I be fifty? Will I feel and think as I do this day? Like a twenty year old gangster who finally managed to learn to listen to the purring of his engine, and not the gravel cracking underneath his spinning tires?

Will I remember our secret body language and the vows of our youth? Will I cry when he beckons me to him with cloudy smoke circling his knees? Will we feel each other's touch or just the memory of it? God, how I wish I knew these things. How I wish he could come back to tell me.

I know things about the Pale Horse. Things I have seen in the eyes of the dying as they drift away from this place. I have watched this mighty God close the book on three people I loved. Watched as the last breath caught in their throat as they stepped away from behind exhausted, spiritless eyes.

One thing I can tell you for certain is that fear was not in the room. It simply waited outside to pounce upon the backs of the living as they entered and exited the dying place. I know some things about this death, but not nearly enough to befriend it. Its uncharted oblivion terrifies me at some level and I am not certain how I shall face its embrace.

I would like to believe I could offer a gracious bow before slipping my foot into its stirrup and mounting its eternal saddle. It would be just like me to scamper away knowing I would not get far.

Maybe I have known him for several lifetimes. Maybe we died together on an ancient battlefield, or chased witches through the boroughs of Massachusetts, holding fiery torches as golden crucifixes bounced like gavels upon our breasts.

Maybe we will fly through space together and watch our Earth roll over and die on some news highlights from another time or planet. Makes me wish I could meet God for coffee, if only for fifteen minutes.

Diresk used to say, "I hope God's a woman, Toph. Or maybe different people get to be God for a while and then give it up when their turn's done. Man, I would hate that friggin' job. Can you imagine how you'd feel if you made a decision about something and the whole damn planet got blown up and shit?"

I too hope God is a woman. I hope she's very upset about how humans are running the planet, but not too upset to give us all a chance to turn it around. Maybe Diresk will put a good word in for us. If anyone could make her laugh it would be him. Or possibly Mark Twain, and he would have had plenty of time by now to get it done.

I wish I knew so many answers to so many questions. I wish I knew what he was thinking right now. God, I hope I get to see him again!

I'm going to visit his grave three days from now. I'm going back to see my parents and to re-walk the streets with my memories of him. I want to see everything again. I want to remove my shoes and socks and wade in the waters we once worshipped and loved. I want to smell the gymnasium and peer into the dingy windows of Bob's Arcade, long since deserted after Bob moved away. I am going to sleep under the stars and sing the songs we swore to live and die by. I shall look for our stain upon this faded fabric, and I will wave at every driver I see.

I will tell my mother and father how much I love them, and I will linger past our usual embraces. I will kiss my mother's cheek and find her silver hair so appealing this time. My father's face will be much softer, and I will go with him to check the mail. And I will drive.

I will visit Jake and Celia Webster and tell them of my life and job when they ask, but I will hurry through, as such delineations often unnerve me so. I will force them back against their cushions with undermines and excavations of truths none of us will really wish to address, but I will dig just the same. And I will eat her cookies and he will walk me to my truck when we have completed our melancholy dance around each other. They will be glad to see me drive away, but will miss me as they fall asleep holding hands.

I hope I will cry. I know I will cry.

It's so hard to lift the needle now, but I must now spend time with the hauntings this will bring. These months have taken him from me again.

I simply wished to share a stunning melody within a particular piece of music as it continues to play on. I shall treasure always the simple chime and resonance as I continue to return to this hook in my song. I guess it would be a chorus. Yes, it would.

I'll always bring him a new poem when I visit. Sometimes I'll read it to him. Sometimes I'll just leave it under some paperweight upon his stone.

The first time I brought flowers, but the idiocy of that one struck me like a truck and I laughed and laughed as my knees rested above the rotting bones that once carried his heavy heart. He really had a wonderful heart! One of the best ever.

One time I brought him a pizza.

The last time I visited him I was joined by a butterfly. A blue butterfly with orange wings. It let me touch it and I could not help but wonder if it was somehow Diresk, reminding me of why we are here. We are here to serve and help each other on our paths. To shine each other's wings and to point back towards the sky. I always wish it would rain when I visit, but it never does. But then again, butterflies never fly in the rain.

Dear Readers:

Thank you for purchasing **Butterfly Pit Crew** and for spending your time with my book. Please feel free to leave a review on the website where you purchased the book. I hope you find love and I hope you find your wings.

Shawn Michael Bitz
December 2015

About the Author

S hawn Michael Bitz grew up in the Black Hills of South Dakota and played music professionally for twenty-two years before retiring in 2009. He has worked in the mental health field for over twenty-five years and has written three novels of fiction. He is the son of internationally known comedian, Gary Mule Deer. Shawn lives in Rapid City, South Dakota with his lovely lady, Julia and their boxer, Prozac where he is at work on another novel.

Made in the USA
San Bernardino, CA
13 May 2016